THE CHASTITY OF GLORIA BOYD

THE CHASTITY

of

GLORIA BOYD

by

Donald Henderson Clarke

THE BLAKISTON COMPANY

Philadelphia

TO GLADYS

*A sweet face was needed for
the jacket of this book—so we
borrowed hers*

Chapter 1

MA BRENNAN clutched her son Edward's arm, and shook it.

"Don't lie to me!" she cried. "What's that you said?"

Edward gestured aimlessly with a right hand which held a half-burned five-cent cigar.

"I'm not lyin', Ma," he replied. "Ernie's gone off with a blonde, and he ain't comin' back."

Ma Brennan released Edward's arm, and put both hands to her throat. She made noises of strangling.

"For God's sake, don't make a scene now, Ma," Edward urged uncomfortably. "I was wonderin' the best way to break it to Josie."

Ma transferred her hands from her wrinkled neck to her untidy, gray-blonde hair and dug the nails in her scalp, staring at Edward from tired blue eyes.

"That's right, Ma," Edward said. "Don't fly off the handle. Ernie and me was over in Sullivan's back room after dinner; and this blonde was there. She makes a play for Ernie, and Ernie—he makes a play for her. When I asked him was he comin' along home, he said he wasn't comin' home any more; he was goin' away with Rose. That's the blonde's name— Rose. Kind of hard-boiled dame, but Ernie seemed to fall for her. They got in a cab and went away, and I come along home."

Ma balled her hands into fists and thumped her son's chest. Her voice was hoarse.

"And you just stood there and let your brother-in-law go off with a prostitoot?"

"Be calm, Ma, for God's sake! I don't know if she was a

prostitoot. What was I goin' to do? Ernie said he an' her was goin' away together and they went. An' I come along home."

"And Ernie had his pay with him," Ma quavered.

Then she began to scream, long shrill blasts, one after the other.

"Aw Cheese!" Edward protested, unheard. "What's the good of that, Ma? Now you've spilled the beans. Here comes Josie."

Josie Boyd, blonde hair in disorder over her shoulders, comb in her right hand, soiled gray woolen kimono gathered together in front with her left hand, hurried into the narrow, red-carpeted hall of the Jersey City tenement.

"What's the matter?" she cried. "What's the matter, Eddie? Has something happened to Ernie?"

She let the kimono fall open disclosing a glimpse of plump bosom in corsets, wide white cotton panties with a coarse lace fringe, and shapely legs in black cotton stockings; and pressed her left hand over her heart.

"It's all right, Josie," Edward said. "Ernie ain't dead."

Ma Brennan stopped screaming abruptly.

"It would be better if he was dead," she sobbed, turning to Josie. "Oh, my poor daughter!"

The color left Josie's cheeks.

"Quick, tell me," she gasped. "Has something happened to Ernie?"

"He's run off with a prostitoot," Ma Brennan bawled.

Josie laid her right hand, still grasping the comb, on Edward's shoulder.

"You tell me, Ed," she begged, blue eyes on his. "What has Ernie done now?"

"Aw Cheese, Josie! I wanted to break it to you gentle."

Josie stamped a foot in worn, wool house-slipper on the red, figured carpet.

"For God's sake, tell me everything, Ed! Can't you see you're drivin' me crazy?"

"Well, Josie," Edward said, "Ernie met a blonde in Sullivan's, and he and her went away together; and he said he wasn't comin' back, ever. That's what Ernie said."

Josie made word forms with her lips, but no sounds accompanied them.

"Aw, now, don't you start screamin', Josie," Edward pleaded. "I can't stand much more to-night; I'm all upset."

Tears gathered in Josie's blue eyes. First one big, glistening drop, then another, and after them others in rapid succession rolled down her cheeks. She took an edge of her kimono in both hands and worked it into a knot. Her mouth strained like a child's in pain.

"He had his pay with him, too, Josie," Ma Brennan wailed.

"Ernie always was funny," Edward observed. "You know that. If it was any one else I'd think he might be back—but not Ernie."

"The rat!" Ma Brennan screamed. "The little no-good rat! If I could only get my hands on him! We'll notify the police; we'll have him arrested. I'll show him. He'd look good in jail."

Josie gulped hard, and shook her head.

"No, Ma," she said, stifling sobs, "there won't be any police or any jails. If Ernie has gone he's gone."

Ma Brennan whirled on her daughter.

"Are you crazy, too?" she panted. "Your no-good husband has run off with a trollop, out of the back room of a saloon, and left you—only twenty-six years old yourself—with six young ones, and one of 'em just weaned. Are you goin' to be a ball of putty all your life?"

"Ernie is my husband, Ma," Josie said, "and I'm not one who'll have my husband in jail."

"Getting elegant, ain't you?" Ma Brennan sneered. "Like your Grandma Haskell that eloped with Father when he was a Sergeant-Major in the British Army. A lot of good her airs did her. Airs don't pay the landlord or the butcher."

Josie choked a sob.

"Oh, Ma," she whispered, "I feel so terrible."

3

She began to wail softly, shaking her head from side to side.

"Oh, dear! Oh, dear! Oh, dear!"

Ma Brennan poked an unaccustomed arm around her daughter's shoulder, and began to cry louder.

"Aw Cheese!" Edward exclaimed, shuffling his feet uncomfortably. "Don't do that, will you?"

Ma Brennan raised her free arm and made a red fist of her hand.

"You get out of here," she said. "You've caused trouble enough."

"What did I do?" Edward asked.

"You get out!" Ma Brennan screamed. "You didn't do nothin', and that's the trouble."

"That's the thanks I get," Edward mumbled as he opened the door and stepped out into the cool April evening.

"Oh, I feel terrible," Josie moaned. "I feel it right in my bowels—sick like."

"I don't know what we're going to do," Ma Brennan cried. "You with six young ones—"

Josie raised her head with a quick movement and held it to one side in the attitude of one listening intently. She pushed her mother away.

"It's the baby," she said. And, catching up her kimono, she hurried down the hall to her room, where Ernest Thompson Boyd, Jr., was squawking.

She had just laid Junior on her lap when the door into the adjoining bedroom opened, and George, ten, brown hair tousled, brown eyes blinking, entered.

"What the matter, Ma?" he asked. "What are you cryin' for?"

Josie dashed moisture from her eyes with the back of her left hand, the large, square gold band on the ring finger flashing yellow in the dim gaslight.

"It's nothin', Georgie," she said, speaking hoarsely, and sniffling. "You get back to bed."

4

"Has Daddy gone away with a blonde?" George demanded in an awed treble.

"You were listening," Josie accused. "How many times have I told you not to listen to other people's business or your ears will grow big like an elephant's?"

"Will Daddy ever come back?" George piped. "Where did he go?"

Adelaide, eight, with her father's brown eyes, and her mother's blonde hair, squirmed past George and ran to her mother, holding her flannel nightdress up from bare feet.

"Why did Daddy go away?" Adelaide asked.

"I'll tell you all about everything in the morning," Josie promised. "Now you get right back to bed and to sleep."

Ma Brennan came in the bedroom.

"Oh, Ma, make George and Addie go back to bed. Please."

Ma grabbed each squirming mite, one in each hand.

"Get in there," she said gruffly, "or I'll make your bottoms smart with a hairbrush."

"Ooh, you hurt, Gran'ma," George protested.

"You're pinchin' my arm," Adelaide said, and began to weep.

Ma Brennan shook her briskly.

"Get along with you," she said, "or I'll give you somethin' to cry for. Stop your snivellin' now. Stop it!"

When the door was opened, Malcolm, six, brown hair and eyes, scrambled back into bed. Gloria, five years old, with her father's dark hair, and her mother's blue eyes, and Francis, four, who had brown hair and eyes, were sitting up in the bed they shared. They promptly laid their heads back on the pillows.

Ten minutes later Josie tiptoed into the kitchen, perfumed with the coffee Ma Brennan was making. Josie softly closed the door into the dining room.

"I figured there's nothin' like a cup of coffee to brace a body up," Ma Brennan said, setting the pot on the bare table, where already were two cups and saucers, a bowl of sugar, and

5

a can of condensed milk, with a jagged hole punched in the cover.

Josie sat listlessly in a cane-seated, curved-back chair. Ma Brennan poured steaming coffee into the cups, pushed the can of milk and the sugar nearer Josie, and dropped her female shapelessness into a wooden-seated rocker, with a high curved head rest. It creaked as she leaned back, and the left rocker slipped off.

"Everythin' around this house is falling to pieces," she said, grunting, as she hoisted herself to her feet, bent over and fitted the rocker and frame back into place.

Josie tilted the condensed milk can over her coffee, added two heaping spoonfuls of sugar and stirred the mixture.

"Ernie always was wild about blondes," she said.

Ma Brennan snorted.

"Where are your guts, Josie?" she demanded. " 'Ernie always was wild about blondes'," she mimicked. "I'm tellin' you he can't do this. You have him arrested! He's got to support you and the children."

Josie shook her head, wiping her red eyes again with an edge of her kimono.

"No, Ma," she said. "I would never have Ernie arrested. He can't help it. He was just sick of everything, I guess— the babies and no money. Ernie always liked parties, and dancin'."

Ma Brennan blew on her coffee, sipped a mouthful and set the cup down. She glared at her daughter.

"Well, what are you goin' to do?" she demanded hoarsely. "The rent ain't paid—nobody's paid."

Ma's voice became shrill.

"If it was me," she continued, "I'd have been to the police before this. And so would you, if you had any pride. And besides, I'd get after those Boyds. I'd make them do somethin'."

"They haven't had anything to do with Ernie since we got married," Josie said. "His father said Ernie made his bed: let him lay in it."

6

"Let me go see the old man," Ma Brennan cried, cords on her neck standing out. "I'll tell him a thing or two before I'm through. Those young ones are his own flesh and blood. Is he going to see them starve to death, and him and his rolling in luxury?"

"You stay away from the Boyds, Ma," Josie said. "He don't even know we're alive, and I guess he don't care. He told Ernie if he married me Ernie wouldn't be his son any more, and I'll never forget what he told me when I was workin' for him in the mill."

"I wish I'd been there," Ma Brennan said. "A fine thing for a grown man to be scaring a sixteen-year-old girl!"

"You know yourself, Ma, he told me if I was figurin' on gettin' money by marryin' Ernie I was foolin' myself—that Ernie wasn't any good."

"What did he think you was goin' to do about the baby you had comin'?" Ma Brennan demanded. "I suppose he didn't figure the Brennans' reputation amounted to anything."

"He didn't say anythin' about that," Josie replied. "All he knew was the talk about Ernie and me."

"This coffee would be more tasty if there was an egg to put in it," Ma Brennan said, pouring herself a fresh cup. "But there ain't any egg. The Lord knows what we're goin' to eat in this house. Have some more coffee?"

Josie mopped her eyes again and Ma refilled Josie's cup.

"Mr. Boyd was all dressed up that day," Josie said. "He had on the suit he used to wear for funerals, Prince Albert with striped trousers."

"It was when President McKinley came to Wilkstown to make a speech," Ma Brennan said. "He stopped at the Boyds. He had a nice face. Eighteen ninety-eight it was."

"I was all excited about bein' married," Josie said. "Ernie was a wonderful dancer, and I loved the way his hair curled on the back of his neck."

A tear dripped from her nose into her coffee.

Ma Brennan pushed back her cup and saucer, arose from

7

the rocker, and leaned with both hands on the deal table top.

"And he come and lived on your Pa, who was makin' good wages then. A bricklayer wasn't good enough for the Boyds, but he was good enough for their son to live off of."

"Ernie never could get along in business," Josie said. "He would be so polite and nice to his boss for a while, and then all of a sudden he would call him the most awful names. He always wanted to be an actor or a poet. Ernie loved poetry. He could recite 'Gunga Din' perfectly wonderful."

"It would have been better for him if he'd liked nailin' up boxes in shippin' rooms, or servin' customers in dry goods stores, or sellin' insurance," Ma Brennan exclaimed, straightening up.

"I thought he liked it in Hanson's, jerkin' soda," Josie said.

"More girls to make eyes at than in shipping rooms," Ma Brennan sneered.

Josie rose, stacked the cups and saucers in one hand, and picked up the coffee pot in the other, and walked across the bare, splintery kitchen floor to the boarded-in iron sink where two faucets, one supposed to be hot and one cold, drooled eternally.

"Let 'em stay till mornin', Josie," Ma Brennan advised.

Josie shook her head, twisted the hot water faucet, picked up a bar of yellow soap and a rag, and began to wash a cup.

"It's hard enough to keep ahead of dirt by cleanin' up as I go along, Ma," she said. "This'll only take a jiffy. Oh, Lord! I can never seem to get used to these cockroaches."

"I don't see what you're goin' to do, Josie," Ma Brennan said. "There's plenty of men would want you, but none of 'em would want those six young ones."

Josie dumped grounds from the pot into the sink and held it under running water, swirling it vigorously. She turned her pretty face, stamped with patient sweetness, to her mother.

"You'd better get up to bed, Ma," she suggested.

"I just can't figure you out," Ma cried. "I declare sometimes I believe you was born just to be walked on."

John Petrolle, the landlord, was about five feet eight inches tall, with wide shoulders, thickset, a broad, dark face, clear brown eyes under thick black lashes. The blood showed through his closely shaved cheeks. Petrolle was a successful man at forty—he built, sold and rented buildings. After a certain amount of red wine he sang love songs in a surprisingly good tenor.

He followed Josie into the kitchen, and closed the door after him.

"Don't close the door," Josie said. "If the baby should cry I might not hear him."

John grinned and propped a chair under the knob.

"This is a hell of a house," he said. "There ain't no privacy, what with kids, and your mother and your brother."

"Now Mr. Petrolle," Josie said, cheeks rosy, "I don't want you to be fresh any more. I told you that before."

John Petrolle turned from his barricaded door into the hall and walked lightly over to the door which opened into the backyard. There was a key in the lock and he turned it. He lifted his shoulders and sighed.

"How can we talk, Josie, if we can't be alone for a few minutes?" he asked.

Josie backed into a corner by the sink. John laughed, revealing strong white teeth and a healthy pink mouth. Moisture gathered in Josie's blue eyes.

"I suppose you think you can be as fresh with me as you want, Mr. Petrolle," she said, "just because I can't pay the rent."

John's smile changed to a frown. He jerked his head impatiently.

"You know that ain't true, Josie," he asserted. "You know as for me I don't give a damn if you never paid the rent. I got plenty of money. And now your husband has run away with another woman you got to do somethin'."

John moved towards Josie, who pressed harder against the wall behind her.

9

"We got to have a little talk, Josie," John said, unconsciously lowering his voice to a husky whisper.

"We can talk sittin' down, Mr. Petrolle," Josie said.

He put his arms around her. She strained against him. He put his left hand under her chin, and pulled it around, and put his lips to hers. She squirmed and struggled against him for a moment and then relaxed.

"What are you goin' to do with me?" she whispered weakly after a minute.

He kissed her ear, her white neck and her breast.

"Call me 'John'," he commanded.

"John," she murmured.

He pressed his left hand on her hip and moved it slowly up and over her swelling breast. At the same time he bent her gradually sidewise and backwards until she was off balance, and only supported by his right arm around her waist. Suddenly she started, and struggled awkwardly.

"The baby!" she gasped. "The baby is crying. Let me go."

She pushed against him with surprising vigor. John held her fiercely for an instant. She pushed a free hand against his freshly shaven jaw. He released her so suddenly that she staggered.

"Damn the baby!" he said.

Josie, panting, eyes suffused, with enlarged pupils, moist red lips partly opened, deftly set in place escaped blonde locks. She caught the bosom of her white shirtwaist together, made a dab at her black skirt, and ran to the door. John pulled away the chair. He was trembling.

"Listen, Josie," he said rapidly in a hoarse whisper.

Josie paid no attention but hurried through the dining room adjoining and into her bedroom. John followed, arriving in the door just as Josie settled on the unmade bed, the baby across her lap. The room was aromatic with the odor of discouraged diaper.

Josie deftly undid pins and mopped at a small pink backside.

"Hand me that diaper there—over the chair," she said.

John gave it to her.

"Look here, Josie," he said.

The front door slammed and Adelaide and George ran in.

"Jesus Christ!" John said prayerfully. "If this ain't a bird of a house!"

"Gimme some gum, Mr. Petrolle," George shrieked.

"Gimme some too," Adelaide echoed.

"If I give you a nickel apiece to spend at Vitale's, will you promise not to come back for an hour?" John demanded.

"Sure," George howled, dancing up and down and showing two big buck teeth.

Adelaide merely held out her hand, dirty face under disordered yellow curls wistfully tilted up to the landlord. He gave them each five cents.

George screeched.

"Look, Ma, what Mr. Petrolle gave us!"

Adelaide held up her coin gingerly between thumb and forefinger, staring at it.

"Now, get out and stay for an hour," John Petrolle roared.

Josie took the last safety pin from her teeth and plunged it into baby's swathing.

"Georgie!" she said. "Addie!"

The children, already headed for the hall door, hesitated.

"What do you say to Mr. Petrolle?"

"Thank you," George replied, grinning.

"Fank you," Adelaide repeated.

Then they ran, screaming.

"Now, put the baby down, Josie," John said.

Josie raised sweet blue eyes, pink cheeks.

"Perhaps we can talk better if I hold the baby, John," she said. "You ought to be ashamed of yourself."

"I'm crazy about you, Josie. You're the prettiest woman in Jersey City—and New York, too."

"That's what they all say," Josie smiled. "Men all want the same thing."

"Aw, put it down."

"It isn't an 'it'; it's a 'him'."

"Put him down, then."

Finally Josie laid the baby in his crib, and John promptly put his arms around her.

"Don't, John. Mother—my brother—some one'll come in."

"To hell with 'em," John said.

"Don't do that, John. Stop."

"Just like a girl's," John said. "And you with six kids."

"Somebody'll come."

John pushed Josie over on the bed.

"Oh, John," she looked up at him from wide, wondering blue eyes.

Ten minutes later Josie came from the bathroom across the hall. John started to put his arms around her. She pushed them away, her face serious.

"Look here, Josie," John Petrolle whispered. "I love you; I'm crazy about you. I never knew a woman like you. Stick the kids in a home somewhere and we'll get married. I'm on the level."

"I'm already married to Ernie; how could I marry you?" Josie asked.

"That's all right," John said eagerly. "I'll look after you till you can get a divorce. With the pull I got we can get it so fast you'd be surprised."

Josie looked at him, her eyes clear and frank, her features, as always, appearing to be about to relax in a pleasant smile.

"You know I can't get a divorce," she observed.

John Petrolle sank into a rocking chair and groaned. Then he rose and walked up and down, two steps each way, cracking his knuckle joints. He stopped suddenly and took Josie by both arms, his fingers sinking into her flesh.

"I've got to have you, Josie," he said. "We'll get the kids in a good home, and get that mother and brother of yours out of the way; and then we can work things out."

Josie looked up at him.

"You're hurtin' me, Mr. Petrolle."

John dropped her arms.

"I'm sorry," he said. "God damn it! Don't call me, 'Mr. Petrolle.' Jesus Christ! You've got me all worked up. That's the way you do."

"I wish you wouldn't swear," Josie said mildly. "I don't like swearing."

He seized her arms again.

"Then it's all settled," he exclaimed. "Put the kids in a home, and I'll take care of everything. You won't ever have to worry about anything any more."

Josie shook her head gently.

"I wouldn't feel right about being separated from the babies," she said.

John Petrolle stared at her; he raised his hands over his head and turned his eyes up, giving a good idea of a man about to throw a fit. He gasped. Then he grabbed her again.

"But look, Josie," he said. "You have no money; your husband has gone away; you owe bills everywhere. Me, John Petrolle, I have plenty of money. I love you. I will pay everything; you will have everything. The only thing, the kids will go to a home. God damn it, where will they go if you don't do what I say? How are you goin' to keep six kids and a mother and a brother? Answer me. Tell me."

"I thought if you would help me, Mr. Petrolle, I could move to a big house and take boarders," Josie said.

"You—" John choked. "You run a boarding house with men boarders? Some boarding house! And don't call me 'Mr. Petrolle'."

"I can cook," Josie said. "I love to cook."

"I'll say you can cook," John Petrolle said. "But it ain't the cooking the boarders you get 'll be interested in."

"Here comes Ma," Josie said.

Footsteps in the hall were followed by the opening of the

bedroom door. Ma Brennan, in little black bonnet and black silk dress, looked in and said:

"Oh, excuse me."

"It's only Mr. Petrolle come about the rent, Ma," Josie said.

Malcolm and Francis squeezed past Ma Brennan's soft bulk and ran to their mother's knee. Malcolm snuffled and wiped his nose on his sleeve. Francis snuffled and lapped a moist upperlip with his tongue.

"How many times have I told you to use a handkerchief?" Josie asked.

"We ain't got none," Malcolm replied.

"How many times have I told you not to wipe your nose on your sleeve?" Josie said, pulling Malcolm gently to her and drying his face on a diaper.

"Come here," she added to Francis. "Come here, Frankie."

Francis began to weep when she applied the diaper to his nose.

"Blow!" she commanded. "Blow hard."

Francis twisted his head vainly, and finally made a faint blowing sound.

"They both have colds," Josie explained to John Petrolle.

"Oh!" John said.

"From not having enough heat in the house in this damp spring weather, and playing out in the wet without rubbers or raincoats," Ma Brennan said accusingly.

John Petrolle looked at Ma Brennan.

"Mrs. Brennan," he said, "your daughter and I was just havin' a business talk to see if we could fix things up for everybody. Will you take these kids out and keep 'em out for a few minutes. Somethin' has got to be done."

"I've got to go in the kitchen," Josie said. "You come with me into the kitchen, Mr. Petrolle, and Ma will take care of the babies in here, won't you, Ma?"

"It won't be the first time," Ma Brennan said.

Chapter 2

"Hello there, Josie—always workin', ain't you? I never saw the equal."

John Petrolle strode into the neat kitchen, blue and white linoleum on the floor, porcelain sink, with nickel taps, and four-burner gas stove. Josie Boyd shut the oven door and straightened up, submitting to John's kiss. He shook her gently.

"What's the matter, Josie?" he demanded. "Ain't you happy to have a nice clean little apartment, and no worries, and me to love you?"

Josie's blue eyes rested solemnly on John's brown ones. She made no reply. He hugged her roughly, burying his face in her neck. Then he held her away from him.

"Still worryin' about those kids?" he asked. "My God! I should think you'd be happy to have 'em in St. Xavier's Home. You're better off and they're better off. How's a woman, without a husband, goin' to raise six kids decent?"

Josie didn't answer.

"Why don't you answer me?" John cried. "If there's anythin' I hate it's to ask some one a question and get no answer at all—only a dumb look. Aw, Josie. Answer me, won't you? Say somethin'."

A tear slipped down Josie's right cheek. She brushed it away with quick fingers, and gazed at John, eyes brimming with tears. But she remained silent.

John threw his soft hat against the Nile green plaster and kicked a combination ladder-and-chair against the ice-box.

"God damn it, Josie," he exclaimed, raising his voice, "why do those damn kids always have to come between us? You're

15

only a little girl, Josie. You and I can have a good time. The kids are all right."

Josie sniffled. John wrapped vigorous arms around her and kissed her mouth, her neck, her ear. She sighed and relaxed against him.

"I love you, Angel," he whispered.

He moved with her towards the door. Josie struggled faintly.

"Not now, John."

He kept moving.

"The cake will burn—a chocolate cake like you love."

"To hell with the cake!" John said.

After Josie had finished the dinner dishes, John said:

"Let's go around to the Star; there's a Keystone comedy there."

"All right," Josie replied.

"Damn it," John said, "I wish you'd show some life, Josie. You just do anything I say without acting as if you cared a damn. What do you want to do?"

"I just as soon go to the pictures."

"You 'just as soon'! That gives me a pain. For God's sake! What would you like to do?"

"Nothin', I guess—anythin' you want to do."

John rose from one of the two stuffed green chairs which went with the living room set. He was in his shirt sleeves. The *New York Journal*, open at the comics, lay discarded on the green and red rug.

"I'm getting fed up, Josie," John said. "I give your brother Edward a job time-keepin'; and I got you fixed up all cosey here in a nice three-room apartment, and you ain't happy. Always those damn' kids are on your mind. You couldn't have kept 'em, could you, after your husband ran away and left you? Why in hell don't you forget 'em and be happy? Come on. Give us a smile."

Josie made a shadow of a smile.

"What would make you happy, Josie? Just tell me and we'll do it. My God! I've stood this moonin' around for nearly three years."

"April 18, 1908, Ernie went away," Josie said.

"You're a wonder on dates."

"And this is December 3, 1910," Josie said. "It'll be two years and ten months on the tenth."

"What do you do—keep it marked on the calendar?" John growled. "Look here; what do you want more than anythin'?"

Josie opened her lips, but before she made a sound John said hastily:

"Except havin' those kids live with you."

Josie's cheeks flushed, and her eyes were bright. She began to speak rapidly, words tumbling over each other, as if long dammed back.

"You say you are tired because I'm not happy. Well, I'm not happy either, Mr. Petrolle. Edward knows a man, a Mr. Fleeter, who is a very fine gentleman, who will board with me if I open a boarding house; and they have another man, Mr. Brady, who will come too."

John Petrolle's lower jaw sagged an inch. His ordinarily high color flamed higher.

"You're tellin' me you'd rather run a boardin' house and slave for a lot of no good bums, your brother included, rather than live with me like a lady? Who is this Fleeter?"

"Edward met him," Josie said. "He is at the Elks with Edward and Mr. Brady. He has a splendid position in New York. He wears vests with white cord on the edges, and his nails are always manicured, and he carries a cane with a solid gold knob on it."

"Where did you meet him?" John roared, moving nearer to Josie, and clenching and unclenching hairy fists.

"Edward brought him up to call," Josie said. "And we played pinochle; and Mr. Streeter said Edward and Mr. Brady and him would be glad to help me with a boardin' house."

John Petrolle roared.

"Your brother brought this bum up here?"

"Mr. Fleeter is not a bum; he is a very fine gentleman. He wears gold eye glasses on a ribbon, very elegant."

John seized Josie by each arm and shook her violently. Her hair came down; she began to weep. Suddenly he dragged her over to the couch, which matched the two easy chairs, sat down, pulled her over his lap on her stomach, whisked up her skirts, and brought his hand down vigorously on her pink silk-covered rump. He was panting, as he continued to thump her, his hand falling with loud smacks on plump, quivering flesh.

"I'll show you," he breathed. "I'll show you just a part of what'll happen if you let bums come up here when I'm away. I'll kill the bums. I'll whip you within an inch of your life!"

He suddenly stopped the smacking and pushed Josie over on the couch beside him right side up, dishevelled and tear stained. Puffing, he straightened his collar and tie. As if he couldn't restrain himself, he slapped her face.

"Don't ever do that again!" he warned.

Josie sat, sobbing quietly, blonde hair falling on gently heaving shoulders. John got to his feet and began to walk up and down the room.

"Nobody's goin' to put the horns on Joe Petrolle," he cried. "I'll fix you. I'll fire your no-good brother tomorrow, first thing."

"You hurt," Josie quavered.

"I meant to hurt," John replied, still breathing hard. "What the hell kind of sap do you think I am anyway? I know you. All a man has got to do is just get his hands on you, and you get hot. Don't I know?"

Josie dried her eyes with a handkerchief and straightened her clothes.

"I suppose the bums 'll take the kids in the boardin' house too," John said.

Josie shook her head, tears still running down her cheeks.

"We didn't talk about that," she confessed. "But I know it'll be all right."

John raised Josie to her feet. She stood, unresponsive, in his arms. He kissed her; she remained limp.

"You need to be taken care of, Josie," John said. "Why, here you've got everythin'; and we're goin' to get married as soon as we can. Don't go and be a damn' fool."

Josie wrote a note in unformed script the next morning, and left it on the bureau of the bird's-eye maple bedroom set. It ran:

Dear Mr. Petrolle: I am going away, and please do not make any trouble about it. I only am taking my own things. You will find everything clean. There is some chicken in the ice-box, and the cake is in the tin on the second shelf. Sincerely, Josephine Boyd.

Edward was waiting at Journal Square. He was five feet ten, slim, and wore a gray suit, with darker gray squares in the fabric, cut collegiate, a blue, double-breasted overcoat, a black and red striped cravat, somewhat worn, a gray soft hat, and tan shoes. A fraternal pin adorned his left lapel. He jumped in the cab beside his sister, his breath steaming in the cold air.

"Court Square, Brooklyn," he said to the driver. "Buh-lieve muh, I was glad to see you, Josie," he exclaimed as the cab started.

He looked out of the windows, side and rear, rubbing off the steam.

"I would've helped you pack," he added, "only you can't tell about those Wops. Hot tempered they are: just as soon pull a knife on you as not."

"Was Mr. Petrolle mad this mornin'?" Josie asked. "Have you lost your job?"

"I didn't go to work," Edward said. "I'm through with that Wop. I'm goin' to work for Julius's firm on the first—

E. Krumfelder & Co., right in Wall Street—their own building and everythin'."

"It was nice of Mr. Fleeter and Mr. Brady to be willing to help me have a boardin' house," Josie said. "Now I can have my babies back with me again. I'm so glad."

Edward turned and looked at his sister. Then he lighted a cigarette.

"It's a good thing you didn't see Mr. Petrolle this morning," Josie continued. "My but he was mad."

"He had a hell of a nerve beating you up," Edward snarled.

"I can hardly wait to get the children home again," Josie exclaimed.

Edward glanced at Josie again, and coughed uneasily.

"Say, Josie."

"What is it, Eddie?"

"Take a tip from me, and don't talk about having those kids to live with us right off the bat."

Josie turned to Edward, opening her eyes wide.

"Why, Eddie," she exclaimed. "You told Mr. Fleeter that the reason I want a house where I can take boarders is so I can have my children with me—didn't you, Eddie?"

Edward coughed cigarette smoke, apparently through the wrong passageway, because he half-strangled for an instant. When he recovered composure he dropped the stub on the floor of the cab and rubbed a shoe over it. Then he lighted a fresh cigarette.

"You smoke too many cigarettes, Eddie," Josie asserted.

"Only two packs a day," Eddie said. "Cigarettes never hurt nobody."

"I don't see why I can't have the children just as soon as we are settled in the new house," Josie said.

"Listen, Josie," Edward said. "You're stuck on those kids because they're yours. You can't expect other people to be stuck on them like you are. Now you got to promise that you won't talk about the kids till we get everythin' straightened out. You'll keep your trap shut, won't you?"

"I don't see why," Josie said. "I won't be happy till I have a home for them again."

Edward dropped a hand on Josie's thigh.

"Look, Josie, I fixed this all up for you, didn't I?"

Josie nodded.

"All right then. Just for me, don't say anythin' about the kids till I give the word. See? Is it a go?"

"I won't say anythin' then, Eddie, till we're all settled, just as you say. But it won't take me long to get settled. Wait and see."

Julius Fleeter was forty-one, six feet tall, and weighed one hundred and fifty on the bathroom scales, fresh from the tub. He had reddish-brown hair, receding at the temples and thinning on the crown, gray eyes, rather close together, a large Roman nose, a luxuriant, straw-colored mustache, just enough chin to get by, and an air of great dignity.

His favorite garb was a Prince Albert coat, a choke collar, an Ascot tie with a pearl stick-pin, gray trousers, patent leather shoes with spats, and a gold-headed snakewood stick. He also wore ordinary blue and black suits, and even a pepper and salt suit once in a while. But he always wore the choke collar. His shoes always were neatly polished, his clothes always pressed; he was shaved to the quick, and the long, peculiarly bulging nails on his thin white fingers, decorated with tufts of reddish hair between the joints, sparkled like semi-precious stones. A white linen handkerchief in his breast pocket radiated an odor of violet water. He did not use alcohol or tobacco.

He watched Josie skip up the front stairs of the newly rented house, ahead of men bringing in furniture, bought at auction, and then turned to Edward.

"Let us step outside for a moment, Edward," he suggested.

"Okay," Edward replied, stopping to light a cigarette.

They went through the front door, down a flight of wooden steps to a brick walk, and along the walk to the tar sidewalk.

"Didn't you think it was odd that your sister wanted such a large house?" he asked.

"Of course not," Edward replied. "I told you she was nutty on the idea of runnin' a boarding house. She wants room for the boarders."

"Edward," Mr. Fleeter said, a chill quality in his tone, "why didn't you tell me that your sister had six young children, now in a home, and that she expects that they all are coming to live with us in the very near future."

Edward coughed, his blue eyes caught Mr. Fleeter's gray ones for an instant, and then shifted away.

"Aw Cheese, Mr. Fleeter," Edward said, "I didn't think."

"You needed that five hundred dollars I loaned you and the new position I secured for you, didn't you, Edward?"

Edward shifted his shoulders uneasily, threw his cigarette away, and blurted:

"She promised me she wouldn't say anythin' about those God damn' kids."

"Not till after the house was all settled. I am afraid you are a mythopoetic type, Edward. And please don't use profanity."

Edward looked blank.

"You aren't particularly addicted to the truth," Mr. Fleeter explained. "You arranged with me to have your sister have me for a lodger, but you neglected to mention the six encumbrances. You were afraid, if you did, the arrangement would fall through."

Edward stopped walking and turned to Julius Fleeter, his hands extended, palms upward.

"Honest to God, Mr. Fleeter. Cross my heart, and may God strike me dead! I figured you had a case on Josie, and that you would be a lot better for her than that lousy Wop; and I was hopin' somethin' could be done about those God damn' kids. You'd never have believed Josie had even one kid, let alone six, to look at her, would you. Huh?"

"Well don't stop here on the street and make an oration, Edward. And I do wish that your vocabulary might be fumigated."

Edward started walking again.

"You're not going to let those kids spoil everythin', are you, Mr. Fleeter?" he asked after a few moments.

"I haven't made up my mind as to the course I'll pursue," Julius Fleeter said coldly. "But you have a long road to travel to restore yourself to my good graces, Edward."

"That's the thanks I get," Edward blurted. "Me, I was just tryin' to do what was best for everybody."

"There is one point I wish to impress upon you, Edward," Mr. Fleeter said, his close-set gray eyes boring into Edward's blue ones, whenever the blue ones would stop shifting long enough to be bored. "Don't say anything to your sister about this, or I promise you that you will regret it."

"Aw, all right, Mr. Fleeter," Edward grumbled.

Josie knocked at Julius Fleeter's bedroom door about eleven o'clock Sunday morning.

"Come in," Mr. Fleeter said pleasantly.

Josie, face flushed from work, blue eyes shining, stood on the threshold. She was wearing a black skirt and a white shirt-waist turned in in front so that her white, blue-veined throat generously was disclosed.

Julius Fleeter, in blue silk pyjamas and brocaded blue silk dressing gown, laid down the news section of the *Times* and arose. Josie's cheeks became even more red.

"I thought you would like your bed made, Mr. Fleeter, but I don't want to disturb you."

"You couldn't disturb me, Josie," Julius Fleeter said, dropping the gold nose glasses on silk cord from his eagle nose. "I think you look more beautiful every day. Are you happy?"

"Oh, yes, Mr. Fleeter," Josie smiled. "And I'll just think I'm in Heaven when I have my babies back with me again."

Josie turned as if to leave.

"I can wait until you're through in your room," she added. "I have plenty to do in the kitchen. I was just worryin' because I thought you might be dressed and your room wasn't tidied up."

"Don't go, Josie," Julius Fleeter said. "Really I would enjoy watching you while you work, if you don't mind."

Josie hesitated for an instant, then smiled, stepped to the bed, and stripped off the clothing. She pushed the bedstead, of mahogany, from the wall.

"Here, wait. Let me help," Julius Fleeter exclaimed, grasping the foot of the bed.

"Oh, that's all right," Josie said. "Mercy! This is nothin'. I'm used to it. I just want to turn the mattress. Please sit down, Mr. Fleeter."

Their arms touched as Julius bent and lifted the mattress. Josie laughed and gave a vigorous pull and heave. The mattress flopped over.

"Seems as if I'd been doin' it all my life," Josie explained.

Julius Fleeter's hand closed over Josie's wrist. She glanced up at him quickly, surprise and timidity mingled in her blue eyes.

"You are the most beautiful creature I've ever seen," he said softly.

Josie's red lips parted.

"Please, Mr. Fleeter," she protested. "Please don't."

Julius Fleeter pressed his lips against hers suddenly. She struggled silently for a few seconds, and then was still. Her eyes, almost black, swimming, stared up at him when he released her.

"My little wife," he whispered. "The most beautiful girl in the world."

"Oh, you mustn't, Mr. Fleeter. I have a husband somewhere."

"We'll find a way, little one," he whispered, kissing her ear, and fumbling at the buttons of her shirtwaist.

"Don't, Mr. Fleeter."

"You are so beautiful, so lovely, so soft—like a baby."

He kissed her breast. Josie trembled, and sighed. Her arms around his neck tightened; her body pressed, involuntarily, against his.

24

Julius Fleeter got out of the hired limousine-with-chauffeur and helped Josie Boyd to alight. Josie was wearing a Hudson Bay Sable coat. Her cheeks were pink with excitement and the cold; her eyes were like sapphires.

"Oh, Mr. Fleeter," she exclaimed. "I know as soon as you see my babies you will want them home with us just as much as I do—or almost, anyway."

Julius took her arm, and helped her up the steps of St. Xavier's Home.

"You really must call me Julius," he said. "And remember I am Uncle Julius to the children."

Josie nodded.

"I'll remember, Julius," she said. "Only it seems strange for me to be calling such a brainy man by his first name—although Ernie's family have brains. His father has a big factory in Pittsburgh."

"Be sure and remember now," Julius warned. "You'd better say 'Julius' once more."

"Julius! Oh, I'll remember all right. I'm not that dumb."

"And remember, Josie, that I am doing everything for you that I can, and don't make a scene because we are unable to take the children home with us to-day."

Josie stopped, raised her eyes to Julius's, and clasped gloved hands together nervously.

"I won't," she said. "But when you see them I know you will love them; you couldn't help it."

Ten minutes later Josie was sitting in the parlor of the home, kissing Ernest, now four years old, whom she held on her lap, and alternately hugging, and smoothing the hair of George, thirteen, Adelaide, eleven, Malcolm, nine, and Francis, seven.

Their Uncle Julius sat, rolling his gold-headed cane between long fingers.

"Aren't they beautiful?" Josie burbled. "Don't you love Addie's yellow hair and brown eyes? It's such a contrast."

"Is that gold?" George asked, looking up at Uncle Julius, and pointing to the head of his stick.

"That's gold, George."

"Why do you carry a cane? Are you lame, Uncle Julius?"

The Mother Superior, vast, imposing, funereal in her mediaeval garb, entered.

"And here is our little Angelica," she said in her subdued voice.

All eyes involuntarily focused on the door behind the Mother Superior, and Gloria Boyd made an entrance. Her dark hair, almost black, hung to her shoulders in wonderful curls. Her blue eyes, harmonizing with the blue of the trimmings on her white middie blouse, and the solid blue of her skirt, were wide with excitement. Pink spots glowed in her white, soft cheeks of a blonde. She walked with the assured carriage of a grown woman, her slim legs, beautifully hinged to her body, straight as it is possible for legs to be.

Julius Fleeter, standing beside his chair, adjusted his gold pince-nez and stared at the little girl, close-set gray eyes eager. He wet his lips under the wide, but carefully trained mustache, with his tongue.

"Yes, we call her Angelica," the Mother Superior was saying, while Josie hugged and kissed Gloria. "We always have one little girl in the home whom we call Angelica. It is our hope that we never may have to lose this one."

"This is your Uncle Julius, Gloria," Josie explained. "Make him a little bow."

Gloria looked at Uncle Julius from wide blue eyes and, without hesitating for an instant, walked to him and held out a tiny white hand. She said nothing, but regarded him, as if fascinated.

Julius took Gloria's hand; suddenly bent and kissed her. She relaxed in his arms, soft and warm and clinging, human putty and disconcertingly lovely. Julius raised his head to the Mother Superior.

"How long will it take to get the children ready?" he asked. "We would like to take them home with us to-day, if it is possible."

Chapter 3

GLORIA BOYD, in a blue and white gingham dress and black patent-leather shoes with blue socks to match her blue hair ribbon, was in the kitchen scraping from a pot the remains of chocolate frosting that her mother had made for a cake. The spoon she was using was big and unwieldy and about as much chocolate lodged on the outside as on the inside of her face.

When Josie returned from the front of the house Gloria rolled up sweet blue eyes just visible over the top of the inverted spoon.

"Well, I never!" Josie cried. "Now look what you've done!"

Gloria dropped the spoon, and her full lips trembled as she gazed soulfully at her mother. Josie swept her into her arms.

"Mother's boo-ful girl," Josie cooed. "Did you get all nas'y chocolate? Come on, and we'll get nice and clean for Uncle Julius."

Josie led Gloria over to the sink. Gloria held up her face and Josie washed it. Then she kissed both cheeks and the mouth. She dried the skin and hung up the towel. Gloria turned around, silently, as on a pivot.

Josie smiled and sighed.

"What is it now, Baby?"

Gloria shook her head, flouncing her long, black curls, which fell over her shoulders.

"Want your hair curled again?"

"Yes," Gloria said, bobbing her head.

"Come here, then," Josie agreed.

She sat down in a chair by the window and began to wind

27

the waving strands over the index finger moistened in her mouth.

"Mama's little doll," Josie said.

"Let me see," Gloria demanded.

Josie put her hands under Gloria's arms and lifted her up to a wooden-framed mirror on the wall beside the kitchen table. She snuggled her face against Gloria's, kissed her neck, and said:

"Isn't she boo'ful?"

"I'm a little doll," Gloria said, gazing lovingly at her reflection—black hair, blue eyes, red cheeks and lips, white teeth.

Josie laughed, kissed her again, and plumped her down on the floor. Gloria smoothed down her skirt and touched her lips with her tongue in exactly the manner of Miss Doherty, her teacher in Grade 3.

"The airs of that one," Josie exclaimed when Julius, arriving home a little later, sat in the living room, Gloria on his lap. "She acts like a woman of twenty."

Julius Fleeter squeezed Gloria closer to his white-edged waistcoat and kissed her cheek. Gloria snuggled closer. Josie laughed, and went back to the kitchen.

"Whose littie girl are you?" Julius asked.

Gloria smiled and punched him gently in the arm with her right index finger. Julius kissed her ear. Gloria squirmed.

"Tickles!" she said, sitting up and rubbing her ear with her hand.

Julius hugged her again.

"You're my little girl, Gloria, and I'm going to wait for you to grow up; and then what are we going to do?"

Gloria buried her face in his coat.

"Get married," she whispered.

"You bet we will," Julius said. "But we're never going to tell any one our secret, are we?"

Gloria wagged her head negatively.

George came home, slamming the door. He had a job as

office boy with Gowan & Gowan, lawyers. He came into the living room. Julius regarded him severely:

"How many times have I told you not to slam doors, George?" Julius asked.

"I forgot," George replied sullenly.

"Well, go upstairs, and wash up for dinner," Julius said. "And brush your hair. You'll never get ahead if you don't keep neat."

"I ain't no dude," George growled.

"Don't answer me back."

"Oh, aw' right."

George slammed out of the room and stumped upstairs.

Josie poked her head in the door, through which came odors of roasting meat, boiling onions and hot bread.

"Was that Georgie?" she asked. "I wonder where Addie is? That one worries me."

The front door slammed again and Adelaide ran in, blonde hair tousled, black eyes sparkling, rosy face smudged, dress shabby, shoes scuffed.

"There's your Addie," Julius said. "A regular little tomboy."

Adelaide stuck her tongue out at Julius.

"What she needs is to have her mouth washed in quinine," Julius said. "And a good spanking might not be a bad idea."

"Don't you know it isn't nice to make faces, Addie?" Josie asked.

Adelaide tossed her head.

"I don't care," she said.

"It's too bad you can't be good like your sister Gloria," Julius said severely, squeezing Gloria.

Adelaide looked at Gloria, and her upper lip curled.

"Teacher's pet," she said.

"I am not!" Gloria cried.

Josie took one of Adelaide's hands.

"Why, Addie!" she exclaimed. "What's the matter with Mother's little girl? Come on and get washed for dinner."

In the bathroom upstairs Josie bustled at the task of before-dinner child cleaning. Malcolm, nine, snatched a comb from Adelaide, eleven. Adelaide pulled his hair. Malcolm kicked her shins. Francis, seven, sailing a boat in the bathtub, wet his shirt sleeves as far as the elbow. Junior, four, howled when Josie screwed the end of a towel into his ears.

Edward stood outside in the hall.

"Aw Cheese!" he said. "What a family."

"If you don't like it, what are you hangin' around for?" thirteen-year-old George growled.

"Georgie! Is that a nice way to talk to your Uncle Ed?"

"Aw shucks!" George exclaimed. "He gives me a pain."

"Georgie!"

"I'll Georgie him," Edward said.

"Just try it and see," George said.

"Give me that soap," Adelaide screamed. "Ma! Malcolm won't lemme have the soap."

"She had it," Malcolm yelled.

"I did not."

"You did too."

Julius sat at the head of the table, Gloria at his right. Julius whispered to her:

"Don't let your fingers touch the blade of the knife. No, Baby. Just hold the handle of the fork like this. Look at me."

Gloria laid her knife and fork on her plate with a clatter and pouted.

"I can't," she complained.

"Yes, you can, Baby," Julius soothed. "Gloria is a little lady: she's so beautiful. She can eat like a beautiful little lady."

"Yah!" George cried, his mouth full of roast beef and mashed potato, not to mention turnip. "Gloria's a little lady."

George had the tines of his fork in one fist, and the blade of his knife in the other. His elbows were squared out for the work of feeding. Adelaide looked at Julius and Gloria, and quickly changed the position of eating tools.

"Take the spoon out of your cup," Julius murmured.

Gloria removed the spoon from her cambric tea—milk, hot

water, and sugar—to the saucer. Adelaide quietly copied her movements, her dark eyes quickly scanning the unconscious, jaw-working, noise-making faces, at the table.

"Some more," George said, holding out his plate.

"How do you ask for it?" Uncle Julius demanded.

"Please," George conceded sourly.

Uncle Edward slapped a hunk of butter on a slab of bread, folded the bread over the butter, and rammed it into his mouth.

"When you're through with Georgie," he said, holding out his plate, and speaking with his mouth full, "I'll have another helpin' too."

"There's chocolate cake and ice cream for dessert," Malcolm piped. "I seen it."

"Oh, goodie!" Adelaide shrieked, bouncing up and down in her chair. "I can eat two plates."

Malcolm and Frank said in chorus:

"Ice cream."

Francis pushed away his plate. Junior beat on the table with his mug.

"There isn't any ice cream," Josie said. "But I made a chocolate layer cake."

Groans and howls of disappointment blended.

"Quiet!" Uncle Julius said sharply. "What is this—a menagerie?"

He glanced at Gloria. She looked wistfully up at him, her lips slightly pouted.

"Would you like ice cream, Gloria?"

She smiled.

"Well," Uncle Julius said, "if you'll all be quiet, you can have ice cream."

He pushed slightly back from the head of the table, and took from his waistcoat pocket a thin package of new bank notes. He removed two one-dollar bills.

"Here, George," he said, holding out the bills, "you run around to Equi's and get two quarts of cream."

31

"Chocolate!"

"Strawberry!"

"I want chocolate and vanilla."

"Coffee!"

Uncle Julius rapped sharply on the table.

"Quiet!" he said.

He looked around the table, suddenly silenced.

"If there is any more noise like that," he said, "there will be no ice cream at all. Get chocolate, vanilla and strawberry mixed," he added to George, "and hurry."

"I love coffee ice cream," Malcolm pleaded. "Can't I have coffee?"

Julius frowned.

"Gloria likes coffee too," Adelaide said.

Gloria nodded.

"All right," Julius said. "Get chocolate, vanilla, strawberry and coffee."

"Can I go with Georgie?" Adelaide piped.

"Me too," Malcolm said.

"No," Julius ordered. "George, you run along."

Gloria was playing horse with Uncle Julius's gold-headed stick in the living room the following Saturday afternoon. Julius was reading the *Evening Sun*. Josie stepped in from the dining room.

"Come on, Gloria," she said. "Come on and get your bath."

Gloria, astride the stick, gazed first at her mother and then at Uncle Julius. Julius dropped the newspaper and raised his eyes.

"I'm sorry to bother you and Gloria, Mr. Fleeter," Josie said. "But I've got so much work to-day, and the children all have to have a bath. I don't know how I'm goin' to get everythin' done."

Julius dropped his gold-rimmed glasses, smoothed his mustache and, leaning suddenly forward, caught Gloria's arm and hoisted her to his knee.

"I'll give the baby her bath, Josie," he said. "Wouldn't you like Uncle Julius to give you a bath?" he asked, kissing Gloria's cheek.

"Ooh! It tickles," Gloria said, squirming.

"I can do it," Josie said. "I didn't mean that. It would be too much trouble."

"No trouble at all, Josie," Uncle Julius announced, arising. "Come on, Gloria."

He lifted Gloria to his shoulders, sat her astride his neck, and clasped her ankles in his hands. Gloria screamed and laughed.

"She'll ride right upstairs to the bathroom," Uncle Julius promised, his face red from exertion.

"All right, then," Josie said. "Give Mama a kiss," she added, putting her lips to Gloria's.

Uncle Julius soaped Gloria all over, and then scrubbed her gently with a wash cloth. The room filled with steam and the odor of violet soap.

"You're the most beautiful little girl in the world," he said, kissing her back.

Gloria giggled.

"It tickles," she said.

He kissed her little girl breasts.

Gloria looked solemnly at him.

"I'm a little doll," she said.

"You are Uncle Julius's little doll," Julius Fleeter said. "And your Uncle Julius is going to wait for you to grow up, and then you will be Uncle Julius's little doll wife."

As he was drying her with a big bath towel from his own private stock, Julius said:

"And what dress do you want to wear for dinner to-night, Baby Doll?"

"The white one with blue ribbins on it," Gloria said. "Blue brings out the color of my eyes."

"My word!" Uncle Julius laughed. "It doesn't take long for the Baby Doll to learn what looks nice on her, does it?"

"An' I'll wear my white socks and white hair ribbin, to match," Gloria asserted.

Julius slid the towel up and down her legs. Then he kissed her legs and her feet. Gloria laughed.

"It tickles," she protested, shivering, and gazing up at him with blue eyes, cheeks red; her black curls twisted to the top of her head for the occasion, giving her a quaint flavor of maturity.

Uncle Julius folded her in the towel, so that there was visible only her head with the face, like a pansy, and with the curls swept up clear of her soft neck. Then he hugged her.

One afternoon Julius came home, and called for Gloria. Josie appeared from the direction of the kitchen.

"She isn't home, Mr. Fleeter," she said. "She has gone to Mabel Kane's birthday party."

Julius's close-set gray eyes frowned, his cheeks whitened and then suffused with blood. His thin frame trembled with rage. He clenched his fists until the knuckles whitened.

"Didn't I tell you to keep that girl home when she isn't in school?" he demanded hoarsely.

"Why, Mr. Fleeter," Josie protested, fumbling at her kitchen apron with damp hands, "I didn't think you meant she shouldn't go to little boys' and girls' parties."

"You didn't think!" Julius sneered. "You never could think. You're not supposed to think. Now you go and get Gloria, wherever she is. That's one of your litter that isn't going to be spoiled by associating with the riff-raff around here."

"But, Mr. Fleeter—Julius."

Josie's eyes under blonde hair were wistful.

"Go and get Gloria from that party," Julius Fleeter repeated. " 'Buts' won't do any good. Some brat may be kissing her and pawing her now."

"Why, Julius, they may play post office, or drop the handkerchief, but all the children do. That's nothin'. They're only babies."

A vein stood out on Julius's left temple. He snorted disgust.

"Well, I'm not going to have Gloria being kissed and hugged. I know what it leads to."

"Why, if it wasn't too silly I'd think you were jealous," Josie cried.

"I'm not jealous," Julius Fleeter asserted violently. "What's the matter with you anyway? You have the most amazing mind. Now stop this nonsense immediately and go and get that girl."

Josie's jaw set in stubborn lines. Her blue eyes rested bravely on his.

"I would do anything for you, Mr. Fleeter. You know. You made it possible for me to have my babies with me. But I can't spoil Gloria's good time at this party. And Mr. and Mrs. Kane are not riff-raff. He is a cashier in the bank and Mrs. Kane is a lovely woman. And what would everybody think if I went and got Gloria right at supper time?"

Julius took three quick steps to the bay window, and three quick steps back again. He looked at Josie more calmly.

"All right," he said. "I see you don't care anything about pleasing me."

"Oh, Julius," Josie breathed. "How can you say that?"

"All I have is the child's best interests at heart," Julius resumed, "and I am accused of being jealous. Did you ever stop to think that you might be the one who is jealous—and thoughtless and ungrateful."

Tears brimmed in Josie's eyes.

"You twist everything so," she said, a catch in her voice. "All—I wanted—was for the children—to have—a good time."

"Well," Julius Fleeter said, "there is no sense of my staying here when you are in this mood. I can see that. I'll have my dinner at a restaurant."

He turned towards the hall door.

"Don't do that," Josie pleaded. "I don't know what I said.

Honest! We are having rare roast beef to-night, and potatoes roasted in the pan, and apple pie—your favorite dinner."

"I'll be home later," Julius said.

He put on his coat and hat and closed the front door gently behind him. Josie lifted her apron, wiped her streaming eyes, and walked blindly back to the kitchen.

When Julius returned at eleven o'clock, Josie, eyes red, was sitting up waiting. She met him in the hall. Julius stifled a groan.

"Will you fix me some powdered ginger and bicarbonate of soda, Josie?" he said. "I have an attack of acute indigestion."

"It'll only take a minute," Josie said, and hurried down hall towards the kitchen.

Josie helped Julius undress and got him a hot water bottle and rubbed his stomach.

"Gloria and Addie and Malcolm had a perfectly wonderful time at the party," Josie said. "And Gloria couldn't understand why you wasn't home to kiss her good night."

Julius sighed.

"I had a rotten dinner," he said.

"How do you feel?" Josie asked.

"Better," Julius replied. "A lot better. Take away that hot water bag and come on to bed."

He pulled Josie's head down and kissed her warm, soft lips.

"Wait till I see if the children are all right."

"Good Lord! Always the children. Well, hurry up."

Josie went to her room and got into nightgown and kimono and returned.

"They are all asleep and so sweet," she whispered.

Chapter 4

LEMUEL KANE, assistant cashier of the Sevier National Bank, his wife, Emma, his daughter, Mabel, just Gloria's age, and his son Thomas, two years older, lived diagonally across the street from the Boyds.

Lemuel was a genial, round-faced man of medium height and impressive abdomen. His round bald head was ringed with blond hair; his blue eyes swam, magnified, behind lenses in aid of farsightedness. He went to the club one night a week and played whist or billiards, and he led his family to the First M. E. Church every Sunday morning. He read the *New York Times* on the Gay Street trolley, which carried him to the bank, and he read the *Brooklyn Eagle* and the *Evening Sun* on his return home from the bank. In Moreno's Barber Shop, where he had a haircut, shave, and shampoo once every two weeks, he read the *Police Gazette* and the *New York Evening Journal*, just as, when he made a business trip to Boston, he went to a beer garden and drank beer and looked over the giddy females.

On Dr. J. L. Pearson's advice, he lately had taken up golf. He played Saturday afternoons. He hadn't been brought up to play games or fish or hunt on the Sabbath.

Mrs. Kane was slim with light brown hair which contained many prematurely gray strands. She also wore spectacles, but the difficulty with her hazel eyes was astigmatism and just a touch of nearsightedness. She never wore the spectacles, rimless with gold temples, when she went to musicales or to the theater, which was once or twice during the year. But she did wear them at the movies, which, slightly shamefaced, she visited at least once a week.

Emma Bisbee and Lemuel Kane had been childhood sweethearts. She frequently said to her friends:

"I suppose some disappointed women would have it that all men are unfaithful. But I *know* that Lemuel could not be untrue to me, even in thought. And when sometimes life brings its troubles I get such comfort as I could not describe from the thought that just as Lemuel and I love each other, and live for each other and our children, that there are thousands of other decent, stay-at-home people, who are the same way. I tell you," she would conclude earnestly, slim body shaken with fervor of conviction, "most people are good; you don't want to believe all you read in the papers."

Thomas and Mabel were slim like their mother, and blond and blue-eyed like their father. They were handsome children and people turned to look at them on the street, particularly after Thomas came through infantile paralysis with his head dropped over towards his left shoulder and his left shoulder sagging lower than the right.

"Isn't it too bad—such a handsome boy!" the people whispered.

At his sister Mabel's birthday party, Tommy Kane attached himself to Gloria.

"You are awful pretty, Gloria," he said.

"I'm a little doll," Gloria confessed.

"You're the prettiest girl in Brooklyn," Tommy said.

Gloria put her arms around him and kissed him. Tommy flushed and pushed her away. Bricky Adams yelled:

"Oh, look! Gloria's kissing Tommy."

A half-dozen boys and girls called:

"Tommy's got a girl."

Crystal liquid welled up in Gloria's big blue eyes. Tommy blushed.

"She's cryin'."

"He's blushin'."

"Kiss 'im again."

"I dare yuh."

"Let's play post office," Adelaide suggested shrilly.

"Drop the handkerchief."

Tommy went into the hall just before supper and Gloria followed him. He stood in front of the mirror in the hat rack and straightened his head and his shoulders.

"What is that for?" Gloria asked, looking at her own reflection over Tommy's shoulder and adjusting one of her long black curls.

"I had infantile paralysis," Tommy said. "And when I think of it I have to go to a mirror and make myself straight the way I should be, and if I keep on doing it before long I'll be all right again."

"Let me see," Gloria said.

Tommy turned from the mirror, standing like a soldier at attention.

"Am I all straight?" Tommy asked.

Gloria nodded, agitating her curls, and getting the effect by a long glance in the mirror.

"We're goin' to have ice cream and macaroons and lady fingers for supper," Tommy confided.

Lemuel Kane later lifted Gloria to his lap.

"I suppose everybody tells you you're pretty," he said.

Gloria smiled candidly.

"Yes," she said.

"Well, you certainly are a picture," Lemuel Kane said. "Are you going to give me a kiss?"

Gloria promptly raised puckered lips.

"What beautiful curls and what a pretty dress," Lemuel Kane said.

"My mama always keeps my hair curled and blue is my color," Gloria explained gravely, wide blue eyes gazing directly up into his. "I like men's kisses better than boys' kisses," she added.

"Great Jehosophat!" Lemuel Kane exclaimed. "You've begun early, haven't you?"

Gloria merely kept on looking at him.

"You know, little girl," Lemuel said, "somehow I think you're going to cause a lot of trouble in the world."

He lifted Gloria to her feet. She smoothed her skirt and adjusted her curls. Lemuel Kane watched her, fascinated.

"Give me one more kiss?" he suggested suddenly.

She immediately raised pouting, moist, red lips, white teeth showing through. Mrs. Kane entered the room during the kiss.

"Caught in the act," she laughed.

Lemuel Kane started and flushed violently. Then he laughed.

"Why, Lem, you look guilty," said Emma Kane.

Lemuel flushed more. Gloria's direct gaze shifted from Lemuel and focused on Mrs. Kane.

"You're as red as a beet, Lem," Emma Kane accused.

"Everybody is always kissing Gloria," Malcolm Boyd piped.

"I don't know what's the matter with me," Lemuel Kane said. "I feel foolish."

When they were getting ready for bed that night Emma Kane said:

"Oh, Lem."

"What?"

"I wonder about those Boyds."

"Why?"

"I don't know. I just wonder, that's all. There are six children, and that awfully pretty mother who is always working, and that old dude of an uncle of theirs."

"Well, why should that make you wonder?" Lemuel asked, dropping his second shoe on the floor and standing up in his socks and union suit.

"The father went away and left them," Emma continued.

"Well, they seem to be getting along all right."

Emma, in corsets and balloon drawers, was braiding her hair in front of a cheval glass.

"I think the uncle is horrible," she announced, shivering. "He is one of those men whose eyes seem to be looking right through your clothes when you meet him. He reminds me of a snake—or something slimy, I don't know."

"The type with an eye for a pretty ankle, eh?" Lemuel said carelessly, slipping down the top part of his union suit and insinuating himself into a flannelette night shirt. "Well, Em, there are plenty of those, and some of them mighty decent men, too."

"Oh, I don't mean that," Emma exclaimed, getting behind a closet door and stepping out of her balloon drawers and beginning to unhook her corset. "He's the lewd kind that seems to try to see every woman naked. And, besides, he seems to be a man of more education than the mother and her brother. The brother is a very common type."

"Well, I guess they can't harm us much, Em; and they may be all right at that."

Emma hung up her corset and stood rubbing the red creases its impress had made in her soft sides, still screened from her husband by the door.

"Men are so dense," she exclaimed. "What I mean is I would hate to have anything serious develop between that little Gloria and our Thomas."

Lemuel switched down the bed covers, sat down on the side of the bed and stripped off his socks. He grinned at the door which concealed his wife.

"I pass," he called pleasantly. "You women have me beaten. Why those two are only babies."

With a flurry of arms Emma dived into a linen nightgown, of modest thickness, and appeared from behind the door.

"I'm afraid, Lem," she said, "I just couldn't bear the thought of Thomas marrying a girl that wasn't worthy of him."

Lemuel laughed.

"Maybe you're just jealous because I kissed her. Lord! But she's pretty, isn't she?"

41

Emma didn't laugh.

"You wouldn't notice it, Lem, but that girl has a provocative look. When she looks at you those eyes of hers are inviting people to admire her and kiss her. And that is all wrong."

"Well, I kissed her," Lemuel said.

"And you blushed over it, too. You can't tell me. There is something about that little girl that makes me have to keep reminding myself she is only a child and not a woman. I felt it before you got all red when I came in the room when you were kissing her. You tell me why you should get all flushed up and guilty-looking for just kissing a little girl."

"Aw, Em, you're crazy. It wasn't like you say at all."

Emma sniffed.

"You're making it look as if there was something to feel guilty about. I think that's awful."

"She's just the kind men all go wild about—doll face, curls, and simper," Emma said. "Can't pass a looking glass or a window without admiring herself. I think Mabel is *much* more beautiful. She has spirit and character and intelligence in her face."

"Well, you've got to admit Gloria has *something* to get you all stirred up like this," Lemuel said.

"She's as spoiled as all get-out," Emma said. "I'd like to give that too-pretty mother of hers a piece of my mind. Did you see the curls and the sheer linen dress? Spoiled, that's what she is."

"She's only a baby," Lemuel said.

Madame Cele, Lord Frederick, seven dogs—a French Poodle, weirdly clipped, with a red ribbon around his neck, two wire-haired fox terriers, one smooth fox terrier, two French Bulls, and a Pekingese—two parrots, and a monkey, lived in a yellow frame house just around the corner from the Boyds.

Nobody knew just how old Madame Cele was, but it was

said that she had been a toast at Monte Carlo when she was the premier lion tamer of Europe. She was just over five feet tall and a trifle on the plump side, but amazingly active. She had astonishing red hair, like a flame, and terrible eyes that sometimes looked green and other times looked yellow. They blazed out of her rouged wrinkles like witch's fires. Her teeth were beautifully white and even; when she was excited she made them click. Animals and people all minded when Madame Cele snapped an order in her husky gutturals.

Madame was marching up and down in the yard in front of her house one afternoon, a parrot on each shoulder, and the seven dogs trotting abreast one pace behind. Gloria Boyd and Thomas Kane were passing, homeward bound from school.

"Halt!" Madame Cele barked.

The seven dogs froze in their tracks. Madame showed her shining teeth in what clearly was intended for an ingratiating smile.

"Come here to me," she said to Gloria and Thomas.

Gloria looked at Thomas, and he looked at Gloria. They hesitated, Gloria trembling a little. Madame said nothing more—merely waited. Gloria and Thomas turned in at the curleycue iron gate which, like the adjacent fence, showed traces of red paint, and stopped, silent, in front of Madame. She raised both hands in an outlandish gesture and brought them down on her red skirt in the neighborhood of her knees. Then she laughed hoarsely.

"You are afraid of Madame Cele," she cackled. "Ho! Ho!"

She stretched out a small hand, tanned and freckled, and with work-roughened fingers tilted up Gloria's chin. Gloria's blue eyes, wide and dark, gazed straight back at her—waiting.

"Ha! SoooOH! A real beauty!"

The old lady nodded her flaming head so vigorously that it seemed like three or four heads painted in a blur. Gloria's cheeks were pale, the pupils of her eyes dilated; her teeth looked white through slightly parted lips.

43

"A girl for the men to go carazee about," Madame Cele said. "Already the men love to kiss and hug you—do they not?"

Gloria flushed faintly. Her lips murmured:

"Yes."

"Oh, you don't have to tell me," Madame Cele cried in stentorian tones. "I know."

She laughed again. And when she was through, the two parrots, one on each shoulder, croaked:

"Ho! Ho!"

"I was such a girl," Madame announced. "I never was a little girl at all; and if ever I was a virgin I don't remember that."

Madame laughed harder than ever and stopped abruptly. The parrots still laughed.

"Shut up!" she ordered.

They cocked their heads and looked at her from bright eyes, silent.

"Marchons!" she shouted to the dogs.

"Come with me," she said to Gloria and Thomas. "We will go in my house."

Madame Cele, green shirtwaist and red skirt, walked up the walk, swinging her hips. The seven dogs followed in a line. After them trudged the children.

Madame opened a screen door.

"Single file, you," she ordered.

The dogs dropped one by one into a column and marched in the door. She said:

"Disperse! Beat it! Go to hell."

The dogs scattered. She took the parrots, wings fluttering, from her shoulders, stepped into the living room, and set them on top of a big cage. Lord Frederick, in red smoking cap with tassel, worn house suit of black brocaded silk, with maroon silk collar and pipings, arose and bowed, a fat white hand on his fat stomach.

"Children, this is Lord Frederick," Madame said.

"It is a very great pleasure indeed to meet such charming young folk," Lord Frederick said, bowing again and smiling with big, black, moist eyes, one misty behind a monocle.

Lord Frederick was six feet tall, but he didn't look it, because he was almost six feet in circumference. He had a round head, on which closely cropped hair was brushed pompadour, a round face under a narrow forehead, great bushy black eyebrows, nose, mouth and chin of one of the plumper of the Roman emperors. His hands were balls of white fat.

Gloria and Thomas stared up at Lord Frederick.

"This is the little girl I have told you about," Madame Cele said, taking Gloria's arm and dragging her closer. "I know a beauty when I see her."

Lord Frederick cleared his throat and peered at Gloria. Then he reared his head and cleared his throat again.

"The child is indeed very lovely," he said in the full round tones of an orator. "She reminds me of Cleopatra, whom I knew well."

"But Cleopatra had red hair," Madame interrupted. "Haven't I heard you say that often enough. Mon Dieu!"

"If you had not interrupted me," Lord Frederick resumed, bowing at Madame, "you would have heard me continue to say that while Cleopatra's coloring was different, the beauty is the same—the beauty that may wreck an empire in one case, or the green grocer's domestic happiness in the other."

Lord Frederick cleared his throat.

"Hotsy Totsy!" Madame Cele exclaimed, kicking high with her left foot.

Lord Frederick frowned, without dislodging the monocle.

"Helen of Troy had the same appeal," he continued. "She was a very charming girl. She used to visit our place in the north of Africa—we had a farm of five thousand square miles there in those days—when she was a lass. Many is the apple tree I have climbed with little Helen."

Gloria turned her head towards Madame Cele for a moment,

just as Madame dropped a withered lid over one wicked eye in an elaborate wink.

"But I thought Helen was a blonde," she said.

Lord Frederick looked pained.

"My dear Madame," he said, bowing again. "I fear you failed to notice that I said 'same appeal', not the same coloring. And I might say the same about the Queen of Sheba—I happened to be in Jerusalem at the time she visited King Solomon, whom I knew well. And if there is any one man about whom history is more wrong than about Solomon, I haven't good sense."

Lord Frederick fixed Gloria and Thomas with his big, glowing eyes.

"Most of history is a lie," he asserted vigorously. "Solomon—a sweet man, and with far too much good sense to accumulate eight hundred wives—was incarcerated in an institution, and held there incommunicado while an impostor sat on his throne. I wish you would always bear that in mind. I spent millions of shekels, and fifteen years and three months of my time, trying to free him and restore him to the throne, but without avail. It was no use."

Lord Frederick pulled a fine linen handkerchief from his breast pocket, applied it to his nose, and made a trumpeting noise.

"Solomon preferred the quiet and peace of the insane asylum to the bother of being a king," Madame Cele explained to the children.

Lord Frederick nodded ponderously.

"That is quite correct," he said. "And it was Solomon who discovered the secret of perfection, and set me on the road to approximating it."

"The nearer you can get to being a perfect ball," Madame Cele said, "the nearer you get to perfection."

"A perfect sphere is the most perfect thing in the universe," Lord Frederick said. "King Solomon was the nearest to a perfect sphere of any one I ever saw—except myself. He

46

carried on the first great experiments with bread and milk, drinking forty gallons of milk and eating sixty-three loaves of bread daily. If the terrestrial globe on which we now are whirling through space were a perfect sphere it would be a perfect world. But the globe is flattened at the poles, and that has its baneful effect on all of us."

Lord Frederick drew a gold watch from his pocket.

"My word!" he exclaimed. "It is time for my bread and milk now."

Madame Cele kicked up her left foot.

"Hotsy Totsy!" she cried in her harsh voice. "We will have some pickled herrings and beer while Lord Frederick is having bread and milk."

She led the way from the living room, which was a clutter of tarnished gold furniture, including a battered white and gilt grand piano, through a dining room, in which was a glass case full of porcelain figures and watches in strange shapes—apples, peaches, rings, skulls, crystals—through a musty hall, in which the odor of dogs and parrots became more pronounced, and into the kitchen. A monkey jumped on Madame Cele's shoulders and put his arms around her neck.

Gloria screamed.

"It's nothing but Fritzee," Madame Cele said. "Shake hands with the little girl, Fritzee."

Fritzee dropped to the floor and held up a cold, skinny hand, twitching his nose and glancing first at Gloria and then at his mistress from shoe button eyes. Gloria timidly held out her hand and Fritzee put his cold one in it. Unexpectedly he clutched Gloria's skirt, and in a jiffy was perched, chattering, on her shoulder.

"See?" Madame Cele cried delightedly, extending both hands, with palms upward, at girl and monkey. "See? Fritzee he only likes me until you come. Fritzee knows what is good, don't you, Fritzee?"

Gloria, cheeks pale, stood motionless, head twisted awkwardly.

47

"Take it off," she pleaded.

Madame Cele drew herself up and filled her lungs with air.

"Attention!" she called, giving the word its French pronunciation.

Fritzee jumped to the floor and stood with right paw to right eye, facing Madame. A scurry of claws sounded on linoleum, and the seven dogs lined up behind Fritzee, all sitting on their tails with left paw dropped and right paw raised.

Madame Cele turned proudly to Gloria and Thomas.

"See!" she said. "I am Cele, the g-r-reatest tamer of lions of all. Look!"

Unmindful of the animals, who began to teeter and now and then dropped a paw to maintain balance, she lifted her skirt, pulled down a stocking, and pulled up a yellow silk panty's leg, baring a great, jagged scar on her thigh.

"And look."

She pulled open her waist, and pulled down a yellow silk undervest baring her right breast. What was left of it was scar tissue.

"Oh!" Gloria moaned.

"Gee!" Thomas exclaimed, wide-eyed.

"Oh, I have more souvenirs from my pets," Madame Cele said. "They were jealous, just like men, my pets. They knew if I was in love. And I was always in love. I am in love now. When I am no longer in love let me die. I have the heart and the body, the passion of a girl. Do you see often legs like those?"

Up went her skirts, disclosing legs well calved and muscular.

"Me, I was a dancer, too," she said.

She pirouetted and kicked.

"Hotsy Totsy!"

"The dogs," Gloria said. "They are getting tired."

"Disperse, babies," Madame said, waving her hands.

Fritzee leaped on the sink. The dogs trotted away. Lord

Frederick was sitting at the kitchen table eating bread and milk, which he had got for himself from the ice-box in the back hall, just off the kitchen.

"And we will have pickled herrings and beer. I make these herrings myself."

"I don't think my mama wants me to have beer," Thomas said.

"What would your mama like you to have?" Madame Cele asked.

"I think she would prefer me to have milk; and please I am more used to bread and butter and sugar than to herrings."

Madame Cele ha-hawed heartily. She wiped tears from her eyes with the back of her hand.

"Pardon," she cried, "but you see I forget. I never drank water when I was young. I was told the water would make me sick. But that was in Germany and in France."

"Never drank water?" Gloria asked.

"No!"

Madame shook her head.

"But perhaps you too, little girl, would prefer the bread and butter and sugar and milk."

A slow smile illuminated Gloria's face.

Madame Cele groaned.

"Such disrespect for my lovely herrings that I pickle with these hands. Look!"

She picked up a dangling, dripping object from a dish on the sink shelf.

"Does not that make your mouths water?"

She looked at the two blank faces.

"No? I am desolated. Well, come on. You will have your wish. I myself will eat those herrings, and drink the beer."

After the herrings and beer and bread and butter and sugar and milk, Madame played an old music box and danced, and then went to the door with Gloria and Thomas. She put her rough fingers again under Gloria's chin.

"You are coming to see Madame Cele whenever you can, Little One," she said. "You should know some things."

She bobbed her head up and down with great vigor.

Julius Fleeter met Gloria in the hall. He stood in silence till she hung her blue felt hat on the rack. Then he said:

"Come in the living room, Gloria."

Gloria walked in ahead of him and he closed the door after her. The door into the dining room already was closed. Julius had the appearance of chief mourner at a funeral. He said:

"Won't you sit down, Gloria?"

She sat down in a stuffed rocking chair, covered with red silk. It squeaked as she sat. She looked at Julius breathlessly. He took two steps to the bay window and two steps back. He stopped in front of her, close to her chair, and looked down.

"I am very disappointed in you, Gloria," he said sadly.

"Why? What did I do?"

Gloria looked innocent as a dove.

"You know very well what you did. You stopped somewhere on your way from school. You didn't meet me at the corner as you always do. You have upset me very much."

Gloria slid out of the chair, causing it to rock back and forth with more squeaks, and went over to Julius.

"I suppose you know you should be punished for this," Julius said.

Gloria gazed at him silently with big blue eyes, and laid her hand on his coat sleeve.

"Where were you?" he demanded.

Gloria climbed into his lap, put her arm around his neck, and held up pouted lips.

"Gloria is sorry," she said, tightening the arm around his neck and moving her mouth nearer.

Julius groaned and pressed his mouth against hers and hugged her.

"Where were you?" he repeated.

50

Gloria put her index finger through the buttonhole in his lapel, bent her head to one side, and dropped her eyelashes.

"I was at that house where Madame Cele lives with all the dogs and parrots and monkeys and a big fat funny man. And I had some bread and butter and sugar and milk. I wasn't bad."

"Those lunatics!" Julius exclaimed. "Do you wish to please your Uncle Julius, Gloria?"

Gloria nodded, still twisting her finger in the buttonhole.

"Well," Julius said, "you keep away from that house and those people in it."

"What are lunatics?" Gloria asked.

"Crazy people," Julius replied. "They're dangerous. If you are going to be my little girl you must promise me never to go to that house any more."

"It was fun," Gloria said. "We laughed."

"Who laughed? Who are 'we'?"

"Thomas Kane, the little boy that lives in that house over there," Gloria said, pointing. "He's a blond," she added.

"Do you like him?" Julius asked.

Gloria bobbed her head slowly, her eyes on Julius's face. When he looked displeased, she wrapped both arms around his neck.

"No I don't, Uncle Julius," she said. "I don't like anybody —only you."

After Gloria went to bed that night, Julius, in his room, told Josie the adventures of the afternoon.

"Gloria has got to come right home from school," he asserted. "And she must be kept away from the bad influences in this neighborhood. Now I'm going to hold you responsible."

The next evening, just before dinner, Martin Brady, about forty, five feet nine and thickset, with straw-colored hair and eyebrows, pale blue eyes under white lashes, was in the living room when Julius Fleeter and Gloria entered hand-in-hand.

Martin arose, adjusted a lavender tie against a pink shirt, brushed an imaginary speck of dust from the sleeve of a crisply pressed blue suit, and showed two rows of solid, yellowish teeth in a grin that distended his pink, clean-shaven cheeks.

"Here I am, Julius," he said, pale eyes resting on Julius's close-set gray ones. "If you hadn't neglected to give me the address after inviting me to be a member of the establishment I'd of been here sooner."

"Hello, Martin, I'm glad to see you," Julius said evenly. "I would have given you the address, only as it turned out there isn't any extra room."

He turned to Gloria, just behind him in the doorway.

"You may run along, Gloria. I am going to have a talk with this gentleman."

Martin Brady's gaze encountered Gloria's curious eyes. He took a deep breath and turned to Julius.

"Why, Julius," he said pleasantly. "Don't you think it would be nice to introduce me to the little girl?"

He stepped forward, took Gloria's hand, and bowed slightly over it.

"I'm Martin Brady, Gloria," he said. "Who's pretty little girl are you?"

"I'm Gloria Boyd," Gloria said, her dark blue eyes solemn.

"Jumping Catfish!" Martin Brady exclaimed, looking up at Julius quickly. "Eddie's little sister."

"You may run along now, Gloria," Julius Fleeter exclaimed.

Gloria took a step to Julius and held up her mouth for a kiss. Julius hesitated and bent and pressed his mustache against her lips. She looked at Martin Brady again, and then skipped from the room. Julius closed the door.

"Why, you bastard," Martin Brady said, fingering his lavender tie again with a hand on which shone a big diamond. "Up to your old tricks—robbing the cradle."

Julius Fleeter clenched his hands until the knuckles were white. Then he relaxed.

"Not so loud," he cautioned. "And be more careful of the names you apply to me."

"You son-of-a-bitch," Martin Brady said pleasantly, pale

eyes resting on Julius's face speculatively. "You homely old son-of-a-bitch. Some day you'll hang, and I hope I'll be there to see it."

Julius Fleeter's face became bleak. Lines usually obscure suddenly dominated his face—evil lines of stealth and cunning; vicious lines of self-indulgence and deceit. He took one step forward.

"That's enough, Martin," he snapped.

Martin Brady grinned again, but without mirth.

"The mother was the game; and now it's the daughter," he said. "A verr-rry prett-tty little arrangement."

"I'm not responsible for any construction you may choose to apply to the situation," Julius said.

Martin, lighting a cigarette which he had taken from a gold case, puffed a haze of smoke, waved his hand, sparkling with diamond glitter, through it and shook his head.

"Still talk like a schoolmaster, don't you, Julius? You get hold of a little girl that's the whole damned Ziegfeld Follies rolled into one—for what? Sure, I know, just for the pleasure of hearing her call you 'Uncle.' You are 'Uncle', ain't you? Uncle Julius! Holy Jumping Catfish! It's lucky I have a strong stomach."

"If you've finished with your nonsense, Martin," Julius Fleeter said severely, "perhaps you'll allow me to talk for a moment."

"Go ahead," Martin said, sitting down again. "Take your time. Talk a lot. It's always a pleasure to listen to you—even if it's impossible to believe you."

Julius remained standing.

"This is the situation," Julius said. "Edward's sister, Josephine, about whom you know, wanted to have her six children with her. Well, I am very fond of Josephine; in fact, between you and me, I may say we are contemplating marriage."

"The old army game," Martin interjected. "Go ahead." Julius frowned.

"I am telling the plain truth," he continued. "And none of your remarks, engendered of a dirty mind, can change the truth."

"Hear! Hear! The schoolmawster is talkin'."

"The six children are here, and Edward and I are living with them and Josie, and paying for our board and room. I am interested in all of the children, naturally."

Martin rose to his feet and shook down his trousers.

"Where's an ash tray?" he asked, looking around.

He went over to a fern in the bay window and crushed out his cigarette end in the loam.

"Anyway," he said, "it's going to be a damned interesting place to live. I'm going to like it."

"We'd be glad to have you, Martin," Julius replied. "But there's no room—all the rooms are taken. I'm sorry."

"Don't be sorry," Martin Brady said. "Josie has fixed me up fine. My room ain't as good as yours, but it'll do."

Julius balled his hands into fists again.

"I'm Uncle Martin," Martin Brady said, lighting a fresh cigarette.

Chapter 5

UNCLE MARTIN BRADY slipped easily into the family life of the Boyds. He rose about noon and Josie served coffee and orange juice in his room. Then he left the house, returning when every one else was asleep.

One day he left with two bags in a cab, and did not return for two months. After that he was away frequently. He talked of Saratoga, Belmont, New Orleans, Havana, Louisville.

"Is Uncle Martin a traveling man?" Gloria asked after he had been living in the house a year.

"He's a bookmaker," Uncle Edward said.

Gloria looked puzzled.

"How does he make books?" she asked.

Uncle Julius frowned at Edward over the top of the *Evening Sun.*

"Of course, he doesn't make books, as you understand it, Gloria. But he is interested in books. That is what Edward meant."

"Oh," Gloria said, glancing from Edward to Julius, dubiously.

"What do you do, Uncle Julius?" she asked. "You own a bank, don't you?"

Uncle Edward said:

"He shears lambs and spears suckers, Baby."

Then Edward snickered. Uncle Julius tossed his newspaper aside and took Gloria on his lap.

"Your Uncle Edward doesn't know it," he said, "but unless he is careful he is likely to lose his position—and what do you think the pool parlors and the dance halls would do then?"

"Aw Cheese, I was only foolin'," Edward said.

Julius paid no attention to him.

"Your Uncle Julius deals in stocks and bonds, Gloria," he said. "He buys for some people and sells for others; and he is paid a fee for doing it. Now that is all."

"What are stocks and bonds?" Gloria asked.

While Julius was trying to explain, Edward, clad in a gray checkered suit cut in the latest collegiate fashion, according to Broadway, arose and went out. Edward never read anything except the sports pages and dramatic columns. He knew all the vaudeville headliners and motion picture stars, pugilists and baseball players by name and family as well as professional history. But he thought Willie Hoppe was the greatest genius of the age. Hitched to the butt end of a billiard cue, Edward became for the moment the outward presentiment of a man with a purpose.

Gloria didn't learn much in school. Immaculately dressed, black curls flowing over her shoulders, placidly lovely, she arrived early at the red brick building four blocks away. She had blue, green and yellow hair ribbons with socks to match, and always wore patent leather pumps. Usually she carried with her an apple or an orange for her teacher. In the spring and fall she gave her teacher flowers. She sat quietly during recitations, blue eyes directed affectionately on the teacher. When the blue eyes looked eager the teacher called on her. The women teachers through the grades up to the last in the grammar school, where the teacher was Thaddeus Coffee, all loved her. Gloria came under Mr. Coffee's supervision in 1916 when she was thirteen.

Thaddeus Coffee had a small round head covered with silky, black hair, parted neatly on the left side, almond-shaped hazel eyes, big shoulders which he shrugged nervously during conversation, twisting his head over to one side at the same time. He wrote a very fine script, marvelously neat and legible. He went to concerts and lectures, where he took notes. He was thirty-eight and a bachelor. His library included Dr. Eliot's

Five Foot Shelf, *In His Steps,* the Charles Dudley Warner Library of the World's Best Literature, Henry Van Dyck's *The Other Wise Man,* the *Oxford Book of English Verse,* the *Rubaiyat* (in limp leather), James Whitcomb Riley's *An Old Sweetheart of Mine,* a set of Dickens, a set of George Eliot, a set of Shakespeare, the *Decameron,* and a set of Balzac, including the *Droll Stories* in two volumes, illustrated. He subscribed to the *Atlantic Monthly* and the *National Geographic Magazine,* smoked a cigar rarely and inexpertly, and took great interest in the moral welfare of the boys and girls in his public school class and the boys in his Sunday School class.

He invited the boys to visit him at his parlor, bedroom and bath, or rather, study, bedroom and bath, and asked them in a high, husky tenor if they had anything on their consciences; if they had any problems in which they needed sympathy and help; if, in other words, they indulged in any boyish habits that might be undermining their health. To sum it all up, did they play with themselves.

He never invited the girls to his rooms, naturally, but he kept them after school in order to have intimate little talks with them about morals and religion; about kissing each other and allowing boys to be too familiar with them. His eyes always shone and his brown cheeks always flushed with holy zeal during these interviews. He made no secret of his belief that it was a splendid idea to promote the growth of the mind, but that the chief duty of a teacher charged with the sacred task of caring for the immature was to safeguard the morals, to stimulate the immortal soul.

Thaddeus Coffee was to a great extent self-educated. He had suffered a great deal to obtain his bachelor's degree, and had just won his master's. At the moment he was taking outside courses at Columbia University on the trail of a Ph.D. Being principal in a grammar school in Brooklyn was only a step on his road to the more lofty peaks of pedagogy. He had waited on table at the University of Michigan and at Harvard, and knew men, and above all, women chiefly from books.

When Gloria left an apple on Mr. Coffee's desk one crisp morning in November, he smiled, twitched his head, shrugged his shoulders, and said:

"Thank you, Gloria. I wonder if you could arrange to remain after the other young people have gone this afternoon. I should like to have a little talk with you."

Gloria's eyes, clear and dark and blue, strangely giving the effect of expectancy and promise, met his hazel ones squarely. A faint additional tinge of red showed in her cheeks.

"Yes, sir," she said.

Gloria put on her hat and coat with the other girls, but returned to the classroom instead of going home. Thaddeus Coffee was waiting. The white shades had been drawn; he closed the door.

"Sit right here near me," he said, "where we can talk more comfortably. I like to know my pupils."

Gloria sat down quietly gazing at him.

"Perhaps you had better take off your things," he suggested. "It is hot in here and cold out-of-doors."

Gloria obediently rose and let him help her with her coat. He laid the coat on his desk, cleared his throat and smiled.

"You have two brothers and two sisters, have you not, Gloria?" he asked, as soon as they were seated close together, he at his desk, she beside him.

"I have three brothers and two sisters, Mr. Coffee."

"Oh, yes. I only knew of the two—George and little Malcolm."

"My big brother George works in New York."

"I understand your father is dead," Mr. Coffee said, sympathy in his tone.

Gloria shook her head from side to side.

"He ran away with a blonde," she replied, "when we were living in Jersey City."

"And who looks after you all?" Mr. Coffee asked, jerking his head to one side and shrugging his shoulders.

"My mother," Gloria said. "And my Uncle Julius and my

Uncle Martin live with us, too, but Uncle Martin goes away a lot."

"Are these uncles your mother's brothers or your father's brothers?" he asked.

Gloria looked puzzled and uncomfortable. Mr. Coffee repeated the question.

"I don't know," Gloria said, flushing, her lower lip trembling a little. "They are just my uncles."

"I see," Mr. Coffee said vaguely, leaning forward in his chair. "I don't want to make you nervous or to seem to be prying into your affairs, my dear child. I only want to help you in any way I can. You know that, don't you?"

Gloria nodded affirmatively, eyes, big and dark, on his.

"Are your uncles kind to you?" Mr. Coffee asked.

"Yes, sir, specially my Uncle Julius."

"Do you play with the other little boys and girls?"

Gloria hesitated and made a faint negative gesture with her head.

"My Uncle Julius doesn't like me to play with boys," she said. "And I went to the Kanes' camp last summer and he made me come home. He likes me to be home when I'm not in school. And I shouldn't stay after school too long either, because he likes for me to come right straight home."

"Well! Well! Your uncle is pretty careful of you, isn't he?"

Gloria didn't answer this question—merely kept her eyes on Mr. Coffee's, her red lips parted just enough to show white teeth. Mr. Coffee moved his head and shoulders in characteristic gesture.

"Do you help your mother with the housework?"

"No, I don't," Gloria said. "Uncle Julius says I am not to work and my mama doesn't want me to."

Mr. Coffee looked at the blackboard and then back to Gloria.

"I suppose many people tell you you are pretty?"

"Yes," Gloria said. "They do. My Uncle Julius says I am a little doll."

59

"Do boys kiss you?"

"No, but my Uncle Julius does all the time," Gloria said. "I had better be going now."

She slid out of the chair and stood up, a tall little girl, slim, but oddly mature physically, her breasts standing out clearly under her waist. Mr. Coffee also stood up, straightening his trouser legs awkwardly. Gloria's face, white and rose, was almost on a level with his; her breath, sweet and warm, reached him. Her lips were soft; her eyes invited. He put his arm around her and kissed her. She pressed her body against his.

Shouts of a boy in the street came dimly through the closed windows, the honk of an automobile horn. Footsteps sounded loudly in the hall. Mr. Coffee suddenly released Gloria and stepped back. His eyes glassy, his hands trembling. He picked up Gloria's coat and held it for her.

"We will continue our little chat at another time, Gloria," he said.

Gloria's breath was hurried, her pupils dilated. She started slightly when the doorknob rattled and the door opened to reveal Prescott, the janitor.

"Oh, I didn't know you were still here, Mr. Coffee," the janitor said.

"We were just leaving, Prescott," Mr. Coffee said, smiling. "Come right in."

If Julius Fleeter took a taxicab instead of the trolley from his office at night he always got out of the cab at the trolley stop where Gloria met him. On her daily trips to meet Julius Gloria became great friends with Policeman Michael James Duff.

Mike Duff was just six feet and weighed one hundred and ninety pounds, stripped. He was thirty-six, and had been a policeman four years. He had mouse-colored hair, slate-gray eyes, a broken nose, a crumpled right ear, of the type called cauliflower in the athletic set, and a solid, wide jaw like a

60

granite rock. White seams of old scars marred his cheeks. He was unmarried and lived with his mother.

"Me mother," he told Gloria, "is a grreat, big Irish lady; an' th' reason I'm so shtrong mesilf is doo t' th' fact me mother suckled me at th' breast until I was two-year-old."

Mike Duff had fought in Mexico and in Central America. When he bared his head one afternoon to put in his hat a cigar just given him by a citizen, Gloria exclaimed:

"And how did you get that scar in your hair, Mr. Duff?"

"Sure, Darlin'," Mike Duff said, "that's where a Colonel av th' Forin' Legin slapped me over the head wit' a sabre."

"Didn't it hurt?" Gloria asked.

"God bless ye, Darlin', I was so plased wit' havin' socked th' Colonel in th' jaw I didn't notice at th' time. But it ached me some later. They put me in jail after that, but I escaped two days afther an' it was in th' Turkish Navy I got this wan."

He turned his head and pointed with a big finger to a long white line down the side of his face.

Mike told Gloria of his escape from prison in a few words.

"There was nothin' to it," he said. "Th' shtories av th' Forin' Legin arre mostly th' bunk."

Mike preferred to tell Gloria fairy stories, which began "Wanst upon a time." He and Dr. J. L. Pearson were the only men Gloria admired and with whom she came in daily contact who hadn't kissed her, or felt of her legs and arms and breasts.

Her Uncle Julius kissed her, and hugged her, and rubbed her gently; and even had started slipping to her room after she was in bed and Adelaide hadn't come in, and lying down with her and hugging her.

Her Uncle Martin Brady made no secret of his pleasure in kissing her and hugging her. He always smelled of whisky and cigars, and he made Uncle Julius mad by snatching her up and kissing her cheeks and eyes and mouth.

Even Edward, her real uncle, pawed her and kissed her

whenever he could find her alone. But she always ran away from her Uncle Edward.

"I hate you," she told him.

When Gloria was sick, which was infrequently, Josie called Dr. J. L. Pearson. He was only forty-two but already looked tired from getting out of bed in the middle of the night and climbing interminable flights of stairs day and night, and working through influenza epidemics when he had a higher fever than any of his patients. He was of medium height, compactly built, with black curly hair, beginning to recede at the temples, brown eyes with dark pouches under them, and one of those beards which show like a blue smudge under the skin after a close shave and resemble a shoe brush a few minutes afterwards. When Dr. Pearson told Gloria to take cascarets she promised she would, and then threw them under her bed when no one was looking.

Adelaide, who was only one grade ahead of Gloria, stopped going to High School and went to work as a model in New York. Adelaide smudged dark make-up around her dark eyes, tinted her blonde hair even lighter than nature had, and added red to her cheeks and lips.

When Adelaide came home, mostly after midnight, and sometimes slightly unsteady on her feet, Gloria lay in bed and watched her undress. Adelaide bound her breasts in tight brassières.

Gloria appropriated a brassière one morning and smothered her breasts, naturally full and elastic and magnets for men's eyes, in it. She looked at the result in the mirror, and her eyes beamed satisfaction. At breakfast Josie exclaimed:

"Why, Gloria, what have you done to yourself? You've been using rouge—that's what you've been doing. You go straight upstairs and wash it off."

Gloria pouted. Uncle Julius looked up from his breakfast *Times*. Gloria gazed hopefully at him. Julius smiled.

"Don't be harsh with the Baby, Josie," he said. "She didn't know she was using too much of the stuff, or that she is still too young. She'll go upstairs and wash it all off before she goes to school—won't you, Beautiful?"

After that Gloria was more cautious with the rouge.

When Julius stayed in New York one Saturday afternoon in January, Gloria went with Thomas Kane to the Parkview Theatre. They held hands in the dark. Gloria leaned gently against Thomas and looked at him more than she looked at the screen. She turned her face up, lips slightly parted, waiting. Thomas stirred uneasily and took his hand from hers. Gloria pouted. On the way home, Thomas said:

"What are you mad at me for, Gloria? Did I do anything?"

"No," Gloria said.

Thomas was one of those humans who fail to realize that not doing anything is one of the most heinous offenses possible. He and Gloria always wrote each other notes in school and met whenever they could secretly. But except once, when Gloria kissed him unexpectedly, the nearest they got to close communion was holding hands.

Gloria never failed to run in to see Madame Cele and Lord Frederick whenever Uncle Julius was away on business, which was at irregular intervals. On one such occasion Julius kissed her good-by at the cab in front of the house and handed her a dollar.

"Promise me you'll be a good little girl," he said.

"Yes," Gloria replied, eyes wide and full on his.

As soon as the cab was out of sight, she walked quickly down the street, asphalt paved, tar walked, with straggling young maple trees set in round holes in the tar. At the corner she turned, and continued to Madame Cele's.

Lord Frederick was on the front porch, collarless, in shirt sleeves, suspenders, trousers and bedroom slippers, mopping sweat engendered by August heat from his forehead, and waving a palm leaf fan. The parrots in their cage beside him cocked shining eyes at Gloria.

"How do you do?" Lord Frederick said. "I trust you will pardon me if I remain seated."

Gloria smiled, and walked up the steps.

"You are very beautiful, Child," Lord Frederick said. "Very beautiful. You remind me of Dido, who had black hair and blue eyes, too. My friend Aeneas made a great fuss over her and then sailed away and left her inconsolable—poor creature. We all did our best to comfort her, gave her sweetmeats and flowers and mirrors and what not, but she was one of those one-gentleman ladies, which, alas, grow scarcer with the years. She was really a cultured gentlewoman."

Lord Frederick sighed. Gloria looked blank.

"Speaking of Aeneas made me think of Rome," he explained. "Aeneas had two sons, Romulus and Remus, who history says were nursed by a she-wolf, but I happen to know were nursed by a healthy, red-cheeked peasant girl, whose name I forget for the moment. But I knew her well. And Romulus grew up and had Rome named after him. But Rome didn't last long, my dear. You'll read a lot about Rome if you continue your education and read history; and you'll hear a great deal about it anyway. But, really, my recollection of it, looking back over thousands of years, is that it was just one of those disastrous experiments which man insists on making to prove that art is better than nature, and a steam-heated flat is superior to a cave in the forest. All nonsense, my dear. How much better it would have been for everybody if Aeneas had settled down like a sensible human being with Dido, had children, done a little hunting and fishing, read a little Homer, or listened to Dido play the harp. You wouldn't have had any Neros and Caligulas and Heliogabuluses—horrible specimens of the genus homo."

Lord Frederick shook his head sadly, his monocle gleaming as a stray shaft of sunlight, piercing the honeysuckle vine on the porch, found it.

Madame Cele, orange-red hair in disarray, green and orchid silk dressing gown wrapped around her, popped through the screen door.

"Hotsy Totsy!" she cried. "Come on in the house, Pretty, out of the sun. Has your Uncle Julius gone on a trip?"

"He went to Boston," Gloria said, stepping into the hall.

Lord Frederick with grunts and groans, arose from the chair and bowed.

"Your Highness!" he said.

"Your Excellency!" Madame Cele replied, making an elaborate curtsy.

Lord Frederick smiled happily.

"The old world manners; the old world customs," he said. "My friend—platonic, of course—Madame Pompadour, was not more graceful. I remember . . ."

"You will pardon, Lord Frederick," Madame said, "but I am just out of the tub."

Madame Cele opened and closed the dressing gown rapidly.

"Oh! Fie! Fie!" Lord Frederick exclaimed. "Little Salome dancing for Herod—a pretty enough girl, but disgustingly sadistic. I caught her several times pulling wings and heads from flies, and laughing at her poor victims' uncouth antics."

"Come on, Dolly," Madame Cele said, letting the screen door slam shut. "We'll get you some ginger ale and me some beer, and then we'll go upstairs. I must get dressed because Croquet is coming to call this afternoon. I've had my bath, and I'll get all perfumed and powdered and my silk panties and stockings on. That's what the men like, my dear."

She went to the kitchen, Gloria trailing. From the ice-box she took two bottles, from a cupboard two glasses.

"Now to find the damn' opener," she exclaimed.

Gloria sat in a kitchen chair, seven dogs poking cold noses at her. Fritzee was chained out in the yard.

"Is your Uncle Julius still playing his monkey tricks?" Madame Cele asked, rumpling hardware in a drawer.

"Yes," Gloria said.

Madame Cele snorted.

"Touching you all over, I suppose, just like they do?"

Gloria remained silent. Madame Cele turned around and took her by both arms and looked down into the blue eyes.

"Look here, Dolly," she said. "You promised me you would make that old degenerate behave himself. Does he still sneak into bed with you at night?"

Gloria's lips quivered but she didn't answer.

"And your other uncles—I suppose they are after you too. Dogs! Pigs! Oh! I could shake you. Why do you stand it? Tell me. Why don't you tell your mother? And that school teacher. He kisses and has his hands everywhere. Poor little girl. Poor little Dolly!"

Tears gathered in Gloria's eyes.

"I'm afraid," she said. "But Uncle Julius is going to marry me."

"That," Madame Cele cried, letting go of Gloria's arms and striking a dramatic pose, "that is what they all say. Listen! I myself will tell your mother."

"Oh, no. No! You can't! You promised!"

Madame Cele took a deep breath and spoke as if she were declaiming lines on the stage.

"You are *afraid?* Afraid of what? It is they who would be afraid if anybody knew of it. I told you everything so you could know what to do. And what do you do? *Hein?* Nothing! That's what you do. Nothing."

Suddenly, she relaxed, bent close to Gloria, one hand gentle on her shoulder, mouth close to Gloria's ear.

"Perhaps you like it when he makes love—NoOH?" she breathed, with a pleasant lingering on the word "like" which magically intensified its meaning.

Gloria raised her eyes to Madame, and then dropped them again. Madame Cele stood off a pace and gazed down, head to one side.

"Ahah! You do. I know. You lie there dreading, fearing that he will come—and afraid that he will not come. It is terrible; it is tragic, it is life. I understand. I have been like that my own self.

"I have known this was wrong. I have made up my mind I would not do it. But when he came, with his soft voice, his hot lips, his heart beats that I could hear, his hands—I did not think any more. It was just feeling with me—a singing in my head, red and black and gold, and the beeg river had little me. It is from that come the babees. I told you that before."

"I can't help it," Gloria said.

"You are only a little girl now, even if you are beeg. You should be playing games, dancing, singing, swimming, playing. You should not have this life. You should be with boys —not with old men. I will myself do something. You wait."

"I don't like boys," Gloria announced, wrinkling her nose. "They are dirty and sweaty. I like men who have manicures and shoes shined and have nice clothes."

Madame Cele tossed up her hands and did a dance step, with side kick.

"Hotsy Totsy!" she cried. "The poor little girls who are pretty that the men all hunt! Where is that damn' opener I wonder."

She pulled out another drawer.

"Ha! Here it is."

She pried caps from bottles, screwing up her mouth.

"We will have ice, *n'est-ce pas?*"

She went to the ice-box and chopped at the ice with a pick, took pieces to the sink, washed them, and dropped them into highball glasses. She filled one with ginger ale, and the other with beer.

"I like ice in my beer," she said, handing the ginger ale to Gloria, and lifting her glass.

They drank.

"Look at me, Baby," she said.

Gloria obeyed.

"I have told you everything about life—everything. But I do not think you understand—here."

67

Madame Cele pressed her left breast.

"You are very spoiled. You just sit and look pretty, and everything is done for you. But you are so sweet, I myself like to kiss you too. See?"

Madame Cele set her beer down on the sink board, and kissed Gloria resoundingly on each cheek, and then on the mouth.

"You are in the hands of Life," Madame said dramatically. "If there is trouble you must come to me—Madame Cele. Those damn' dogs!"

She gazed down at the seven dogs, nuzzling and pushing at Gloria for more petting. She stamped her foot.

"You bad babies! You all go to your beds and lie down."

Seven pairs of brown eyes focused on her for an instant, and then seven sadly wagging tails departed slowly in seven different directions.

The screen door in front slammed. A baritone voice, slightly cracked with age, but still musical, sang:

"Sola! Whoa Ho! Sola! Sola!"

"Croquet!" Madame Cele exclaimed. "And me that was going to be so all dressed up when he arrived."

She went to the kitchen door.

"I'm in the kitchen," she called.

"My Cinderella!" Croquet replied from the dining room.

He entered the hall, a tall, very thin, very dandified figure, with a perfectly bald, egg-shaped head, high arched black eyebrows under which yellow eyes sparkled, a short upturned nose, an extraordinarily wide expanse of shaven upper lip, and a wide, flexible mouth with thin lips. He wore a morning coat with a red rose in the buttonhole, striped trousers, patent leather shoes and white spats. He carried a bouquet of tea roses, whose dewy fragrance overcame for the instant the smells of dogs, parrots, monkey and pickled herring, which was the normal aroma of the kitchen. Croquet had been advertised as the most famous clown in the world. He now was retired.

"Croquet!" Madame Cele said, extending her hands, but

68

hastily withdrawing them to grab her sagging dressing gown.

Croquet bowed elegantly and held out the roses.

"I brought some posies," he said.

"They are beautiful," Madame Cele exclaimed, taking the flowers. "Give me a good kiss."

Croquet stooped, Cele stood on tiptoe, and they kissed.

"And the little beauty?" Croquet asked, smiling at Gloria.

"Oh, I am so sorry," Cele cried, turning and taking Gloria's hand. "This is Gloria Boyd, Croquet."

Gloria flushed a little, kept her blue eyes on Croquet's, and held out her hand. He took it, bent and kissed it.

"It is a pleasure," he said, "to meet such a beautiful little lady."

"I guess I'd better be going," Gloria said.

"Don't let me scare you away," Croquet protested.

Madame Cele put her head back and laughed.

"That little girl knows, Croquet. She knows more than you think. She is very sweet. Here is a kiss, Baby Doll. She knows I want to be with my Croquet, don't you, darling?"

Gloria smiled and held out her hand to Croquet.

"Good-by, Mr. Croquet," she said.

"Call me Uncle Croquet," he suggested, taking her hand in both of his. "I would like such a pretty niece."

"Oh!" Madame Cele screamed, laughing. "Oh! No, Croquet. No! No! NO! That little girl already has too many uncles. Is it not so, Baby Doll?"

"I guess so," Gloria said.

Chapter 6

ADELAIDE CAME home early one afternoon in the winter of 1917. She had on a new black coat with sable collar and cuffs. She met George in the hall on the second floor.

"Oh, Addie," he said, "just who I wanted to see. I've volunteered. Will you lend me twenty dollars?"

"Not on your life," Addie replied, one hand on the door knob of the room she and Gloria shared.

"Aw, Addie," George said. "Don't be so mean. I'm going to France probably, and I need the money bad."

"Well, you won't get it out of me," Addie said. "I haven't got it anyway."

She opened the door. George drew nearer. His eyes fell on the coat and roamed over it.

"Where did you get that coat?" he demanded.

"Don't you wish you knew?" Addie snapped, and would have closed the door except for the intervention of George's knee.

"You leave me alone now, George," Addie cried, her voice becoming shrill. "You get out of here. I've got to dress in a hurry."

George pushed the door open and followed her into the room. She tore the coat off and threw it on the bed, and began unhooking her dress, red silk.

"I've got to have twenty dollars, Addie," George said.

Adelaide was pulling the dress over her head. Curvy legs, plump backside, laced-in breasts—headless for a moment—she made a last wrench and tossed the dress on a chair. Slip, brassière, undershirt followed. Adelaide, in pink silk panties, black silk stockings, and patent leather pumps, faced her brother. She never had worried at all about whether or not she had anything on when appearing before members of the household.

"You get out of here, George," she said. "You make me sick. You're nothing but a bum. You never paid back five cents you owed anybody in your life."

George's pale cheeks remained sallow, but his eyes became bloodshot.

"Why, you God damn' little whore!" he shouted, clenching his fists. "A fine sister you are! Chasing around with men and getting money and diamond watches and fur coats out of 'em, and then tellin' your brother he's a bum. You dirty little whore! I've half a mind to knock your block off."

Adelaide screamed, the cords on her neck standing out. She picked up a hairbrush and threw it at George. It hit the panel of the door and clattered to the floor. George advanced towards her.

"You whore!" he sneered. "Comin' home cockeyed mornings. Why you're no more a model than I am, you dirty little bitch. Walkin' around the house with no clothes on. I'll teach you."

Adelaide picked up a nail file.

"You touch me and see," she panted.

Josie's voice came from the hall.

"Georgie! Addie! Please! What's the matter?"

Josie appeared behind George at the door.

"What's the matter, George?" she repeated.

"Matter!" Adelaide cried hysterically. "He wanted to borrow money from me, the dirty bum, and when I wouldn't give it to him he called me awful names."

"I called her a dirty little whore," George said defiantly to Josie. "And I should think you'd be ashamed of yourself to let a daughter live in the house and run around the way she does. Look at that diamond watch. Look at that new fur coat."

"You'd just as soon be a pimp and take my money," Addie screamed. "If you'd got the money you wouldn't have cared. Pimp! That's what you are."

Moisture welled in Josie's still youthful blue eyes. She pressed her left hand, worn with work but still white and shapely, under her plump left breast. She grasped George by the coat sleeve with her right hand.

"That ends it," George said. "Nobody can call me a pimp and get away with it."

He struggled, with outward ferocity, to pull from his mother's grasp.

"Ha! Ha! Ha!" Adelaide laughed with mirthless venom. "You make me laugh. You hate to hear the truth. That's the trouble."

"Oh, Georgie," Josie pleaded. "Please, Georgie. Your own sister Addie—my babies."

"A fine mother you turned out to be!" George stormed, weak face wearing a wild expression. "Look at your daughter. Look at the fambly! I suppose Gloria'll be on the turf next."

"Oh, Georgie," Josie panted. "Please stop. You're out of your head."

"A fine example you set," George raved. "First it was Julius Fleeter and now it's Martin Brady. Maybe it's both of 'em. This is a hell of a fambly."

Gloria stood down in the front hall listening, face pale, eyes dark and wide, lower lip trembling. Malcolm came from the direction of the kitchen and stood close beside her.

"What is it?" he whispered. "Addie and George havin' a fight?"

"Mama is there," Gloria whispered. "I'm so frightened. What'll we do?"

Malcolm, fifteen, and tall for his age, grew tense. Josie's voice came down the stair well.

"Don't, Georgie! Please *don't.*"

Her plea ended in a wail and the sound of a falling body. Malcolm laid one hand on the newel post and ran upstairs three steps at a time. Gloria began to weep silently. Josie was lying on the threshold of the bedroom. George was bending over her, a scared expression on his face. Malcolm hit George in the chin, sending him off balance.

"Hit Mama, will you?" Malcolm cried. "Hit Mama, will you?"

He began to sob and kneeled down beside Josie. She looked at him, face pale and contracted.

"Don't cry, Malcolm," Josie said. "George didn't hit me. I have such a terrible pain—my indigestion."

"I'll get the ginger an' soda for you, Ma," Malcolm said. "What was George doin'?"

He glanced up and saw Adelaide.

"Aw, for cripe's sake!" he exclaimed. "Why don't you keep covered up, Addie?"

"What do you all come runnin' in my room for?" Addie asked. "That's what I wanta know. My God! If I can't have any privacy I'll move."

Josie moaned, her eyes rolled, and she moved her body stiffly as if in agony.

"It hurts," she gasped.

Malcolm jumped to his feet.

"I'll run and get the soda, Ma," he said. "How do you fix it?"

"A half-teaspoonful in a little hot water," Josie said, rolling her head, and gasping. "Kettle is on the stove."

Malcolm ran out of the room and slid down the banisters.

"Ma's got indigestion," he said to Gloria. "I got to get her some soda."

He ran down the hall towards the kitchen. Gloria waited at the foot of the stairs. When Malcolm returned with a tumbler in his right hand, walking carefully but quickly, she followed him upstairs. George was on the floor, holding Josie's head. Adelaide was standing, looking down.

"Here's the soda, Ma," Malcolm said.

"Gimme it," George directed, reaching for the glass. "This'll make you feel better," he said, raising her head with his right arm and holding the soda to her lips with his left hand. Josie drank, made a face, gasped:

"I—never—was—so—sick."

"Want us to carry you to your room?" Malcolm asked.

"I—just want to—be left alone, thanks."

Tears dripped down Gloria's face. She caught her breath heavily. Josie saw her for the first time and smiled.

"I'm—all right—Baby," she said. "Don't cry."

"Oh, Mother!" Gloria wailed and plumped down beside her.

"Aw, criminy!" Malcolm said. "Women're a mess."

"I should think you'd get a doctor, Ma," Adelaide said. "Those attacks might be dangerous."

"What was you eatin'?" George asked.

"I bet it was those pork chops for dinner," Malcolm said. "Pork is greasy."

"She's been havin' gas bad," George said. "There's somethin' she eats that don't agree with her, all right. You should be more careful what you eat, Ma."

Josie looked at them from beneath partly closed lids, face gray, looking almost as young as, and more helpless than her children. She was thinner than she had been ten years before, but still pretty, kind eyes, smooth face, sweet mouth—a creature made for love and cheerful service.

"Go call the doctor, Malcolm," Adelaide said. "That's the only thing to do."

Josie shook her head painfully.

"No," she said, "I'll be all right. I'll take an enema."

Five minutes later, George and Malcolm helped her to her feet.

"You'd better go in your room and go to bed," Malcolm said.

"I'm all right," Josie said in a stronger tone. "I can't go to bed. Who'd get the supper? What time is it?"

"It's twenty minutes to six," George said, after glancing at his Ingersoll.

"Mercy!" Josie said, hands going instinctively to her blonde and still luxuriant hair. "I had no idea it was so late. The men will be home any minute."

"And for Christ's sake, here I am late for my date," Adelaide cried. "Come on! Get out of here, will you, everybody? Give me a chance. And keep out of the bathroom for five minutes."

She stepped out of her pants, kicked off her pumps, and began to peel down her stockings.

"Hey wait a minute, can't you?" Malcolm yelled. "For criminy sake!"

"Keep the hell out of the way then," Adelaide retorted.

"I wish you would be more modest, Addie," Josie said, speaking with an effort.

"Modest, hell!" Addie replied. "What would that get me—the city hall steps?"

Josie sighed as Adelaide, snatching fresh underwear from a dresser drawer and holding it in front of her, pushed through the doorway, stepped across the hall to the bathroom, and slammed the door.

"Don't mind her, she's a bum," George comforted.

"Oh, I wish you wouldn't speak that way of your sister, Georgie," Josie said. "Why can't all my babies be sweet to each other?"

A scream came from the bathroom, mingled with the sound of water running in the tub.

"A towel," Adelaide yelled. "My God! I never come into this God forsaken can without finding myself without a towel or toilet paper or something. Ma! Ma!"

She opened the bathroom door, letting steam trickle into the hall.

"Don't you ever think anybody might want to take a bath?" she exclaimed.

"I'll get you one, Addie," Josie said. "I guess I must of been busy."

Gloria ran to a closet down the hall and came back in an instant with a towel. Adelaide snatched it and slammed the door again. The others went downstairs.

"Nobody seems to care if I'm going away to-morrow," George said. "I could get killed in France and a lot this family would care."

Josie's eyes filled with tears. She stopped in the hall and put her arms around George.

"How can you talk that way, Georgie?" she asked. "My first baby! I had an awful hard time having you, Georgie."

"Aw, tie that stuff, Ma," George protested. "All you dames had an awful time, but you kep' right on doin' it."

"I love you to death, Georgie," Josie said, hugging him. "Give your mama a kiss."

George kissed her hastily on the cheek.

"Love is all right, Ma," he said, "but what I need is twenty bucks. This is my last night."

"And you're goin' to stay home with me, aren't you, Georgie?"

George laughed uneasily.

"What would I do at home?" he asked. "Fight with the rest of the fambly? Naw! I gotta go out, an' I've gotta have twenty bucks."

"I wish you'd stay home just to-night, Georgie," Josie said. "It would make me feel happy."

"Aw, you're always workin', Ma," George said, "in the kitchen, or sewin' somethin', or darnin'. You'd never know I was around."

"I won't do anythin' to-night after the dishes—and you could help me with those."

"Yes, I could," George said, grinning for the first time. "You caught me that way once or twice when I was too young to know better. But no more. Gee! I gotta get twenty bucks somewhere."

"I'll give you the twenty dollars, Georgie," Josie said. "I've got some money saved."

"Oh, Gees, Ma!" George said, kissing her heartily and hugging her. "I always says you're won'erful. You couldn't make it forty, could you, Ma?"

"I haven't that much, Georgie," Josie said. "I was savin' up for a new suit for Ernie and a birthday present for Adelaide."

"A birthday present for that bum. My God!"

"Please, Georgie!"

"Well, gimme the twenty then, Ma. I can make it do."

"After supper, Georgie."

"For cripe's sake! I need it now, Ma. Get it now, will you, Ma?"

"But you're goin' to eat supper home, ain't you, Georgie? Your last night? I'm havin' roast chicken and giblet gravy, just on your account, Georgie."

"I'd like to, Ma, but I gotta be out—it's my last night. Hustle and get the twenty, Ma."

"I've got it hid out in the pantry, Georgie."

"You'd better hide it with that little sneak, Frank, around. He'd swipe the gold outa your teeth."

"Frank is your brother, Georgie."

"Cripes! That's your fault, not mine."

Josie sighed again and opened the door at the end of the hall, which led through the pantry to the kitchen. She took a tea tin from a shelf, opened it, and took out some bills.

"You got more than twenty there, Ma."

"But that's all I can spare. I wish it was a thousand. Here, Georgie. And be a good boy, won't you?"

George took the money and stuffed it into his pocket. He kissed Josie hastily.

"Thanks," he said. "So long."

"You'll be home early, won't you?"

"Oh, sure," George replied, grabbing his hat from the rack and opening the front door.

Frank, thirteen, ran in at the same moment.

"Oh, Ma," Frank said. "There's a big automobile just stopped in front. It's an old man after Adelaide. Gee! It's a big one. Come on and look."

"That's where your daughter gets her fur coats," George called back over his shoulder. "My God! I'm glad I'm gettin' outa this."

As he walked down the front steps, a distinguished-looking, gray-haired man in black derby, black overcoat, and black shoes, carrying a malacca stick, was just getting out of the car. George looked back as the black derbied one ascended the Boyds' steps.

"You answer the bell, Gloria," Josie said. "Tell the gentleman Addie will be right down."

"I don't want to," Gloria said.

The bell rang and Frank opened the door. The visitor removed his derby, and bowed to Gloria. He was slim, of medium height, with grizzled hair, a long, thin, red face, a long curved nose, and predatory dark eyes. The eyes glowed as they rested on Gloria.

"Good evening," he said, stepping across the threshold. "You are Adelaide's younger sister, I presume," he continued, addressing Gloria. "She hadn't told me that she had such a beautiful little sister concealed around somewhere. My name is Cooper Patten."

"Pleased to meet you, Mr. Patten," Gloria murmured, big eyes on his. "Won't you step into the sitting room? My sister is getting dressed. She'll be right down."

Malcolm and Frank stood a few feet away, staring, while the man with the derby, by dropping back politely, arranged it so that Gloria preceded him into the living room.

"What is your name?" Mr. Patten asked.

"Gloria Boyd."

"A beautiful name for a beautiful girl," Mr. Patten said, smiling. "And just sweet sixteen."

"No, I'm not," Gloria said. "I'm fourteen."

"Won't you sit down, Gloria?" Mr. Patten said.

78

Gloria sat down and ran her tongue over her lips in the manner of her mother meeting strangers. Mr. Patten pulled off his overcoat, revealing a fur lining. He had a fur-and-silk appearance: very smart, much more elegant than Julius Fleeter. His suit, his shirt, his cravat, his shoes, his socks all looked as if they had been made for him at great expense. Gloria was wide-eyed.

"You are only fooling when you say you are fourteen, aren't you, Gloria?" Mr. Patten asked, after a quick glance around the room, with the fern in the bay window, the mahogany finish bookcase holding a half-dozen standard sets of classics, and odds and ends of novels, the big green velvet chair in which Julius Fleeter always sat, the red silk-covered chair in which Gloria now was seated, the mahogany rocking chair with the doily, the green velvet couch on which Mr. Patten and his marvelous overcoat were resting, the love seat near the folding doors which shut off the dining room, the three straight-backed chairs upholstered in red, the card table on which Martin Brady played solitaire, and the black marble mantelpiece and fireplace with gas logs.

"I will be fifteen next February seventh," Gloria said. "But everybody thinks I am older. I even get taken for eighteen."

Mr. Patten's eyes ran over Gloria's dainty ankles, slim, shapely, straight-hung legs, and returned over the same route, past her vigorous young bosom and white neck to her face, with red cheeks, red lips, white teeth, and dark blue eyes, shadowed by black hair. He took a deep breath.

"By Gad!" he ejaculated. "But you *are* a beauty. I guess it would be impossible to hide you anywhere except in Brooklyn, People that live here don't seem even to know the name of the street a block away from the one they live on."

"Oh, I know all the streets," Gloria said, blushing a little, and at the same time making a little pout of her lips at his admiration for her.

"Would you go for a ride with me some time?" Mr. Patten asked, lowering his voice and glancing into the hall.

Gloria shook her head.

"Oh, I couldn't," she said. "Adelaide will be right down."

One of Mr. Patten's predatory eyes vanished under a quickly lowered eyelid. The other eye gave an impression of four times as much boldness.

"We can fix it so Adelaide won't know anything about it," he said hurriedly in a whisper and looked at her with both eyes again.

Gloria moved uneasily in her chair, her cheeks pink, eyes starry. Quick steps sounded on the stairs.

"Here's Adelaide now," Gloria said, rising nervously.

Adelaide, plenty of artificial shadow around her dark eyes, plenty of rouge on her cheeks, and lipstick on her lips, blonde hair showing under a little black hat, ran into the room in an aura of perfume. She flashed a venomous glance at Gloria and showed Mr. Patten a dazzling smile, as she held out an ungloved hand to him.

"Hello, Cooper," she said in her throaty voice. "I hope you'll excuse me for bein' late, but mother had indigestion, and the fambly was upside down."

Cooper Patten took her hand and smiled.

"I didn't mind at all, Addie," he said pleasantly. "Gloria entertained me while I was waiting, didn't you, Gloria?"

Adelaide strained a smile at him, and shot a hateful glance at Gloria.

"I trust your mother is feeling better," Cooper Patten said politely.

"Oh, she's all right," Adelaide replied. "She's gettin' supper ready now. Let's get a move on, Cooper."

She took him by the arm and smiled promisingly at him. Cooper turned, picked up his overcoat, and slid an arm into a sleeve. Adelaide held it for him. Both faced Gloria, standing by her chair. Adelaide scowled at Gloria; Cooper Patten winked solemnly at Gloria. While Mr. Patten was buttoning the coat, Adelaide took his arm again and urged him towards the door.

"Wait till I say good-by to Gloria," he said.

He stopped, hat in left hand, took Gloria's fingers in his right and bowed.

"Thank you for entertaining me while I waited, Gloria," he said, "and *au revoir.*"

"Good-by, Mr. Patten," Gloria said.

A moment later the motor roared outside, and all that was left of the visit was the odor of the heavy perfume Adelaide used.

With thousands of other last-minute volunteers George Boyd landed in New Rochelle, New York, next afternoon, and joined with them in piddling thousands of fanciful designs in the freshly banked snow along the sidewalks of that city—an unheralded preliminary of their approaching task of making the world safe for Democracy.

Chapter 7

GLORIA BOYD lay silently in her bed while Julius Fleeter, beside her, talked in whispers.

"You'll have to do it for both of us, Baby," he asserted. "All you've got to do is lead him a little and he will do the rest. And then you can tell him you're going to have a baby and he will marry you."

Gloria stifled a sob.

"There's nothing to cry about, Baby," Julius said. "You just wouldn't let me be careful. You had your own way, and now I've thought of a way out of it for us. If any one ever even dreamed of the truth we'd both go to jail."

Gloria moaned into her pillow.

"This Tommy Kane has been in love with you for years, hasn't he?" Julius asked.

Gloria's head moved uneasily in the darkened room.

"Well, he's a fortunate young man," Julius pointed out. "He doesn't know how fortunate he is. If it hadn't been for this accident—your getting in this condition—you never even would have considered him for a moment, would you, darling?"

"I—I—c-can't," Gloria whispered.

"Now listen, Gloria," Julius Fleeter rumbled in heavy undertone. "It's your fault, isn't it, that we have to face this situation? You tried to make me lose control of myself, didn't you? Tell me! Didn't you?"

"Yes," Gloria replied faintly.

"And you trust your Uncle Julius, don't you? You know if

you do what he says everything will come out all right, don't you?"

"Yes," Gloria said.

"All right," Julius Fleeter announced firmly. "You do what I say then. You'll find it won't be half as difficult as you think. You just give him the chance, and then I'll tell you what to do next."

"B-but why don't you m-marry me—like you always said, Uncle Julius?"

Julius Fleeter sighed resignedly.

"I've already explained to you, Gloria, a half-dozen times, that while you are as young as you are such a thing is utterly impossible. Don't you realize, Baby, that I love you more than anybody or anything in the world? And haven't I always told you that when you got older you and I would be married—that I was waiting for you? But you couldn't wait."

Gloria stirred in the sheets and drew a long, shuddering breath.

"I'm afraid," she whispered.

Uncle Julius took her in his arms and kissed her.

"You haven't anything to be afraid of, Baby," he said. "Uncle Julius will look after you. You trust Uncle Julius, don't you?"

Gloria put warm, sweet-smelling arms around his neck, and kissed him with moist lips.

"You're so beautiful," Julius Fleeter said, kissing her harder.

A half-hour later when he heard Adelaide's key in the lock of the front door, Julius Fleeter rose silently.

"Good night," he said softly. "You'll see everything will be all right. Don't worry."

Then he pushed the door open gently and stepped into the hall. Adelaide already was half-way up the stairs, so he quietly went into the bathroom. An aroma of alcohol surrounded Adelaide. She stumbled at the top step and giggled. She entered the room she and Gloria shared and bumped against a chair.

"Ouch!" she cried.

She switched on a light over the dresser, took a key from her bag, and after three unsuccessful attempts pushed it in the lock of the top drawer. She drew some bills from the bag, hesitated, took a step and swung shut the bedroom door, and then put the bills in the drawer, closed it, and turned the key. She winked at herself in the mirror. Gloria watched her through drooped eyelashes.

As soon as Adelaide closed the door, Julius Fleeter went silently from the bathroom to his room in the front of the house, the best room of all, and went to bed.

Adelaide rose first in the morning, pressed her hands to her head and groaned. Gloria opened her eyes and smiled at her.

"That's right—laugh!" Adelaide said. "Oh, Christ! My head. I'll bet I never drink any ginger ale highballs again. I never drink ginger ale without feeling terrible in the morning."

"I wasn't laughing at you, Addie," Gloria said.

"I wouldn't blame you if you was," Adelaide said. "The life of Riley you have. Don't go to school any more and don't go to work."

Her face hardened.

"And don't you be stealin' my perfume an' wearin' my clo'es," she exclaimed, in sudden anger. "You leave my things alone. Do you hear?"

"I just tried a little bit of the perfume," Gloria said, "and I only wore your brazeers twice."

"Well, don't do it any more; that's all I've gotta say," Adelaide snapped. "This is a hell of a fambly. My Gawd!"

Gloria lay silently watching Adelaide with enigmatic blue eyes. Adelaide, in her underwear, suddenly ran from the room and immediately sounds of retching came from the bathroom. When she returned she said:

"It was that chicken à la king I ate. I feel better."

She was just leaving the room when Josie entered with a

breakfast tray, orange juice, coffee, hot biscuit and boiled eggs.

"Good mornin', Addie," Josie greeted her cheerfully. "It's a beautiful day, isn't it?"

Adelaide stood at one side, straddled her legs apart, and set her hands on her hips.

"It'd be a beautiful day all right if I ever saw you lugging me up my breakfast on a tray like that," she snapped. "Little Angelica there," tossing her head in Gloria's direction, "sure always knew how to get service."

"Why, Addie," Josie protested. "You know I was always glad to bring up your breakfast. Gloria hasn't been feeling well, have you, darlin'?" Josie added, smiling at Gloria.

Gloria, black curls on white pillow, blue eyes sober, moved her head the slightest fraction of an inch to one side and back again.

"'Darlin' hasn't been feelin' well'," Adelaide mimicked. "Well, darlin' 'll be feelin' a hell of a lot worse unless she leaves my things alone after this, I can tell you that."

"Why, Addie," Josie said, laying the tray down on Gloria's lap. "Is that a nice way to talk about your own baby sister? You should be glad to share your things with her."

Adelaide laughed raucously.

"I got a head I'd like to share with her," she said. "Well, give her a kiss for me, Ma—and make it a bite for luck."

"I'll be right down and boil your eggs for you, Addie," Josie said.

"Eggs—Ug-Up! Don't make me sick again. I'll just grab some black coffee."

"You know I'd be only too glad to fix you somethin'."

"I know," Adelaide said. "But what you can fix ain't what I need. So long."

Adelaide started downstairs. Josie shook her head.

"Addie is a sweet girl," Josie said, "but she gets impatient sometimes. I wish she didn't have to work so hard."

Gloria sipped orange juice, blue eyes gazing straight at her mother.

"You look so serious this mornin', darlin'. Have you got anything on your mind?"

Gloria made a barely perceptible movement of negation with her head.

"Do you want Mother to fix your eggs?"

Gloria repeated the movement of her head, this time in the affirmative.

"What's the matter, Baby? Why don't you talk to Mother?"

Gloria smiled a sad little smile, moisture gathering in her eyes. She blinked hard, but the tears kept coming faster. Josie whisked away the tray and took Gloria in her arms.

"Mama's Baby Doll," she crooned. "Tell Mama what's the matter."

Gloria sniffled two or three times, and began to grope with her right hand over the bedspread.

"Lookin' for a han'kerchief?"

Josie felt in her waist and in her belt, and then turned and took the napkin from the tray.

"Here. Use this."

Gloria kept her eyes on Josie while Josie deftly used the napkin.

"Your Uncle Julius didn't go to the office to-day," Josie said. "He had his breakfast and he's downstairs now."

Gloria's eyes widened, tears already made clinging to her lashes but no new ones appearing.

"Come on, let Mama feed you a little at a time, just like she did when you were a little bit of baby."

"Just some orange juice," Gloria said, "and some coffee."

"And just a teeny bit of egg, if I fix it," Josie wheedled.

She was feeding Gloria egg from a spoon when Julius Fleeter walked upstairs and entered the room.

"Good morning, Gloria," he said, rubbing his hands together.

"Good morning, Uncle Julius."

"You run along now, if you want to, Josie," Julius Fleeter said. "I'll feed the baby."

"Oh, I love to do it," Josie said.

Julius made no reply, merely stood aside, waiting at the door. Josie sighed, leaned over and kissed Gloria, and rose.

"I've got a lot of work to do to-day," she said.

After Josie had gone, Julius said:

"You know there's no time to waste, Baby. You get your breakfast into you and get dressed. The sooner you get hold of Thomas the better."

"I can't," Gloria said.

"You're going to do it, Baby. And what's more you're going to eat that breakfast and pull yourself together and get dressed without any more nonsense. What would your mother think if she knew?"

Gloria began to eat her egg.

"That's better," Julius Fleeter said. "What dress are you going to wear? You look like a little doll in the blue one."

Gloria, wearing her blue dress and blue hat, curls freshly made by Josie hanging on her shoulders, met Thomas Kane on his way home from high school that afternoon. Thomas was nearly six feet tall, lean, and blond. He played end on the football team. No one would have believed that he had once had infantile paralysis.

"Hullo, Gloria. Will you go to a movie with me?"

"I don't care much this afternoon."

"It's great to bump into you like this. Gosh! Seems as if the more I try to see you the less I see you. What did you leave school for? Why don't you come back, so I can see more of you?"

Gloria smiled and looked up at Thomas.

"I like to see you too," she confessed shyly.

Thomas flushed.

"You do!" he exclaimed, delighted and awkward. "Aw, come on. Let's go to the movies."

He took her arm. She walked beside him, close.

"Will you?" Thomas said. "Go to the movies, I mean?"

Gloria looked at him quickly and looked away again. Thomas's grip on her arm tightened.

"You can't run away from me to-day," he said. "You've got to come to the movies."

"Anybody'd think the movies were the only place," Gloria said nervously. "Anyway, I'm tired of the movies."

"Well, where else can we go?"

"We could go to my house," Gloria said. "Uncle Julius and Mama have gone out. The kids are all out."

"Come on then," Thomas said.

Gloria sat on the sofa, blue eyes darkened, looking quietly at Thomas's face, close to hers.

"I love you, Baby," Thomas said.

Gloria moved her head back a little, and held up her lips, parted a trifle, her eyes, pupils widened almost to the limits of the iris, on his. Thomas hesitated. Gloria leaned against him and sighed. He kissed her; she clung to him. Seconds passed— a minute. He released her, staring wildly down into her still face.

"I locked the doors," she whispered. "Kiss me, Tommy."

Frank rang the bell and kicked on the door an hour later. When Gloria opened it, he said:

"What's the big idear? Where's Ma? Where's everybody?"

"They're out," Gloria said.

Frank saw Thomas. He grinned, and glanced wickedly at Gloria.

"Hello, Frank," Thomas said, nonchalantly.

"What you lock the doors for?" Frank asked.

"Were they locked?" Thomas inquired, reddening.

"Of course, you didn't know it," Frank said. "Stop blushin'. It's lucky for you Uncle Julius wasn't the one that came home and found the doors locked, and you two on the sofa. Didn't even hear the bell. I almost had to kick the door down."

Gloria's cheeks were wet with tears when Julius Fleeter went into her room that night.

"You ought to be smiling instead of crying," Julius whispered. "Everything will be all right now."

"I—f-feel terrible," Gloria sighed.

"There's nothing to feel terrible about. Everything's all right."

"Oh, I wish I was dead."

Julius Fleeter patted her gently. Gloria moved restlessly, and snuffled.

"I wish things were different," she said.

She began to beat futilely on the pillow and on the bed with her hands.

"You stop this," Julius whispered sternly. "Stop it right away. You're a big girl now; you're a woman, Gloria. You've got to control yourself. Stop it!"

Gloria choked back sobs.

"I don't want to be a woman," she whimpered. "I just want to be little."

"You've got to control yourself," Julius warned her. "If you don't something terrible will happen. If you just do what I say we'll all be happy. Why, you'll forget all about this in a little while. You and I'll be laughing about it. It seems serious right now, and it could be very serious if we didn't use our brains. But you do what I say and see what happens. Now be a good girl. Sssh! Some one's coming."

Gloria and Julius became silent. Not even the sound of a drawn breath broke the stillness for several seconds. Then the bedroom door opened and Josie entered.

"Are you all right, Gloria?" Josie asked in a low voice. "I thought I heard you cryin'."

"I'm all right, Mother," Gloria replied in the tone of one who had been weeping, or who suffered of a cold.

"I'm here, Josie," Julius announced.

"Oh!" Josie cried, startled, pressing her left hand against her heart in a characteristic gesture.

"The baby was feeling a little blue, so I stopped in to talk with her."

Josie went to the bedside and put her hand on Gloria's head.

"Do you want Mama to give you a good rub?" she asked, smoothing the hair from Gloria's forehead.

Gloria remained silent.

"I think she'll be all right, Josie," Julius said. "The best thing for her is to get to sleep. You're feeling better now, aren't you, darling?"

"Yes," Gloria said, hopelessness in her tone.

"Come on, Josie," Julius said. "We'd better let her sleep."

"I'd love to give her a good rub," Josie protested wistfully. "All the children love my rubbing. They say no one has such a light touch."

Julius touched Josie's arm, and Josie obediently stood up. She paused a moment and then bent over and kissed Gloria.

"Mama's little doll," she soothed. "Mama loves the baby."

She straightened the bed clothing and kissed Gloria again.

"Good night, Baby."

"Good night."

Josie went into the hall with Julius, who carefully closed the door.

"You should have let me rub her," Josie said. "The poor little thing!"

"She'll be all right," Julius said. "There's nothing the matter with her—just feminine vapors. You'd better get to bed. You're not looking so well yourself."

Behind the closed door of her room Gloria was whispering:

"Mama. I want my Mama."

But she called so softly that only her pillow heard. When Adelaide came home at three o'clock the next morning and stood swaying in front of the dresser, Gloria was moaning faintly in her sleep. Adelaide leaned against the dresser and stared at her face with blurred eyes, the lids heavily tinted with shadow, lashes thick with mascara.

"Bitches—they're all bitches!" she murmured, and giggled.

Gloria moaned. Adelaide turned unsteadily around.

"Shut up, Bitch," she said hoarsely. "Go to sleep."

She sank heavily on a chair and began to tug at her shoes, head wobbling uncertainly on her shoulders. Something wet splashed on her wrist. She stared at it. She was weeping. She rose, one shoe off, and fell against the dresser. She stood there watching the tears fall, till suddenly the running mascara began to burn.

"Ouitch! Damn! Jesus! That damn' stuff."

She groped her way, stumbling, to the bathroom and began to wash her eyes.

When Gloria went downstairs at eleven o'clock next morning, Uncle Edward, thin, awkward, ineffectual, approached her in the hall. He took one of her hands clumsily, and tried to kiss her. Gloria pushed him away.

"Stop it," she said. "I'll tell Mother."

"What's wrong in me kissing you? I'm your uncle, ain't I?"

Edward spoke in a low voice, glancing uneasily over his shoulder.

"I hate you," Gloria exclaimed. "I hate everybody that touches me."

"I thought you might kiss me once before I go away," Edward said.

"Where're you going?" Gloria asked indifferently.

"I got called in the draft," Edward said. "They don't care who they have in the army—me with feet I never could walk on much, and weak lungs."

Gloria smiled involuntarily.

"I'm glad you're going, Uncle Edward," she said. "Always sneaking around after me like you are."

"Aw Cheese, Gloria. Can't you take a little fun?"

"Maybe you call it fun."

She raised her voice.

"Mama!"

Josie's voice answered from the kitchen:

"Yes, darling, what is it?"

"I just wanted to know where you were."

Josie came into the front hall, wiping her hands on a kitchen towel.

"My, but you're lookin' sweet enough to eat to-day, Baby. Did Eddie tell you about it?"

"About him in the draft?"

Josie nodded.

"It seems a shame," Josie complained. "Eddie's never been strong, and he has to be awful partic'lar about what he eats. He can't eat any cookin' except mine without gettin' his death with indigestion."

Edward, dressed in his best blue suit, with a stiff collar and a new blue tie with white dots, looked gloomy.

"They's somethin' the matter with a gover-mint that does things that way," he said. "They's nothin' but graft. Don't I know? I just didn't have pull. That's all. They'll have good, well men stayin' at home, and me in the front lines. It's all part of the system."

"You want to be sure and take some soda with you, Eddie," Josie said. "I'll fix you some with the powdered ginger in it."

"If I was runnin' things they'd be different," Edward said. "What's a guy's stummick to them guys in Washin'ton? It ain't their stummick that's achin', an' it ain't their feet that get walked on. A guy's gotta have pull, an' I ain't got it. Tha's all."

Martin Brady returned from one of his absences two weeks later. He went straight to the kitchen, put his arms around Josie, and kissed her back of the ear.

"Oh, Martin!" Josie exclaimed. "You scared me."

Martin kissed her again and stood her off and looked at her. She was making pies and her hands were covered with flour. She held them away from him.

"Look out, Martin," she said. "You'll get all mussed up."

"You're one of the seven wonders of the world, Josie," Martin announced. "You're as pretty as a baby, as unselfish as a saint, and a harder worker than a gang of coal miners."

"That's more of your soft soap, Martin," Josie said, smiling.

"And look at the break you get," Martin continued, after kissing her again. "Everybody takes advantage of you—your kids and everybody else, includin' me. Any one of the bums that live on you can come home at three or four in the mornin' and do you give 'em hell? You do not. You ask 'em if they'd like to be rubbed, or wouldn't they like a little bite to eat."

"Everybody is nice to me," Josie protested. "I have my babies and I have my work."

"They're a fine gang—the babies," Martin said sarcastically. "But," he added seriously, "you think they're the finest kids that ever walked, don't you, Josie? They are wonderful kids, ain't they?"

"I think they are, Martin," Josie admitted, flushing proudly. "I often think I'm mighty fortunate. And did you ever see healthier, prettier babies?"

Martin looked hard at Josie, took a hand from around her waist, and tucked a middle finger into his collar, which he tugged as if it were choking him. He swallowed hard. Then he hugged her again.

"It's no use, Josie," he said. "No use at all. Anybody should be shot that ever told you there's no pot of gold beneath the rainbow or that the world ain't all it's cracked up to be."

"What do you mean, Martin?"

"Just that you're the most wonderful female woman I ever knew in my life, and I get wilder about you every week or so."

"Now, Martin," Josie protested, "you know that's more soft soap. I don't do anythin'—just cook, and do the housework."

"And a little sewin', and mendin', and darnin', and dressmakin', and hairdressin', and bed makin', and furnace fixin'. I don't see any one else around here even offerin' to wash a dish."

"I never wanted 'em to," Josie said, pulling away. "I always wanted my babies to have things easy just as if we had money. You'd better go away now, Martin; I've got to finish these pies. I've got a lot of work to do."

"To the devil with the work, Josie. I haven't seen you for a month. Give me a kiss."

Josie shook her head. Martin took hold of her again and kissed her—a long kiss this time. Josie sighed and snuggled against him. One of her flour stained hands marked his jacket with white. He kissed her ear and she pressed closer to him. He lifted his head and looked down at her, an outline of rosy cheek, softly curving, stray lock of blonde hair, humid blue eyes.

"I'm certainly stuck on you, Josie," he whispered. "Come up and get me unpacked."

"I can't, Martin—the pies."

"The pies can wait," Martin Brady said. "You're goin' to settle me first."

He took her wrist, and led her to the door and into the hall, kissing her on the way.

"Behave," she whispered.

"I'll show you."

Gloria and Thomas met in the home of Bessie Mayfield. Bessie lived with her widowed mother and her younger brother Harold in an apartment two blocks away. Mrs. Mayfield, who had prematurely gray hair, was a buyer in a department store in Manhattan. Harold was in high school. Bessie stopped going to school at the beginning of her first year in high school and did nothing except go around with men and boys. Her mother, thin, highly excitable, with brown, nervous eyes, intelligent face, and quick gestures, never seemed to mind how many admirers Bessie had. But every so often she had terrible, hysterical outbreaks, in which she wondered what in the world was going to happen to her daughter. She threw herself on the floor and shrieked. The same night, with Bessie out somewhere, she would wind the alarm clock, put out the cat, see that the key was under the mat, and go to bed and to sleep. Harold was studious and quiet. She never had to worry about him.

Bessie, Gloria, and Thomas's sister, Mabel, had been as friendly at grammar school as it was possible for three girls to be. Bessie was slim and brown-eyed, brown-haired, brown-skinned, vivacious, full of ideas and deviltry. She looked much more mature than she really was, and spoke of, and to, men as if she knew all there was to know about them. She smoked cigarettes and drank cocktails. She had tried vainly many times to get Gloria to go joy riding with her, or to meet boys at her home.

"Well," Bessie said, blowing out a stream of cigarette smoke, "you don't want to take my advice, so I suppose you might as well get married. At that, it's a thrill. I'll bet your father and mother'll be pleased, Tommy."

Tommy looked serious.

"I haven't dared say anything to 'em yet," he admitted. "But I can't see what they're going to do if I show up all married and everything."

"They might throw you out," Bessie laughed. "That would be a thrill. Do you want me to be best man—or flower girl?"

Tommy and Gloria looked at one another. Gloria was quiet.

"You tell her," Gloria urged.

"Sure, there's nothing to that," Tommy agreed, turning to Bessie. "Gloria is afraid she looks so young that they might ask her a lot of questions down at the License Bureau. She was wondering if you would go down with me and take her place, signing the papers and everything. Gloria's bashful anyway."

"Sure," Bessie cried, jumping to her feet from the couch on which she had been perched. "I'd love it. Do you want me to get married for you too, Baby?" she asked Gloria. "I'll do that, too."

Gloria shook her head.

"We can fix up the getting married part of it with the Reverend Mr. Paxton, around the corner. Gloria's been to his church enough."

"She seems to go to any church that her friends go to,"

Bessie said. "Well, she'll learn no new creeds from me. When do we start for the license, Tommy?"

After the marriage ceremony in the parsonage, Thomas gave the Reverend Mr. Paxton an envelope. In the envelope was a five dollar bill, which Thomas had been saving towards a radio set.

"I kiss both the bride and groom," Bessie said, kissing them both. "How do you do, Mrs. Kane?"

Tears gathered in Gloria's eyes. Thomas stood looking down at her helplessly.

"What's the matter, Honey?" Bessie demanded. "Isn't the bride happy? Why, you ought to be so glad the old janitor who was your marriage witness smelled bad and wrote well, that you'd laugh yourself to death. Did you see how nicely he wrote his name on your certificate? Look."

Bessie took the certificate from its envelope.

"What if the janitor had smelled sweet and written hen tracks? What kind of a souvenir would you've had then?"

Gloria smiled through tears.

"That's right, laugh!" Bessie ordered. "Kiss Tommy. Look happy."

"I always thought I'd be m-married in a big church, with bridesmaids and everything. And look at t-this."

Gloria moved the hand which held the license in a gesture which included a bit of the corner of the little wooden church, a dusty maple tree, a brick walk, and a section of street corner, in which was a sewer grating. Bessie laughed again:

"That's what all girls think," she said. "Let's go to my place first, and have a little wedding drink."

Bessie carried a bottle into the parlor where Gloria and Thomas were sitting self-consciously on the sofa.

"Weddings mean wine," Bessie said, "and the only kind of wine I could find in the house is some port wine. I guess it's left over from the mince pie last Christmas. Or do they use brandy?"

Bessie laughed and filled three egg glasses with the dark fluid.

"These are the best wine glasses we have," she explained. "Here's long life to the newlyweds."

She raised her glass.

"Come on, you two sticks," she said. "Show some signs of life and try to look happy even if you aren't. Clink glasses."

Gloria and Thomas held out their glasses and Bessie bumped hers against them. Gloria choked over her first swallow. Her eyes became teary. The hand which held her glass was shaking.

"It's awful strong," Gloria said.

"Drink it," Bessie said, winking. "You may need it later. Who knows?"

Bessie persuaded Gloria and Thomas to drink two glasses of the heady vintage. Their faces flushed. Thomas began to talk louder than usual.

"We'd better get along," he said. "I've got to break the news to the family."

"I don't want to go," Gloria said. "Let's wait till to-morrow. We don't have to tell them yet."

Thomas ran his arm around her and squeezed her to him. Bending over he pressed his mouth against her unresisting lips.

"We're going now," he asserted. "Who's afraid?"

"Attaboy," Bessie encouraged. "Have another little drink of wine, Sweetheart, and you'll win the war."

Thomas walked rapidly towards his home.

"I'm afraid," Gloria moaned.

"There's nothin' to be afraid of," Thomas said. "A family has got to expect people to get married. That's no crime."

"Your father and mother don't like me."

"Of course they like you," Thomas lied. "Nobody could help liking you, Darling. Buck up, Baby."

The more Gloria protested her fears, the louder and more

confidently Thomas talked. In front of the house Gloria dragged Thomas to a halt.

"Please let's wait," she begged.

"We got to do it some time," Thomas said.

"I can't go in," Gloria said. "I just can't."

"They're not going to eat you."

"I'd die. I can't."

"All right then," Thomas said. "You wait here for me. I'll go in and tell them and then come out and get you."

Gloria stood in the dusk of the late April evening, shivering in a southwesterly breeze off the bay. Thomas walked up to the door, opened it, went in, and closed the door after him. Gloria bowed her head and looked up and down the street. She walked swiftly a half-dozen paces up the street, hesitated, and then walked back. She choked. Salt drops began to fall from her eyes; moisture gathered uncomfortably in her nostrils. She felt for a handkerchief in vain.

Thomas stepped into the warm, familiar home atmosphere. The old place was strangely unchanged. It was just as if he hadn't been out getting married and drinking port wine to celebrate it. The smell of cauliflower came from the kitchen. His mother's voice floated out from the library:

"Is that you, Thomas? Well, run straight upstairs and get yourself ready for dinner. You've got only a minute."

Thomas hung his hat on the hall rack. It looked small and inadequate beside his father's hat. In the hall mirror he caught a glimpse of a boyish face with a pimple or two. His father had no pimples. And when his father shaved you could hear the hard, adult beard rasp under the singing steel. His school books, bound with a skate strap, were on the settle. Thomas paled, took two hesitating steps towards the library door, and stopped. His shoes squeaked. Sweat began to trickle down his back. His mother's voice sounded again.

"Thomas! Where in the world is that boy?"

Sound of a newspaper rustling came from the library. His father was reading the *Brooklyn Eagle*. Thomas suddenly straightened his shoulders and walked into the library. Mrs. Kane glanced up from a heavy book. She read papers on books for the Twentieth Century Club. Lemuel Kane thrust his opened newspaper aside and looked past it at Thomas over the tops of his glasses.

"Well, what has my young hopeful been up to now?" Lemuel asked.

"Why, you haven't washed this quick, Thomas," his mother said.

Thomas looked desperately, first at his mother, and then at his father.

"I'm married," he said. "Gloria Boyd. She's outside now. Will I bring her in?"

Emma Kane stared at her son, slowly lowering the book to her lap. Her lips trembled.

"Oh, Lemuel," she cried, as if for help.

Lemuel Kane folded his newspaper, features hardening.

"You what?" he exclaimed.

Thomas stood in the middle of the room, looking pitifully young and helpless. He swallowed hard and appeared about to burst into tears.

"Gloria's outside," he said helplessly.

Lemuel rose to his feet with astonishing speed. Thomas ducked instinctively, raising his arm as if expecting a blow. But Lemuel went straight to his wife and put his arm around her. She made a sound as if all the wind had been violently expelled from her lungs by a blow, and sagged down in her chair.

"I can't stand it," she said. "I can't stand it. Oh, God, why did this have to happen? I can't stand it."

Lemuel paid no attention to Thomas, who began to suffer of long, dry, racking sobs. Lemuel smoothed Emma's forehead with his hand.

"It'll be all right, Emma. Don't take it too hard. We'll find a way."

"I can't stand it," Emma said. "I can't stand it."

Lemuel looked over his shoulder at his son.

"Look what you've done to your mother, young man," he said. "I hope you're satisfied."

"I didn't mean to, Dad. Honest, I'd rather be dead than make you or Mother feel bad. Honest! Please, Mother! Please, Mama! Don't feel bad!"

Thomas moved, trembling, towards his mother.

"Keep away now," his father commanded. "Wait right there. Close that door into the hall."

Light footsteps sounded in the hall. The doorknob turned.

"Lock the door," Lemuel whispered.

Thomas turned the key. Knuckles rapped on the panel.

"It's me," Mabel's voice announced. "What's the matter? Has something happened?"

"Everything is all right," Lemuel replied. "You go back upstairs for a minute and wait."

Mabel's voice sounded excited and tearful.

"Let me in. I know something has happened."

Lemuel's voice was sharply authoritative.

"You go upstairs, Mabel, and wait there. Everything is all right, I tell you. We are just discussing something with Thomas."

Mabel returned upstairs. Mrs. Kane suddenly began to weep.

"Oh, dear!" she sobbed. "Oh, dear! Oh, dear! Oh, dear!"

"That's better, Em," Lemuel said. "It's better to cry and get it all out. But it isn't the end of the world. The boy has been a damned little fool, but we'll find a way out."

After Mrs. Kane had wept for two or three minutes, Lemuel said to Thomas:

"Now open that door, and I'll take your mother upstairs. You wait here."

Thomas walked up and down the room, eyes blurred with moisture until Lemuel walked in, shutting the door again behind him, just as a fresh burst of sobbing came from the bedroom overhead.

"Now, Thomas," Lemuel said sternly, "I'm not going to order you out of the house, and I'm not going to make that poor little girl suffer any more than I can help. Naturally, this has been a terrible blow to your mother and me—more to her."

Thomas looked his father in the eyes, blinking back tears.

"I suppose you got Gloria into trouble and thought you had to marry her?"

"Yes, sir."

"Well, I can understand that. But your mother can't. Now, quick! Tell me about it."

Thomas stumbled through the story. His father nodded.

"It's just as well that you did it this way," he said. "Apparently you've saved a scandal. Thank God, you didn't elope to some place and make a romantic story of it."

"I thought it was the only thing I could do, Father, and I was so worried, I was almost crazy. I don't know how I dared tell you and Mother. I guess it must have been the port wine we had at Bessie Mayfield's."

"So you had wine too? We'll discuss that later. For the present you go out and bring Gloria in here to the library."

Thomas led Gloria in by the hand. She was holding back tears.

"Here's Father, Gloria," Thomas said.

Lemuel stepped over to Gloria, took a clean linen handkerchief from his breast pocket and put it in her hand.

"Well, you must have had a pretty exciting day, Gloria," he said.

Gloria glanced quickly up at him, laid her head against his sturdy chest, and began to weep.

"Oh, Mr. Kane," she wailed. "I feel terrible."

Mr. Kane smiled grimly.

"For a pair of newlyweds you two are pretty sad specimens," he said. "The first thing you'd both better do is go upstairs to the bathroom and get washed up; and the next thing you'd better do is eat dinner. And after that we'll try to see where we are at. What do you say?"

He put a hand under Gloria's chin, and tilted her face so that he could look in her eyes. It was a pathetic face, but beautiful. Lemuel sighed, as he touched his lips to her forehead.

"You poor baby," he said. "Run along now with Thomas. Everything'll be all right."

"Your father is the most wonderful man in the world," Gloria whispered to Thomas on the way upstairs.

"I'm glad you think so, Baby."

"But I hate to meet your mother. Where is she?"

Thomas hesitated.

"I think she isn't feeling very well and is lying down in her room," he explained. "One of her headaches, I guess."

After dinner Lemuel Kane said:

"You young ones had better go over and break the news to Gloria's family."

Gloria ran into the kitchen, where Josie, as usual, was washing dishes. She threw herself into Josie's arms.

"Well, well, Baby Doll," Josie exclaimed, wiping red eyes. "I was so worried about you. Where on earth have you been?"

Gloria pressed her head against Josie's bosom, and said nothing—merely hugged her more tightly. Thomas walked into the kitchen.

"Why, Thomas!" Josie said.

Tommy stammered a moment, and then blurted:

"Gloria and I got married this afternoon, Mrs. Boyd, and we're going to live at my house."

Josie pressed her hand to her heart.

"My baby," she exclaimed softly. "My poor little baby lamb."

She hugged Gloria fiercely, work-reddened fingers sinking into young flesh of her flesh.

"Does your Uncle Julius know?" she cried, as one afraid.

Julius Fleeter appeared in the doorway.

"What is all this," he demanded. "What's the matter, Thomas?"

"Why, Mr. Fleeter," Thomas said, "Gloria and I got married to-day, and we're going to live at my house."

Josie stared with wide eyes at Julius Fleeter, unconsciously moving so that her body shielded Gloria from him. Julius smiled a purely surface smile. He extended a long, claw-like hand. Thomas took it.

"I suppose then congratulations are in order, Thomas," he said, giving Thomas's hand a quick light pressure, and then dropping it. "But wasn't this rather sudden?"

"Yes, sir," Thomas said, "although I've been stuck on Gloria ever since we were little."

"What are you hiding your head for, Gloria?" Julius Fleeter asked. "Let me see the bride."

Gloria kept her face buried in her mother's breast. Josie lifted her face up with some effort.

"Look up, Baby," she insisted. "Look at your Uncle Julius."

Gloria met her Uncle Julius's gaze, and her face suffused with crimson. Julius Fleeter looked old and tired. Gloria re-buried her head. Julius hesitated for a moment.

"Well," he said uncertainly, "let us hope it is all for the best."

Then he walked out of the kitchen. Josie gazed after him wonderingly. She shook her head.

"I was so worried about what your Uncle Julius would do," she said to Gloria. "He's been like a father to this baby," she explained to Thomas. "If she was out of sight for a moment he acted like a crazy man. She couldn't play with the boys, and she couldn't play with the girls; and she had to come right home from school; and she couldn't do this; and she couldn't do that. And now when she runs off and gets married he takes it as cool as a cucumber. I can't make head or tail of it."

Ernest galloped into the kitchen, stuck out his tongue at Thomas, and ran over and hit Gloria on the hip with his hand.

"Now you stop," Gloria said.

"Why, Ernie!" Josie said. "Is that nice?"

"Don't care," Ernest said, and slapped Gloria again.

"Make him stop, Mama," Gloria begged.

Josie reached for Ernest, but he dodged and ran to the door. He stopped a minute, and yelled:

"Toot! Toot! Look out for the train."

Then he ran through the pantry and into the hall. An instant later he howled:

"Ow! Ow! Wanh-wANH!"

"Cut it out then," Malcolm said. "I told you to keep away from me or you'd get hurt."

"You big bastard," Ernest cried.

Came the sound of a slap from the front hall, louder howls from Ernest, and Malcolm's voice:

"I tol' you not to call me those names."

"Ernie, Malcolm!" Josie called, and hurried into the pantry. "Malcolm, do you think it's very nice to strike your baby brother?"

"Well, he keeps bumpin' into me, and callin' me names."

"I don't know why he uses those words. But you should be nice to your baby brother. Ernie! Come here to Mama."

Josie stooped over Ernest, still yelling.

"Your sister got married to-day, Malcolm," she said, head over shoulder. "There she is with her husband."

"Gee!" Malcolm exclaimed. "Tom Kane!"

He turned around, put his hand beside his opened mouth as a sounding board, and yelled:

"Hay! Frank-ee! C'mere, quick. Gloria's got married. C'mere!"

When Gloria and Tom returned to the Kanes, Mabel met them in the hall.

"Father's upstairs with Mother," Mabel said. "Mother's having a terrible time because you two went and got married. Father said to take things easy and everything will be all right. I'm so excited. You're to sleep in the guest room to-night—I guess because it's furthest away from Mother's and Father's room."

"You know what?" Gloria said. "I think I better go back home and sleep."

"Like heck you will," Thomas cried.

"With your mother feeling like she does and everything, I feel terrible," Gloria said.

Thomas kissed her.

"Women are like that," he said. "Anyway, it's too late for you to back out now. You got to stay here. You're my wife, ain't you?"

"Oh, she'll stay," Mabel exclaimed, eyes dancing. "Are her things in that suitcase?" she added, pointing to a suitcase Thomas had set down in the hall.

"I brought some things," Gloria said.

Mabel put her lips to Thomas's ear.

"Let me take her upstairs, and get her settled, Tommy," she whispered. "You wait here."

She caught up the suitcase and took Gloria's hand.

"Come on, Gloria," she invited. "Let's you and me go upstairs. I'll help you get settled. Come on."

At about the same moment that Gloria and Mabel went upstairs, Julius Fleeter put on his hat and a light overcoat, and went out. He walked down the street, taking long strides, shoulders hunched, and hands clenched in his coat pockets.

Chapter 8

COOPER PATTEN stopped his roadster and blew the horn. Gloria, walking swiftly down the street, didn't look around. Patten jumped out, slammed the door, and walked swiftly after her.

"What's the matter, Baby?" he asked, when he had caught up with her.

She turned around, startled.

"Oh, it's you," she said, flushing.

"Don't tell me you didn't know who it was," he laughed. "I'm not very flattered."

"But I didn't," Gloria asserted. "Honest."

She swung a mesh bag on a chain, glanced at Cooper Patten, and up and down the street, and next at the sky. Then her blue eyes returned to Patten's, and finally to the sidewalk.

"Marriage certainly agrees with you," Cooper Patten said. "You grow more beautiful by the minute."

Gloria smiled and involuntarily patted a curl.

"Men are all the same," she said.

"So are girls," he laughed.

"What do you mean?" she inquired doubtfully.

"Why, they all say men are all the same."

Gloria smiled again and became serious.

"Well, they are," she insisted.

"If they all tell you how beautiful you are, they're all sensible," Cooper Patten asserted solemnly. "Are you happy?" he added suddenly.

Gloria gave him a quick flash from her blue eyes, and then

bent her head while she outlined a brick in the pavement with the toe of her patent leather pump.

"I tell you what," he urged. "Get in my car, and we'll ride for a few minutes. We can talk more comfortably that way."

Gloria shook her head slowly from side to side, her eyes solemn.

"I couldn't do that," she said. "I'm married."

He laughed again.

"So you are," he agreed. "But it's so easy to forget it looking at you," he explained.

"Why?" she asked, glancing up from the erratically moving pump.

"Because you look like a little schoolgirl—the prettiest little schoolgirl there is," he replied. "I tried hard to see you after that night in your house when you entertained me," Cooper Patten added. "Did you get any of my messages?"

Gloria glanced quickly at him again.

"My brothers told me you were asking for me," she said, "but that was all." She took a deep breath, and gazed straight up into his eyes. "Addie was awful mad at me for that night," she confessed.

"Oh, she was?" Cooper Patten said.

"I should be going now," Gloria said. "I don't feel right talking to you, as it is. I'm married."

Cooper Patten laughed again.

"I see you're not going to let me forget that," he said. "But surely," he continued more seriously, "there is no harm in a lady who is married talking with a friend on the street. Is there?"

"I don't know," Gloria said soberly. "But it doesn't seem quite right. I ought to be going now."

"Well," Cooper Patten said, "I'm going to tell you something now that I have the chance, Gloria. And that's this. I think you are the most beautiful little girl I've ever met, and I'd be glad to do anything for you—just remember that, will you? Anything."

Gloria's gaze hung on his, as if fascinated.

"I have money and influence," Cooper Patten said. "If you need either, if you are unhappy, let me know. I think you are wonderful. I'll be seeing you again soon."

"Good-by," Gloria said softly.

"Not good-by," he corrected. "You'll be seeing more of me. Until we meet again, then, Baby."

He raised his hat and bowed. Gloria flushed, nodded, and walked briskly down the street. Cooper Patten made a very impressive figure. He breathed of money and influence. The very way in which he walked back to the roadster and swung into the seat might have indicated to any observer that he was used to success and that failure was not a part of his character.

Gloria was getting dressed for dinner when Thomas entered the room, locked the door, grabbed her in his arms, and kissed her.

"Not now," Gloria said, pushing futilely against him.

He laughed, lifted her up and dropped her on the bed.

"You make me sick," Gloria said, half-tearfully. "You've mussed my hair and everything. Look at my dress. You're always after me."

"Oh, bother with that stuff. Give me a kiss."

He took the kiss by force, twisting Gloria's face around so he could reach her mouth. She kicked slim legs.

"Don't, Tommy," she protested. "I'm tired."

"You don't love me any more," Thomas accused, still wrestling with her.

She was panting, hair dishevelled.

"It isn't love; it's only one thing you want."

"We're married, ain't we?"

Gloria held him off for a moment, bending her head away from him and groaning with the effort.

"You're after me all the time," she wailed. "I can't stand it. What'll everybody think? And I was getting all dressed for dinner and everything."

108

He forced her back on the bed roughly.

"You like it all right," he said.

"That's right, tear my underwear," she sighed wearily, tears running down her cheeks. "You've got me all black and blue."

The clothing fell away from her breast. One of his hands pressed hard against it.

"You'll give me a cancer. Ow! Let me up."

She kicked ineffectually and bit at his wrist without violence. After five minutes he rose.

"Well, let's get ready for dinner," he said. "Come on, Baby. Make it snappy."

Gloria lay panting on the bed.

"I hate you," she said.

Thomas laughed, stepped over to the bedside and smacked her on the bottom with his palm.

"Come on, Baby," he urged. "Get up out of that. We're late for dinner."

"I'm sick of everything," Gloria sobbed. "I hate it in this house. Your mother hates me."

"Mother'll be all right," Thomas said. "Give her time. Father likes you, and Mabel likes you, and I'm crazy about you. What more do you want?"

"You—crazy? Huh! You on'y think of one thing, morning, noon and night. You've got me crazy."

"Psst!" Thomas sibilated. "Come on. Snap out of it. We've got to get downstairs."

He tugged at her arm. She kicked.

"I won't! I won't! I won't!"

"Well, young lady, I guess you'll find out there're some things you'll have to do around here," Thomas announced grimly. "I'm not going to stand for any scenes in my own house. Get up out of there."

He yanked her to a sitting position and jerked her roughly to her feet.

"Oh!" she half-shrieked. "You're hurting me."

Mabel knocked on the door, and called:

"Tom! Gloria! What's the matter? Let me in."

"You go away," Thomas replied. "This is our business."

"You'd better be careful or it'll be the neighborhood's business," Mabel retorted tartly.

"If you touch me again, I'll scream loud," Gloria said, pulling a slip over her shoulder and gazing at him from swollen eyes. "Nobody could make me go down to dinner now. Look at me."

She drew a long, shuddering sigh and choked a sob. Mabel rattled the doorknob.

"You'd better let me in," she said. "Father just called from downstairs. Let me in."

"Oh, gee whizz! All right! All right! Have everything your own way."

Thomas turned the key and opened the door. Mabel closed the door after her and hurried over to Gloria, who was lying face downwards on the bed, weeping.

"What's the matter, Gloria?" Mabel asked, shooting a hostile glance at her brother.

"Ev-ev-everything's the matter," Gloria sobbed. "He's mauling me all the time. I was getting dressed in my white dress, and he came in and pulled me around. He's after me all the time."

Mabel turned and faced her brother.

"Tommy," she said, "you'd better go downstairs and tell the family that Gloria is sick. She can't go down like this. Tell them I'll be down later. You make me tired," she concluded venomously.

"There wasn't any reason for all this, Mabel," Thomas protested. "Gosh! I didn't do anything that she hasn't liked before. Just a little fun. My God!"

"Fun!" Mabel sniffed. "It sounded like it. You'd better get downstairs or Father'll be up."

As soon as Thomas had left the room, Gloria jumped off the bed.

"I'm going home," she announced.

Mabel embraced her.

"Now, Gloria, take it easy," she said. "Let me rub your head. I'll get some alcohol and give you a good rubbing, and then bring up something to eat for you."

Gloria shook herself free from Mabel's arms.

"I'm going home," she repeated. "Where's my comb?"

She groped over the top of the dresser.

"Here it is," Mabel said.

Gloria began to comb her hair, yanking the teeth through snarls.

"I never loved Tommy anyway," Gloria said. "I'm sorry I married him. I wish I was dead."

"Why, Gloria!" Mabel soothed.

"I don't care," Gloria said. "Where's my suitcase?"

Mabel went to a closet and got the suitcase.

"I'll do anything to help you, Gloria," Mabel said. "But, honestly, I don't think you should do anything while you're like this. Why don't you wait until you get calmed down?"

"I could never get calmed down in this house," Gloria cried.

She beat on the dresser top with the comb. Then she combed her hair again.

"Everybody with a long face—your mother looking as if she smelled something bad every time I come in a room. I've had enough of it. I can't. I can't!"

Lemuel Kane rapped on the door.

"May I come in?" he asked.

Mabel glanced at Gloria.

"I don't care who comes in," Gloria moaned.

"All right, Father," Mabel called. "Come in."

When her father entered, she added:

"Gloria is all upset. Thomas was a bit rough with her, I guess. She says she's going home."

"I *am* going home," Gloria said.

Lemuel Kane, looking very serious, remained by the door.

"Of course, Gloria," he said gently, "we want you to do exactly as you think you should. But don't you think it would be wiser to wait a little while?"

"I'm going home, Mr. Kane," Gloria repeated. "Nobody can stop me. I don't love Tom; I can't stand him any more."

"Is there anything I can do for you, Gloria?" Lemuel Kane asked, his face serious but kind.

Gloria shook her head vigorously.

"No," she said.

"I hope you'll always remember that I want to be your friend," Lemuel Kane said, after a moment's hesitation.

Gloria turned to him, face swollen from weeping, and eyes red but still pretty.

"I like you," she said. "But I've got to go home."

Lemuel returned to the dining room. During dinner footsteps creaked on the front stairs and the front door opened. Thomas jerked to his feet. Lemuel turned to him.

"Sit down, Thomas," he said sternly.

Thomas hesitated, looking first at his father and then in the direction of the front hall, whence came the sound of a door closing.

"But—" Thomas began.

"Sit down," his father said, "and finish your dinner."

Emma Kane, sitting rigidly at her end of the table, glanced at her husband questioningly. She hadn't spoken to her son, except as a matter of cold politeness, during the two weeks of his marriage. Thomas was nervous, the food in front of him untouched. Lemuel cleared his throat.

"I don't know just how to say this," he announced. "But the idea is that we all are going through a rather trying time in our life together. Tom here is unhappy. You are upset, Emma, and I don't really know where I'm at myself. But really, we all love each other, and we want each other to be happy.

"Now I've just found out that Gloria is just as miserable as the rest of us. She has just gone home, in tears. I must confess that my immediate feeling was one of relief when she said she was going. On the other hand, I can't help feeling mighty sorry for her."

Tom dropped his napkin on the table and rose, pushing back his chair.

"I don't care about all that," he cried. "I'm going to get Gloria. She's my wife."

"Sit down, Tom," Lemuel said.

He waited. Thomas made a furious gesture with a clenched right fist, as if he were striking an enemy.

"Gee whizz!" he exclaimed.

Then he sat down, suddenly relaxed, with scowling, stubborn face.

"I'll get her back; you'll see," he said.

"You wait a minute, young man," his father continued. "It seems to me that we have been very pleasant with you. I don't think you have any kicks coming at the treatment you've gotten in this house."

"You made me stay here when Gloria was going away," Thomas asserted. "I could've stopped her."

"I am not going to try to stop you from seeing Gloria or trying to get her to come back," Lemuel said evenly. "But, now that she herself has raised the issue, I'm going to say for the first time that I think the best thing for both of you would be to have this marriage broken up. You are both too young; you can't support a wife; you don't know, apparently, how to treat a wife. But I know—"

"Yes," Thomas interrupted, raising his voice, "and how about the baby she's going to have? I'd like to know what's going to be done about that?"

He jumped up from the table again.

"I don't care what you say, I'm going after her," he exclaimed.

He rushed out of the dining room. Emma Kane wiped her eyes with a handkerchief. Lemuel gazed anxiously at her over the tops of his spectacles.

"I probably didn't say the right thing, Em," he apologized. "But I've been trying to keep my temper and do my best. I honestly think the whole thing'll blow over."

"The baby," Emma Kane said in the tone of one referring to a polecat.

"That complicates the situation," Lemuel admitted seriously. "But we've got to face it. We can't run away from it. I don't know a way out at this minute, but I honestly believe there'll be one."

"I don't know how I can live through it," Emma said. "I certainly never thought anything like this could happen in my family."

She rose and Lemuel followed suit. He waited until she reached his side and then put his arm around her.

"My old Puritan," he said. "Come on, Em, there's lots of life to be lived yet. Why, we haven't even begun to enjoy ourselves."

Emma stiffly resisted his arm.

"You think I should've been an old-fashioned father and turned them out," he said.

"I could understand if you had," Emma replied.

"Go on! You'd 've been worried sick, then, wondering if Tom had holes in his socks, or changed his underwear, or took his baths regularly, or got to bed on time. I know you."

"I can't believe Thomas is my son," Emma said stubbornly.

"Perhaps he and Gloria'll be divorced before long," Lemuel suggested.

"Divorce!"

Emma's face pinched and her lips narrowed to a thin line.

"There never was a divorce in our family."

She put her hands to her head.

"Sometimes I think I'm going crazy," she said.

When they had reached the hall the front door opened, and Thomas and Mabel came in. Thomas smashed his hat on the rack.

"What's the matter?" Lemuel asked.

"Gloria wouldn't see him," Mabel said scornfully. "And I wouldn't of either. You acted like a fool," she told her brother.

"Shut up," Thomas retorted.

Josie took a lamb chop, french fried potatoes, and ice cream up to Gloria in bed.

"Don't let Tommy in, Mama," Gloria said.

"Don't worry," Josie replied. "Nobody can get in. Poor little baby. Look at the nice lamb chop I cooked for you. I sent Frankie over to Mr. Vogel for it special."

Josie banked the pillows behind Gloria's head, set the tray on her lap, and kissed her.

"I'm glad my baby is home again," she said.

Gloria smiled faintly and looked gratefully at her mother. She cut a bit of chop and chewed it slowly. Then she speared a single piece of potato on her fork and put it in her mouth.

"You're the daintiest thing," Josie sighed, and kissed her again. "You eat just like a little bird. Have you got everything you want?"

Gloria nodded.

"Is Uncle Julius home?" she asked.

An expression of worry showed on Josie's face.

"I don't understand your Uncle Julius, Baby," she said. "I never did. He hasn't been the same ever since you got married, it seems to me. He has stayed away from home four different nights, and he hardly touches a bite to eat. He acts as if he had somethin' on his mind. I dunno."

Gloria stopped eating, her eyes resting in the direct, appealing way which was their characteristic, on her mother's face.

"He was so fond of you, too. Ever since you was a baby he was that wild about you. I thought he would've given you a handsome present. I can't make him out for the life of me. There's somethin' on his mind."

Gloria looked suddenly sad; her eyes sparkled with still tears.

"Now don't you be sad," Josie cried, agitatedly. "You go right ahead and eat. And as soon as your Uncle Julius comes in I'll have him come up and see you."

"I don't want to see him," Gloria said, wiping her eyes with a napkin. "I don't want to see anybody ever. I wish I was dead."

Chapter 9

JULIUS FLEETER arrived early next afternoon with a tall woman, about thirty-five. She had dark-brown, crinkly hair, which had a red glint in certain lights, big slate-colored eyes, a generous, upturned nose, a wide, full-lipped mouth, a good chin, and a great many freckles. She had a generous bust and hips, and walked with an air of confidence.

"This is my wife, Josie," Julius Fleeter said. "Mrs. Fleeter, this is Mrs. Boyd about whom I've told you so much."

Mrs. Fleeter's wide lips parted to reveal sound, large teeth, a space between each tooth.

"I'm delighted to meet you, Mrs. Boyd," she said, rather kittenishly for such a large person, and held out a firm hand.

Josie's chin dropped a trifle. She wiped her hand, damp as was not unusual, on her apron, and took the one proffered her.

"Pleased to meet you, Mrs. Fleeter," Josie said.

"Fanny has been my secretary for years," Julius Fleeter explained. "We were married yesterday afternoon. We came over here to see you and to get a few things packed."

"Oh, that's all right; you're perfectly welcome, I'm sure," Josie said nervously. "You aren't going to live here any more then, Mr. Fleeter?"

"He couldn't very well," Mrs. Fleeter said, showing her gap teeth again. "We are planning to live in uptown Manhattan."

"I see," Josie said. "That'll be fine. Gloria's upstairs in bed, Mr. Fleeter."

Julius glanced at her quickly from close-set eyes.

"Upstairs?" he repeated. "I thought she was living with her husband."

116

Mrs. Fleeter looked alternately at Josie and her husband, her lips raising and lowering, so that now she showed her teeth and now she didn't. She took a deep breath as if she were about to say something, but expelled the breath soundlessly. She repeated this procedure.

"She came home yesterday at supper time," Josie said. "Poor baby, she's in a state. She says she doesn't love that boy and'll never live with him again. I want to have the doctor, but she won't hear of it."

"Oh, I'm sorry," Julius Fleeter said, glancing at his wife. "Gloria's the little girl I told you about, Fanny," he explained.

"Oh, yes, indeed," Mrs. Fleeter nodded. "A sweet little thing with a pretty face."

She nodded her head again.

"Perhaps you'd like to go up and see Gloria, Mr. Fleeter?" Josie suggested. "I can be showing Mrs. Fleeter your room."

"Go right ahead, Julius, don't mind me," Mrs. Fleeter said.

"Perhaps I could offer you a cup of tea," Josie said. "It would on'y take a minute."

"No, thank you," Mrs. Fleeter said. "I really don't care for anything right now."

"I know Mr. Fleeter don't drink tea," Josie said, cheeks pink with excitement, hands nervously twisting and untwisting her apron.

"We can all go upstairs, Josie," Julius said, "and I'll stop in and see Gloria. How will that be?"

"I'll go first, and tell her you're here," Josie volunteered hurriedly. "You don't mind, do you, Mrs. Fleeter?"

"Why, no," Mrs. Fleeter said, with her somewhat superior air. "Why should I mind?"

She laughed as if the idea were ridiculous.

Josie stepped gently into Gloria's room. Gloria was in a blue dressing gown, sitting in an easy chair by the window. She had a pad of paper on her lap and was drawing girl faces with a lead pencil. A big doll sat stiffly in a straightback chair beside her.

"Look at this one, Mama," Gloria said, turning the pad. "Isn't she pretty?"

"Sweet baby," Josie said, kissing her forehead. "She's beautiful, just like you."

"I draw pretty good, don't I, Mama?" Gloria asked, smiling.

"You're what I call a real artist," Josie said.

"I always could draw," Gloria said. "I used always to get a hundred for drawing in school."

"Baby?"

"What?"

"Guess who's downstairs?"

"I don't know. Who is it?"

"Uncle Julius is down there."

Gloria's face lost all expression; her eyes were big and blue and still.

"And he's got his wife with him," Josie blurted. "He married his secretary."

"Is she pretty?" Gloria asked.

Josie began to laugh and cry at the same time.

"No, she isn't pretty, you little tyke," she replied. "But you'll see for yourself."

Gloria looked through the open window. It was a hot day. Sweat gathered in tiny drops on her forehead. Her breast rose and fell rapidly. In the backyard children were playing and shouting stridently.

"I just wanted to tell you before I brought them in," Josie said nervously.

Gloria's head revolved slowly, bringing the big eyes to bear on her mother.

"I want my blue dress then," she said.

"Why, you don't have to get dressed, Baby."

"But I want to, Mama—please."

"All right, Baby."

Josie went to the door.

"Just a minute," she called, "and you can come in."

Julius Fleeter entered alone. Gloria was standing in front

of the dresser. She took a last glance at herself and then faced him. She raised her face and Julius bent and kissed her forehead.

"You're looking fine, Gloria," he said.

"I'm all right," she said.

"She's all right, except she seems kinda spiritless," Josie said. "Maybe what she needs is a tonic. I wish you'd make her have the doctor."

"I don't want the doctor," Gloria said, looking straight at Julius Fleeter.

"I'll run and see how Mrs. Fleeter is comin' out," Josie said. "And you two can talk."

Josie went out, closing the door. Julius stepped over to Gloria.

"What happened to the Baby?" he asked. "Wasn't the young fellow nice to her?"

Gloria kept her eyes on his, and very slowly shook her head. She was solemn.

"I didn't love him anyway," she said. "I hate him."

Julius cleared his throat.

"But, Baby! You both are young; perhaps after you get used to him you will learn to love him. He always seemed to be a nice boy."

Gloria continued to keep her gaze fixed on him. Julius took her hands. He cleared his throat. When he spoke he lowered his voice.

"Everything went wrong, Baby," he said. "I couldn't do anything else. I had to think of us both. You know what I've always thought about you."

He groaned.

"Don't worry; I'll help you with—with the baby."

He coughed awkwardly and took both her arms in his hands. Her eyes never left his. His voice was serious, even menacing.

"Remember, Gloria. You've given me your solemn promise never while you live to tell any one. It would be terrible for both of us if you did."

Gloria began to breath faster, but she remained mute. He shook her gently, but with nervous force that was compelling.

"You understand, don't you, sweetheart?"

Gloria winced.

"You hurt, Uncle Julius," she said. "Where is your wife?"

"I can explain that too," Julius said, "when I have time. You will understand I had to do it."

"She isn't as pretty as me," Gloria asserted.

"Nowhere near as beautiful as you," he admitted.

"And she's old," Gloria said.

"She's thirty-five, Gloria."

"That's old," Gloria said.

Julius pulled a handkerchief that smelled of violet water from his breast pocket and wiped his forehead.

"You know our secret," Julius Fleeter said softly. "We must always act so that no one ever suspects us."

"Do you love her?" Gloria demanded, looking in the direction of Julius Fleeter's room.

"I respect her," Julius Fleeter replied. "She is a very fine woman."

Gloria sighed.

"You always said you were going to marry me when I grew up," Gloria said. "You said you'd wait till I was twenty-three."

Julius Fleeter adjusted the pearl pin in his Ascot tie, and pulled the points of the poke collar away from his Adam's apple.

"And I would, darling," he said, "only you know what happened. And we have to be careful. It would be terrible if anybody knew."

"I wish I was dead, Uncle Julius," Gloria said mildly.

"Don't talk like that, Baby. Why, you have everything to live for. Some man that you will love will come along, and you will be happy. You haven't even begun to live yet, child. You have all your life before you."

Gloria looked at him.

"I know what men want," she said, eyes of a child earnest,

lips trembling the least bit. "That's the trouble with him. He was pulling at me all the time. I hate him."

"But, Gloria, I can't understand. You—"

"I guess I don't like boys," Gloria continued evenly.

"Gloria," Julius Fleeter said seriously, "we haven't any more time. You'll always remember I'm your best friend, and that I will help in every way, won't you?"

Gloria's eyes were troubled. She nodded, undecided.

"Well, you'll find out," Julius Fleeter exclaimed hoarsely. "You're the only girl in the world I ever lost my head over. And remember our secret."

"I'll remember," Gloria said simply. "Can I see your wife?"

Julius wiped his forehead again with the handkerchief.

"Why don't you come with me?" he asked. "Come on."

They walked down the hall together and into the big front room in which Julius Fleeter had lived so long. Mrs. Fleeter was sitting in a Morris chair, looking through a photograph album.

"Fanny, this is Gloria," Julius Fleeter said. "This is my wife, Gloria."

Gloria gazed quietly at Mrs. Fleeter, who showed her teeth in a smile and held out her hand.

"I've heard enough about you, Gloria," Mrs. Fleeter laughed, "and I've seen so many pictures of you in this album here that I think I know you fairly well already."

"I look awful in those," Gloria said.

Julius Fleeter and his wife stayed for dinner, which was a constrained meal. They left immediately afterward.

"I haven't given up my room yet," Julius whispered to Josie while his wife was upstairs in the bathroom after dinner. "Here's two hundred dollars now; and I'll have a long when I come over again."

Josie wiped her eyes with her apron.

"Everything is happenin' so sudden," she exclaim don't know where I'm at."

She put her hand to her left breast and gasped.

"He gave me that," she said. "Real jade. Ain't it pretty? Well, that's just for sayin' I'd help him meet you."

She handed the necklace to Gloria.

"Feel how cold it is," she continued. "You can tell its real jade by the cold feel, if you can't tell it from the looks of it. Isn't it lovely?"

"It's sweet," Gloria said, sitting up, and handling the bauble tenderly.

"Go ahead, try it on," Adelaide urged. "Here, I'll hand you a mirror. See, it makes your eyes look green. It looks perfectly lovely on you."

Gloria took the mirror and studied the effect of the necklace.

"It's awfully pretty," she sighed. "I bet it cost a lot."

"A thousand dollars, I guess," Adelaide said. "Cooper has got millions; he builds ships. I'll bet he gets you diamonds."

Gloria's face clouded, and she removed the necklace. But her eyes lingered on its green luster as she handed it back.

"I don't want any diamonds," she asserted.

Adelaide laughed.

"Now you're on'y talkin' through your hat," she chided. "There isn't any girl that doesn't want jewelry. And you with all those paste buckles and pins and everythin' that you keep. There's nobody likes flash any better than you, and you know it."

"He's an old man, and he's married," Gloria said.

Adelaide laughed. She snapped the necklace around her neck again, and turned to the mirror, looking at her reflection from various angles.

"He may be old but he's got young ideas," she said. "And he hasn't lived with that old hatchet face, foreign missionary wife of his for years. He's awful good to girls he likes. He kept Minnie May Wall for five years till she got married; and he sees her yet, now and then. He likes 'em young, Cooper does. Any girl would be glad to get him."

"I don't want to see him," Gloria repeated.

"I guess I'll wear this while I go to the bathroom," Adelaide

123

said, turning to the door. "He'll call to-morrow, and if you know what's good for you you'll have your hair curled and your blue dress on, waitin'. They don't grow Cooper Pattens on every tree."

"I'll stay here," Gloria said. "I won't see him."

"I told him Ma loves everybody," Adelaide said. "She'll think he's fine because he wears swell clothes and takes off his hat when he talks to a lady. You wait."

"He wears nice clothes," Gloria said, "and his nails look awfully nice. I certainly respect a man that takes care of himself."

When Cooper Patten rang the bell the next afternoon at four o'clock, Josie went to the door. Mr. Patten removed his derby and bowed.

"How do you do, Mrs. Boyd?" he said. "Perhaps you remember me—Cooper Patten?"

"Oh, yes, Mr. Patten. Of course I do. Won't you step right in?"

Josie blushed and pulled together her white shirtwaist, open at the bosom.

"I didn't know who it was," she explained, flustered. "I was workin' in the kitchen when I heard the bell, and I came just as I am. I hope you'll excuse me."

Cooper Patten stepped inside.

"Why, I wouldn't have you look any different," he assured her. "You look charming. Perhaps you'll be surprised," he continued, smiling pleasantly, "but I called to-day on the chance that I might be able to see your daughter, Gloria. I think she is one of the loveliest little girls I've ever met. I'd be so proud if she were my own daughter."

Josie blushed with pride.

"She is lovely," Josie exclaimed, "and just as lovely in her actions as in her looks, Mr. Patten, though I, her mother, shouldn't say so."

"I had heard she has a—well—a not happy experience,"

Cooper Patten said. "I thought perhaps a ride in the fresh air might do her good. I have nothing to do. And if she'd go, it would give an old man great pleasure."

"You're too kind, Mr. Patten," Josie said. "I'm sure Gloria'll be only too glad to go for a ride—poor little doll. She hasn't been feeling well. I want her to see a doctor, but she won't hear of it. She just moons around the house. It worries me. I'll call her right away. You can sit right there," indicating the green upholstered chair. "I won't be a minute." ‑

Josie returned within the minute with Gloria, who entered the room with her head held a little forward and down, as if timid, but with her blue eyes raised to Cooper Patten's dark ones. He rose and held out a carefully tended but square, firm and hairy hand.

"Hello, Gloria," he greeted her. "I just thought I'd stop by and take you for a ride in the country, if you're willing. We could drive down the Island somewhere, maybe to Long Beach, and have dinner. What do you say?"

He glanced at Josie and back to Gloria. She hesitated, and looked at her mother.

"Of course, she'll go, Mr. Patten," Josie said. "It's awfully nice of you. You'd better take your coat, Baby."

"It's too warm, I won't need my coat," Gloria said.

"You can't tell how it will be later," Josie said. "And if you go to Long Beach it'll be cooler there near the ocean."

"You'd better take the coat," Cooper Patten agreed. "I've got a roadster, and it might be cool before we get back."

Cooper Patten brought Gloria back home at eleven o'clock. She was unusually animated.

"I had a wonderful time, Mr. Patten," she said.

"We'll have many more of them," he promised. "Sleep tight, little Gloria. Good night."

Daily, except on Sundays, for two weeks Cooper Patten took Gloria for shorter or longer rides. Sometimes they had dinner on the road; at other times Gloria returned in time for dinner at home.

One evening, upon Cooper Patten's insistence, Gloria had sipped at a cocktail at Belcher's Inn, in Huntington, and at dinner had drunk a small glass of wine. On the way home he stopped the car and kissed her. Gloria's eyes were sad, her lips unresponsive. Cooper Patten held her from him.

"See here, Gloria," he said. "There's something on your mind. I guess you know that I want to do everything in the world for you. I can't marry you. I've told you all about my wife. But I can give you everything you want, help you study art, which you say you'd rather do than anything. Tell me what is troubling you."

"I can't," Gloria said.

"Oh, yes, you can," Cooper Patten insisted gently. "You not only can, but you're going to, if you and I sit right here for the next two days. I only want to know in order to help you."

"Nothing is the matter," Gloria said.

Cooper Patten put his right arm around her and drew her to him gently.

"Now, Baby," he soothed, "you tell Cooper all about it. Whatever it is, he promises he will help you. You know, Baby, that people often get wrong ideas about what constitutes tragedy. Why, when you've lived as long as I have you'll just smile at things that seem terrible to you now. Come on. Be a good girl and tell Cooper."

Gloria breathed in quick, irregular intakes of air.

"Please don't ask me, Mr. Patten," she said.

"Call me Cooper, Baby. And remember you and I are friends now, and we are going to be much better friends. I'll do anything for you, you beautiful, wonderful little girl. No matter what it is, sweetheart, I'll straighten it all out for you. Now tell me."

"I c-can't."

"Tell me, Gloria."

She was silent.

"Is it something you're ashamed to tell me?"

Her eyes, eloquent of suffering, met his.

126

"You must tell me, Gloria," he said authoritatively, in the manner, if he had known it, of Julius Fleeter.

"I'm going to have a baby,". Gloria confessed, and hid her eyes in a handkerchief and began to weep.

"Oh!" Cooper Patten exclaimed. "Is that all? Why, my dear. That may be a slight inconvenience, but it's nothing to cry about. Isn't your husband doing the right thing about it? Well, don't you worry. I'll see you through, Baby. And we can make him do whatever is right."

"I don't want to," Gloria said.

"Don't want to what?"

"Have him do anything," Gloria replied.

"Well, he'll probably want to have something to do with it anyway," Cooper Patten said. "After all, darling, it's his baby as much as it's yours."

"No, it isn't."

"What?" Cooper Patten demanded.

"He didn't have anything to do with it," Gloria asserted.

"Why, Gloria, Baby," Cooper Patten exclaimed. "Do you mean that it was some other man?"

Gloria nodded and sobbed restrainedly.

"You won't like me any more, but you made me tell you, and I got so tired keeping everything to myself. I feel terrible, Mr. Patten."

"Well, who is responsible, Gloria?"

Gloria made no answer.

"Who is the man?"

A half-hour of questioning failed to make Gloria reply to that question. Finally she said:

"I don't know."

She stuck stubbornly to that. Cooper Patten sighed.

"It's a peculiar situation, Gloria," he said. "But there's nothing for you to feel so bad about. Now cheer up. I'm not going to ask you another question ever about this. But I'm going to help you just as I said I would. How would you like to go away somewhere and have the baby, and get a divorce, and come back home and be a little girl without any baby or any husband, just like you were before all this happened?"

"I'd like that."

Gloria took the moist handkerchief from her eyes and looked at him.

"Well," he said heartily, "that's fine then. We'll find the best place for you to go, and I'll give you the money for everything. So smile for me now. Give me a kiss."

Gloria puckered her lips, still trembling and wet, and he bent and pressed his mouth to them. He held her for several moments.

"It wasn't so terrible, was it?" he whispered.

She shook her head, sighing.

"You feel better, don't you, darling?"

She nodded vigorously.

"You don't think I'm so bad, do you, Baby?"

She suddenly kissed him of her own accord.

"I think you are the most wonderful man in the world," she said in a low voice, her warm, sweet breath hot on his wrinkled cheek.

"And you'll be my little Gloria—my little baby—and make me happy?"

"I'll try," she replied faintly.

"You poor, dear, sweet little thing," he soothed. "What a terrible time you must've been having. But now everything is all right, isn't it?"

He kissed her again.

"I'm crazy about you, Baby," he said. "You're the most beautiful little bundle of love I've ever seen. I love your hair, and your eyes, and your nose, and your mouth, and your chin, and the pink in your cheeks. I could eat you all up."

Gloria sighed contentedly, a quivering expelled breath.

"You're a little angel," he said, kissing her again.

"My mother calls me her little doll," she said.

"Now you're going to be my little doll," he announced.

He kissed her again. She pressed against him, relaxed. He

kissed her ear. She shuddered and put her hand up to his mouth.

"That tickles," she said.

He kissed her neck.

"Let's get out of the car for a minute," he suggested. "It's a beautiful night."

"Oh, no," she exclaimed, starting. "Please."

"All right, Baby," he said. "Just give me one more kiss."

Gloria was quiet on the way home.

"You're the most wonderful little love in the world," Cooper Patten told her.

"You're the most wonderful man in the world," she replied shyly.

Josie took breakfast upstairs to Gloria as usual next morning.

"Why, you're lookin' better already, Baby," she said. "It's certainly done you a world of good to go out ridin' with Mr. Patten. I hope you've been properly grateful to him for his kindness."

Josie arranged the tray.

"I wish you'd see Mr. Kane, Tom's father, Baby," Josie continued. "He's an awful nice man, that Mr. Kane. He's asked about you, and asked about you, and he's so disappointed because you won't even talk to him."

"I'll talk to him, Mama," Gloria said.

"When?" Josie asked, smiling happily. "I'm so glad you've changed your mind."

"Whenever he wants to and I'm in," Gloria said.

"You like Mr. Kane, don't you, darling? He was always nice to you."

"I like him all right," Gloria said.

Lemuel Kane saw Gloria the following Sunday afternoon. Cooper Patten spent Sundays with his family. They sat alone in the living room, Gloria perched rigidly on the end of a stiff chair.

"I understand you don't want to live as Thomas's wife any more, Gloria," Lemuel Kane said.

"No," Gloria said.

"You don't think you'll change your mind?"

Gloria shook her head.

"I hope you'll look upon me as your friend, Gloria," Lemuel Kane said. "I'll admit that I was upset when I heard you and Thomas had been married. But I never blamed you. I never blamed either of you. It was just one of those things that happen now and then that can't seem to be helped."

Gloria smoothed down her dress, and examined her pink fingernails.

"It's very hard to understand how you feel or what you think when you don't say anything, Gloria," Lemuel Kane said. "Don't you feel that we should have a friendly talk and see if we can't decide on something?"

"Everything is all right," Gloria said, looking at him with quiet candor. "I don't know what there is to decide."

Lemuel Kane removed his spectacles and began polishing them with a clean linen handkerchief. He rubbed the red mark on the bridge of his nose where the spectacles rested, breathed on the lenses and rubbed them between handkerchief-covered thumb and forefinger.

"Why, Gloria," he suggested mildly, "it seems to me that we have some problem left. So far as the law is concerned you are still Thomas's wife—and there is the baby that is coming. That is a new life in which certainly we must concern ourselves. Of course, we must make some plans, and I want you to consider that I am your friend."

"You don't have to bother, Mr. Kane," Gloria said, moving uneasily on her chair. "Everything is all right."

Lemuel Kane sighed, replaced the glasses carefully, tucked away the handkerchief, and leaned forward earnestly.

"But, Gloria," he insisted. "Arrangements must be made if you are not going to return to Thomas. We must know what is going to be done about the baby—his and yours. I would be very uncomfortable letting matters just drift along. Sooner or later, something will have to be done. Won't you help me?"

Gloria twitched impatiently.

"Everything is all right, Mr. Kane," she said. "You don't have to worry about the baby. And I'll get a divorce from Thomas."

"Well, of course, if you feel that you can't be happy with Tom I guess that's the best thing to do—a divorce," Lemuel Kane agreed. "But the baby is the important thing. I suppose you'll want to keep the baby?"

"I never want to see the baby," Gloria exclaimed, with feeling. "I don't like to talk about it. What do you have to keep talking about it for? Didn't I tell you everything is all right?"

"I'm sorry if I've upset you, Gloria," Lemuel Kane said. "I think you'll find you'll feel differently after the baby comes. Mothers generally do, you know. And, strangely enough, I feel I sort of have an interest in the baby's welfare. I think it is only fair and right that Thomas should make some arrangement for caring for the baby—financial arrangement, I mean. He might even want to have an arrangement made by which he could have a hand in the baby's education later, and perhaps visit it, or have it with him for periods."

Gloria sat up straight in her chair, dismay showing in her face.

"I know it seems as if I were talking about something a long way ahead," Lemuel Kane said, "but my dear, you have no idea how fast the months and the years roll by. When you're my age you'll know. And there is nothing like preparing for every emergency, so far as possible. Some day perhaps you'll appreciate what I'm doing. Friendly arrangements now may prevent heartbreaks later on. And I think you'll understand my interest in the welfare of the child. My conscience would hurt me, Gloria, if I thought the baby were going to be denied a fair chance in life because of any fault of mine, or a member of my family."

Gloria began to breathe fast.

"It hasn't anything to do with your family, Mr. Kane," she exclaimed, speaking fast. "You haven't anything to do with it."

Lemuel Kane made a movement of his body that indicated he was prepared to be patient with youthful stubbornness and ignorance.

"I don't think you understand," he began carefully.

"You don't understand," Gloria cried. "Oh, dear! Why can't you leave me alone?"

Lemuel Kane rose. He stepped over to Gloria and laid a hand on her shoulder.

"Well, I won't bother you any more right now, little girl," he announced. "I'll drop in and see you again in a day or two. I want to help you; I don't want to hurt you."

"It won't do any good to come and see me," Gloria cried. "I don't want to talk about it any more."

"Why, Gloria!" Lemuel Kane exclaimed, smiling down at her. "I guess you're a little excited right now."

"The baby isn't Tom's anyway," Gloria blurted suddenly. "I just blamed Tom."

She sobbed, fumbling around her belt for a handkerchief which wasn't there. Lemuel Kane handed his handkerchief to her.

"There! There! Don't cry, Baby."

"I don't care," Gloria sobbed. "I wasn't going to tell you, but it's the truth. I felt terrible about it, but I had to do it. And now I'm glad I told you."

"But who was responsible then, Gloria?" he asked.

"I'll never tell," Gloria exclaimed. "I couldn't look at Tom. I hate him. I hate him!"

"I think I understand, Gloria," Lemuel Kane said gravely. "It makes things clearer to me. Poor little girl!"

"I'm not poor, and I'm not little."

"Why, you must have been desperate, Baby. I'd like to know what's back of this. Somebody should go to jail, or be tarred and feathered."

Gloria shrank back in the chair.

"Oh, please, Mr. Kane. You've got to promise not to tell anybody. Oh, *please*. Something dreadful might happen to me. Please."

"I'll promise, Gloria. Of course, I'd never say anything unless you gave me your permission. I appreciate your telling me the truth, Gloria. It will take a load from our shoulders, but what about yours? What are you going to do? Even after everything, Gloria, I can't believe that you were a willing party to the deception practiced on Tom."

"I'm all right, Mr. Kane. Honest I am. I'm going away for a while and then I'm coming back again, and I'll get a divorce from Tom."

"Have you the money for all this, Gloria?"

Gloria, wet handkerchief tightly clasped in her hand, talk nodded and snuffled.

"Yes, I have," she said. "I'm sorry about everything, Mr. Kane. I guess I've been crazy."   "I

She smiled, a sad little twisted smile. Lemuel Kane took her hands in his.

"I'm going now, Gloria," he said quietly, "but I'll see you again soon. I want you to know that you can trust me and that if you need any help I'll be only too glad to be of service."

"All right, Mr. Kane," Gloria said.

He picked up his hat and went to the door. There he paused, and stepped back to her side.

"This man," he said. "Is he making the arrangements?"

Gloria raised eyes, suddenly expressionless, a face set in stubborn lines. She softened a little.

"No," she said. "I don't want to talk any more."

Lemuel went out, shaking his head solemnly.

"I can't help feeling that that little girl has been terribly abused by some one," he told his wife a little later.

"Apparently she knows how to pull the wool over men's eyes," Emma sniffed. "Instead of sympathizing with her you should have had her arrested. The little hypocrite!"

133

"It's queer how women's minds work," Lemuel said. "Here you are one of the most sympathetic, loving, helpful persons I know, and yet look at your attitude towards Gloria, and Thomas too."

Emma sat up very straight and stiff.

"I could never compromise with immorality," she asserted with emphasis. "I would rather have a child of mine die than live an immoral life."

"Emma!" Lemuel Kane exclaimed.

"I mean it," she declared. "Why, I always was right about that Gloria Kane. Her whole appearance was, 'Come and get me.' Those preposterous curls, and making eyes all the time. And I do think she paints."

Emma sniffed again.

"I always was suspicious of that family. There was something about it—all those uncles. Of course, I'd report the whole affair to the police."

"And get Thomas and ourselves involved."

"I remember when I caught you kissing that girl and you got red. It's not Thomas you're thinking of, Lemuel Kane."

"Aw, Em!"

"Don't you 'Aw, Em' me. I don't know how I've gone through what I have and lived. Now, if you'll please me, you'll just leave Gloria Kane and her family alone, never see them again, and never mention them again, at least, to me."

"I don't see how you can be so hard on a little girl that doesn't know any better. By your own admission, her beauty is dangerous, and her family is not any help to her—no father."

"Don't talk about it any more. The subject is closed, so far as I'm concerned. I'd like to know what in the world would be the use of us living moral, helpful lives, if flagrant immorality were to be pampered and encouraged. Send the girl to an institution where she belongs. Don't have her around corrupting respectable children."

Lemuel put his arms around his wife. She stood stiff as a poker. He kissed her. "My little Puritan," he whispered.

"There aren't many sturdy oaks like you, Em. I wouldn't have you any different."

She softened and returned his kiss.

"We all have emotions," she said, "but we have to control them. Where would the human race be if we didn't? Why, a family of Boyds can demoralize a neighborhood. You speak as if punishing Gloria Boyd would be thoughtless cruelty. The individual should suffer for the welfare of the community. And you know you feel the same way." Her voice became sarcastically mincing. "Except that this girl has a doll face and a sweet way with her."

Her voice changed to normal tone.

"Well, if you ask me, that only makes her more dangerous. The Lord only knows where she's going to end if she's starting out this way at her age."

Lemuel Kane kissed her again, and hugged her close. "I'm glad I've got you," he said. "Do you love me, Emma?"

"You know I do, Lemuel," Emma replied, kissing him. "I love you and respect you more than I ever thought I could love and respect any man."

"That makes me feel better, Em," Lemuel grinned. "You know for a while I thought I was in your black books too."

Chapter 10

MARTIN BRADY was wearing a yellow shirt and a cerise tie.
His straw-colored hair in which the gray did not show to
casual glance was smoothed down sleekly; his suit in a pastel
shade of green was neatly pressed; his black and doe-skin
sport shoes were immaculate, and the big diamond on his left
hand sparkled as brilliantly as ever. But the pink of his cheeks
had become more of a purple shade, the whites of his eyes
were not clear and dark circles were visible under them. His
hand trembled as he lighted a cigarette before breakfast,
which he was waiting to eat at the dining room table instead
of in his room.

Josie Boyd entered from the kitchen, carrying a large glass
of orange juice.

"Why didn't you let me know, Marty," she said. "I'd 'a'
brought your breakfast up to you."

"No more you won't, Josie," Martin Brady said. "I'll be
God damned if you'll do any more runnin' up and down stairs
for me."

"I love to do it," Josie protested.

"Sure you do," Martin Brady agreed heartily. "You'd love
to break your neck for any worthless bum that came along.
You and I've got to finish our talk. That's a cinch."

Josie set down the glass of orange juice and started back
to the kitchen. As she walked, she said:

"I won't have the doctor, Marty. I told you that. There's no
use havin' the doctor for a little indigestion."

Martin Brady raised the glass in a shaking hand. He pushed

away from the table just in time to avoid spilling some of the juice on his suit.

"It's no go, Josie," he said sorrowfully. "I've got to have a bit of the hair off the dog that bit me. Have you got some of that bum gin out there?"

"I guess there is some," Josie said. "Yes, there is," she added. "Do you want it?"

"Want it?" Martin Brady repeated. "I've gotta have it. I'll shake to pieces if I don't."

He pushed an empty goblet beside his place towards Josie.

"You pour it," he said.

"Say when."

She began to pour. When the glass was a quarter-full she stopped, and looked at him.

"Keep on goin'," Martin Brady directed. "I need a bath, not an eye-wash."

"It'll make you sick, Martin."

"I'd be better off dead than the way I am, Josie."

She began to pour again. He cried:

"Whoa! That's enough."

He embraced the goblet with both hands and raised it to his lips. Tilting his head back, he took a big swallow, choked and gagged a bit, and then took another big swallow. He replaced the goblet on the table and gagged, more purple in the face than ever.

"I don't see how you do it, Marty," Josie said.

He waved his hands at her, grabbed up a napkin, held it to his mouth and coughed and gagged. He put down the napkin and poured a little of the orange juice into what remained of the gin.

"Here's how," he said, and tossed the mixture down his throat.

He shook himself, straightened his tie, and exclaimed:

"Brr! That should do somethin'."

"Don't you think perhaps you drink a little too much, Marty?" Josie asked wistfully.

He turned light blue eyes on her and grinned, showing strong yellow teeth.

"By God! Josie," he said, "you know that may be what's the trouble. I hadn't thought of it before."

"A man don't always stop to think," Josie said, blushing.

"You're right, Josie. And on the other hand, a man might not have anythin' worth stoppin' to think about. Did y' ever think of that?"

"I'll get the coffee," Josie said. "I'm makin' some fresh."

"You would," Martin Brady exclaimed.

He drank the orange juice and a moment later sipped hot coffee.

"I feel better," he said. "Now sit down."

Josie hesitated.

"I've got a lot of chores to do, Marty," she said. "There's the breakfast dishes and the beds and the shoppin' and I've got to bake to-day. You know my family won't eat baker's stuff."

Martin snorted.

"Sit down," he roared, "before I knock you down. My God! It's a life's job to get you to rest for a minute."

Josie sat down sidewise on a chair, wiping her hands on her apron. Her blonde hair ran back from her white forehead in ripples no hairdresser could duplicate; her blue eyes were radiant with good will; her cheeks had lost some roses, but she still had a complexion that a schoolgirl might have envied. There wasn't a line on forehead or cheek. Her expression always was of one about to smile.

"You can't scare me, Marty," she said gently.

"Oh, yes, I can, Josie," he replied. "I could scare you half to death by telling you this coffee wasn't any good."

"Isn't it all right?" Josie exclaimed anxiously, rising. "I put an egg in it, just the same as I always do."

"Sure, it's fine," he comforted her. "I was only teasin'. Sit down and listen to me. There are some questions before the house, and they got to be answered pretty soon. In the first place, what I want you to do is get out of here and marry me."

"I told you, Marty, that I wouldn't leave my babies to marry anybody," Josie said. "I'd just as soon die as be without them. Now don't get mad," she added hastily, as Marty thumped the tablecloth with his fist.

"Mad? It's enough to drive any man with a heart crazy," Martin Brady said. "What in hell do the kids do for you? Do they thank you for all you do? They do like hell! They just holler for more service."

"They're only babies," Josie explained. "They love me."

Martin Brady looked at her, shook his head, sighed, and poured himself another drink.

"I don't like to use it as an argument for myself," he said, "but what in hell are you goin' to do about expenses now that Julius Fleeter has taken a run-out powder? I suppose you expect the dough is just goin' to fall off a tree, or somethin'? The rent alone here is a hundred bucks a month, ain't it?"

Josie nodded.

"That's right," she said. "It went up on account of the war. But we can manage all right, I guess."

"Don't look mysterious, Josie," Martin Brady said. "I suppose you figure you can get a boarder or two. But you don't know anythin' about it. You might not find 'em that'd be willin' to live here with all these kids."

"You'n Mr. Fleeter lived with me," Josie said.

Martin Brady looked hard at her and lighted a cigarette. He shook his head ruefully.

"Yes, I suppose you'll never want for a boarder or two," he agreed unhappily. "But I told you last night somethin' how I feel. I don't like Addie comin' staggerin' home at all hours, and all the men she's got hangin' around. And I don't like the idear of young Frank stealin' things out of my room; and I don't mind sayin' I hate to watch what's happenin' to Gloria. I suppose this visit she's makin' in Camden is to have a baby, ain't it?"

Josie looked hurt.

"I don't like to hear you talk like that, Marty," she said. "Addie's young and full of life, an' I guess all the girls nowadays 're havin' their fling. She'll be all right."

Josie wiped her eyes with her apron.

"An' how about young Frank stealin' things?"

"He's on'y a baby," Josie said. "I talked to him. He won't do it any more. He's promised."

"Yeah! You talked to him before; and he promised before. And how about Gloria, Josie? This Cooper Patten is payin' the freight, ain't he, for her visit in the country?"

"You seem to know all about it, Marty," Josie said. "And anyhow, I don't see what's wrong with you knowin'. Mr. Patten—"

"Sure, I know," Martin Brady interrupted. "Cooper Patten takes a fatherly interest in her. Well, what puzzles me, Josie, is if that kid across the street that she married is the father of the baby why he's lettin' another guy pay the expenses. There's somethin' rotten in this business. I'm nothin' but a God damn' lowbrow bookmaker, but I don't like it. And what did Julius disappear for after he went and married that laughin' hyena of a secretary of his; and what in hell did he go and marry the secretary for anyway?"

Martin Brady was getting more purple in the face than ever. He began to pound the tablecloth and raised his voice to a shout.

"Please, Marty," Josie said, her lips trembling. "You hurt my feelin's. Please don't shout."

Marty subsided. He reached for the gin bottle.

"I wish you wouldn't drink any more gin, Marty," Josie said.

He pushed the bottle away violently.

"I wish I wouldn't too, Josie," he said. "But God damn it, booze is a good way to get away from troubles. I'm nuts about you, but I couldn't take the responsibility for the whole God damn' tribe."

"I wonder where Mr. Fleeter did disappear to?" Josie said.

"You should've been here the day his wife came over. She was wild. I guess she thought we had him hid somewhere."

"That bastard!" Martin Brady exclaimed.

"I always thought you and Mr. Fleeter were friends."

"We were business associates, as you might call it," Martin Brady explained. "But I was never pals with a snake. Not me! I may be a bum bookmaker, but I draw the line somewhere. I'd like to know where he was myself, if it'd be a guarantee that you'll never see him again around here."

"You know, Marty," Josie said. "Gloria says to me that time that Mr. Fleeter brought his wife over here, and they ate supper with us—after they were gone—she says 'Mama,' she says, 'don't you think Uncle Julius looked sad?' And when I said I didn't know or somethin' like that, she says, 'Do you think he's sad because he married that woman?' "

"I'd like to know what it's all about myself," Martin Brady asserted.

"I felt sorry for Mrs. Fleeter—her on'y a bride and everythin'," Josie said. "She took it hard. That's a week ago, an' she's called on the telephone at least twice every day since. She says they don't know anythin' about him at his office except he isn't there. I'd never have taken Mr. Fleeter for that kind of a man."

"You wouldn't," Martin Brady said, lighting a fresh cigarette and arising.

He stretched, shook down his trouser legs, and stepped over beside Josie. He laid his cigarette on a saucer and put a hand on each of her shoulders.

"Look here, Josie," he said. "You'n' me ain't kids. I'm crazy about you, an' I guess I don't exactly make you sick. Now listen. Let's you and me get married. George'll have to look out for himself. Addie's got a job, and 'd be better off away from home anyway. Malcolm's got a job, and c'n live in a Y.M.C.A., or somewhere. Gloria's bein' looked after by Cooper Patten. Besides that, she's married. That leaves Frank and Ernie. My dope is Frank'd be better off in a reform school, but I don't expect a mother like you to feel that way about it. We c'n find some kind of school to put him in—and with me around to put a little pressure on when it's needed, we can handle Ernie. You ain't well, Josie. You should be rid of all these kids and these worries. Come on. First, we can board Frank and Ernie and take a trip. It'd do you good. You're the sweetest dame I ever heard of, Josie, and prettier than you got any right to be. Give me a kiss, and say, 'Yes.' "

Josie let him kiss her, but she shook her head.

"It's just a lot of foolishness, Marty," she said kindly. "Talkin' like you do. I wouldn't leave my babies for anythin' in the world. You know that."

Martin Brady groaned.

"If you think you're doin' those kids any good, Josie," he cried desperately, "you're crazy. You spoil 'em; that's all. All any of 'em have got to do is tease and they get what they want."

Tears gathered in Josie's eyes.

"I do the best I can, Marty," she said quietly.

Martin Brady hugged her and kissed her.

"Excuse me, Josie," he said. "I get so damn mad. Anybody that makes you feel bad is a son-of-a-bitch, and ought to be shot. My God, how could any woman be so sweet?"

Then he added, under his breath:

"And so dumb."

"What did you say, Marty?"

"Nothin'," he replied, kissing her again.

"Well, I've got to get to work," Josie said. "It's near eleven now. I'm 'way late. Let me be, Marty. I've got a lot to do."

She rose and picked up goblet, coffee cup and saucer and spoon. She hesitated, set them quickly down again, and pressed her hand to her left side in the old familiar gesture. Her face was distorted with pain. Small drops of cold perspiration bathed her forehead.

"Another of those damn' things?" Martin Brady demanded.

She looked at him from eyes haggard with agony and nodded.

"I—can't—breathe," she gasped.

He picked her up and carried her into the living room and laid her on the sofa.

"You want the soda and ginger?" he asked.

She was gasping; her eyes were rolling.

"Yes," she panted.

"Right away," he said.

But instead of going to the kitchen, he went to the telephone in the hall, closing the door. He reached Dr. Pearson on the telephone.

"Come over quick," he said.

When the doctor arrived, he examined Josie quickly, and asked questions. Then he gave her a couple of little white pellets and watched her. He popped another pellet in her mouth. She smiled, relieved. When she was resting comfortably, the doctor spoke to Martin Brady in the dining room.

"It's her heart, ain't it, Doc?" Martin Brady asked.

Dr. J. L. Pearson nodded gravely.

"Angina pectoris," he said. "Hardening of the blood vessels. That was nitroglycerine I gave her," he explained. "Now, what she must do," he continued, "is rest, and do absolutely no hard work. In fact, I'd suggest that she sleep on the first floor. When she gets one of these attacks she should take these pills—one or two at a time, with short intervals between—until she is relieved. I'll leave some prescriptions."

"Is it serious, Doc?"

"Well, it's serious, but not necessarily fatal," Dr. Pearson replied. "With proper care many of these cases live for years to die of some other disease. But she will have to be careful. Climbing stairs and doing housework is out of the question."

After Doctor Pearson had gone, Martin Brady returned to Josie.

"I've got to get to work," she said weakly. "I don't know what ails me lately."

Martin Brady grinned, gently pushed her back on the couch and kissed her.

"I've been kickin' because everybody let you do all the work, Josie," he said, "but I never stopped to think I was just as willin' to see you break your neck as they was. You've got to stay right where you are for a while. I'll wash the dishes."

Josie sat up, horror on her face.

"You can't do that, Marty," she cried. "Dishes ain't for men to do. There's nothin' the matter with me. I'm all right. Let me up."

"The doc says your pump has gone on strike," Martin Brady said, "but you'll be all right if you don't work and run up and down stairs. Now, you're goin' to stay right there."

"That's foolish," Josie said. "Who's goin' to do the work if I don't."

Martin Brady held a restraining hand on her shoulder.

"One thing is sure," he asserted. "And that is that you ain't goin' to do any work. And another thing is sure. I've got to stay right here with the gang, an' like it."

Josie ceased mild struggling against him for an instant. Her eyes brightened.

"You ain't goin' away then, Marty?"

Martin Brady shook his head.

"How the hell could I go away without you, Josie? I'll stay here, an' we'll get married anyway."

Josie blushed and smiled.

"Why, don't you know, Marty, that I can't get married? I don't know if Ernie is still alive or not."

Martin Brady's eyes widened.

"But I'm real glad you're goin' to stay, Marty," Josie added.

"You c'd get a divorce," Martin suggested, but not too warmly.

Josie rearranged her hair deftly, smiling up at him.

"I'll never get a divorce," she said, "an' I'd never get married either with my babies to look after."

144

"Well, you stay there, an' I'll take a crack at the crockery," Martin Brady said.

Josie made such a vigorous attempt to rise that he had to help her.

"Look out," he warned. "You're supposed to be sick."

"Don't be silly," Josie said. "I can't afford to be sick, Marty."

Josie compromised by letting Martin Brady dry the dishes.

"It don't seem right," she said.

He kissed her.

"Why holy jumping Catfish, Josie!" he announced. "I didn't know what I was missin' all this time. When do I start on the beds?"

Cooper Patten drove to Camden on Wednesdays and Saturdays to see Gloria, who was living with Josie's oldest sister, Myra, a worn and faded edition of Josie.

Myra was thin and slabsided. Her hair was blonde but dead-looking. Her forehead was marked with many wrinkles. Her eyes were blue but washed out. Her shoulders stooped and her breasts hung down pendulously. She was always ironing, and complaining of the heat of the stove, or of her varicose veins. She always was worrying, either about her husband, Matt Grove, who was a fireman on the railroad, or about her son, Willis, who was with the Expeditionary Force in France, or about her other son, Homer, who was working in a shipyard, or about her daughter, Dorothy, Gloria's age, who was working in a millinery shop.

While Cooper Patten and Gloria were talking for a few minutes in the front parlor, following a short automobile ride, Myra Grove's voice came to their ears, shrill and complaining. She was talking to Ma Brennan, who had lived with the Groves ever since she left the Boyds.

"I always told Matt to be careful about wrappin' himself up good an' warm," Myra said, while she pushed an iron over a shirtwaist, "but that's all the good it did. He goes and gets himself his death of a cold. An' I can't do anythin' with him. He'll get inflammation of the lungs, as sure's you're born . . . those women in France. I warned Willis, but you know how men are . . . I'll certainly be thankful when this war is over . . . of course, with Homer so good lookin', and makin' such good wages . . . all the girls are after him. . . ."

Cooper Patten glanced humorously over his shoulder in the direction of the kitchen, and winked slowly at Gloria.

"I guess your aunt has been carrying on the same conversation for years, hasn't she?" he asked.

Gloria, cheeks still glowing from the crisp Fall out-of-doors, smiled. Her figure was thicker; her face was rounder; her breasts were more prominent.

"She's always worrying," she said, eyes crinkling. "She fusses over me all the time. She wants me to wear rubbers and carry an umbrella if it looks like rain. But I don't go out except at night any more."

Cooper Patten arose.

"Well, it should be all over before long," he said. "And you're going to be perfectly satisfied to have those people adopt it? You're sure?"

Gloria nodded.

"I don't like to talk about it," she said.

"I understand," Cooper Patten said sympathetically. "And I don't want to talk about anything that displeases my baby, but we've got to be sure."

"I'm sure," Gloria said. "I would never want it."

"I wish you'd tell me what there is back of this, Gloria," he said, suddenly bending over her. "You can trust me. You know that. Why don't you?"

She shrank back from him in alarm.

"All right!" he comforted her quickly. "All right! Forgive me, Baby. That's the last time I'll ever mention anything about it. Honor bright! Cross my heart and cut me in two."

"You promised before," Gloria said.

"Well, this time goes," he asserted. "You can't blame me

for being curious, can you? And your attitude is a trifle un-usual, I think. However, Baby, you're an unusual girl—never was one so sweet and so beautiful. Give me a kiss, and I'll be going."

She held up her pursed lips and he pressed his against them.

"Ah!" he said, "that's worth traveling a thousand miles to get."

Gloria smiled, pleased, and, rising from her chair, glanced in the mirror over the white-painted wooden mantel.

"I'll be down to see you next Saturday as usual; and tele-phone me if you're lonesome. It won't be long now."

Gloria walked with him to the door.

"And I'm going to study art and everything then, aren't I?" she asked wistfully.

He laughed and patted her shoulder.

"You certainly are, Baby," he said. "You're going to have your fling for a change. We'll send you to a good school and maybe to Paris afterwards."

"I think I would love interior decorating," Gloria said shyly, eyes glowing. "I've been making lots of designs."

"That's fine," Cooper Patten said. "Nothing could please me more. You keep right at it. I wouldn't wonder if you'd be famous before you knew it."

"I love beautiful things," Gloria sighed. "And everybody says I have wonderful taste."

"Why, you precious baby," Cooper Patten exclaimed. "Who's going to see that you have everything in the world that you want?"

Gloria smiled happily.

"Well, who?" Cooper Patten demanded. "Tell me."

She dropped her eyelashes, and touched him on the coat sleeve with her forefinger.

"You are," she whispered.

"You can just bet I am, Baby," he said, and kissed her brow and at the same time winked over her head his slow wink with one eye.

"I always wanted to be good," she confessed in a hushed voice. "And now nobody'll know I was ever bad, will they?" She looked up solemnly.

"They certainly won't," Cooper Patten assured her. "We'll see to that. Now, Baby, I've got to be running along. Only a couple of days and I'll be seeing you again."

On the drive back to North River, Long Island, where Cooper Patten lived in his big rambling Colonial house, his eyelid frequently dropped down on his cheek and stayed there for a minute at a time. It lent an expression of malevolence to his long, high-colored horse-face.

When he arrived home, his mother, Mrs. Horace Gordon Patten, was in the sun room in the dark, sewing on uniforms for girls in homes. Old Lady Patten had had a stroke five years before, and since then she mumbled unintelligibly. Members of her family explained that she spoke sometimes in French, sometimes in German, sometimes in Italian, and occasionally in English.

"Since her shock," they said, "she is likely to forget which language she is speaking in. That's what makes it difficult for strangers to understand her. She'll use four languages in the same sentence. But she's in full possession of her faculties."

The old lady, who once had been tall and slim, now was bent over in the shape of a hoop. Her head shook. She spent most of her waking hours sewing on the uniforms, worth about eighteen cents each, and got a great reputation for philanthropy among the well-to-do, but a much smaller reputation with the servants, the grocer's boy, the ice man, the garbage man, the butcher's boy.

"Why doesn't the old dope knit balls and chains for convicts?" the garbage man wanted to know.

Mrs. Horace Gordon Patten rode about the countryside in a limousine, with a very high body, her late husband's ex-coachman on the box. The garbage man, whose name was Randall Smith and who said his father used to own land in that neighborhood as far as you could see, averred that the ex-coachman forgot every now and then that he wasn't driving horses.

"I've seen Old Casey bow the old lady into that hearse of hers and then hop into the driver's seat and start chirruping," Randall Smith said. "He nearly run me down once, comin' into the drive. 'Gee!' he says. 'Haw!' he says. They sure make a hell of a pair on the road. Ten miles an hour they do, with everybody that knows 'em gettin' off the road to give 'em plenty of elbow room."

Cooper Patten had his mother sign legal papers at intervals. Old Horace Gordon Patten had left everything to his widow.

"It'd sure be tough on Cooper if she wasn't in her right senses so she couldn't sign all them papers they say he brings to her," Randall Smith said.

Randall Smith grinned, and looked around the group in back of Johnson's Garage.

"If she was in her right senses she wouldn't sign 'em," he added. "That old lady always had Cooper's number. Right senses? Hell, she's been cuckoo for five years."

"Why don't somebody do something about it?" was asked.

Randall Smith lighted a cigarette.

"What's there to do?" he demanded. "Cooper's got high-priced doctors, an' high-priced lawyers around all the time. I'm just tellin' you the lowdown. D'you expect I could be heard sayin' my opinion in court against half a dozen experts? Ha! Ha! Son, when you get as old as I be, you'll know the best job a man c'n do in this life is mind his own darned business."

Chapter 11

Cooper Patten drove Gloria home from Camden in a limousine.

"This is my wife's," he smiled. "Some day I'll have to get you one like it."

"It's wonderful," Gloria said.

"Everything's going to be wonderful for you after this," Cooper Patten assured her. "You didn't have much trouble having the baby, did you?"

Gloria shook her head impatiently. She was wearing a new black felt hat and a new black coat with fur collar and cuffs. Beneath it was a blue dress. A string of blue beads was around her neck. Her pretty legs were in sheer black silk, and she had new patent leather opera pumps. She looked like a little school girl.

"The doctor gave me something and next I knew it was all over," she said. "You know that. I don't like to talk about it."

"You don't even realize you have had a baby, do you?" Cooper Patten persisted, looking at her curiously.

"I don't feel as if it belonged to me," she said. "Please. I don't want to talk about it."

"Well, we won't talk about it any more," Cooper Patten promised. "We'll just consider you were sick, and now the doctors have made you all well again."

"That's the way I feel," she said. "When will I go away to study interior decorating?"

"Very soon now," Cooper Patten assured her. "We've got to take time to look around and find the best way to do it."

"I'm so anxious. I want to work hard and earn money and make beautiful things."

"You will, Baby. Don't worry."

He accompanied her into the house. Josie met them at the door.

"I'm so glad, Baby," Josie cried, kissing and hugging her.

Josie held Gloria away from her.

"Why, you dear, sweet baby," she said. "Mama's little doll hasn't changed. What a pretty hat—and coat. Why, you have everything new. Aren't they lovely?"

Gloria flushed and turned around so that her mother could view her wardrobe better. She opened the coat and showed the figured satin lining.

"And who got you all these beautiful things?" Josie asked.

Gloria pointed to Cooper Patten.

"He did," she replied.

"Oh, Mr. Patten," Josie exclaimed. "You shouldn't 've. You shouldn't spend all that money. You're too good to Gloria."

Cooper Patten grinned.

"She's a sweet little girl," he said, "and it's a great pleasure to do things for her. Isn't she pretty though?"

"She's her mama's little doll baby," Josie cooed, kissing Gloria again. "Won't you come in, Mr. Patten? We're just going to have Sunday night supper—baked beans and brown bread and ham. We'd love to have you."

"I don't think I will to-night, thank you," Cooper Patten said. "I'll be dropping over to-morrow to see how Gloria is. I'm going to keep my eye on her from now on."

"That's wonderful, Mr. Patten. We never can thank you for everything you've done. I'm awfully sorry you can't stay."

When the door closed behind Cooper Patten and his chauffeur, who had brought in two suitcases for Gloria, Josie said:

"This is too wonderful. Georgie and Eddie 've just got home from France. It seems so nice to have everybody home again."

Gloria took the news calmly.

"I guess I'll go up to my room first, Mother," she said.

"I'd carry up your suitcases," Josie said, "on'y the doctor says I have to be careful on account of my heart."

"It must be terrible to have something the matter with your heart, Mama. I'm so sorry."

Gloria kissed her mother. Josie called:

"Malcolm, Georgie, Frankie!"

Malcolm yelled from the kitchen.

"What d'y' want?"

"Come and help your sister upstairs with her suitcases."

"Aw, heck! Why can't she lug 'em up herself?"

"Why, Malcolm, is that the way to act, and your sister just back from a long visit. Haven't you got a kiss for her?"

Malcolm stumped into the hall with a long face.

"Gee whizz!" he whined, "ain't there nobody else around except me? Always pickin' on me."

"You didn't say hello to Gloria," Josie pointed out.

"Hello," Malcolm said, making a quick dab at Gloria's cheek with his mouth. "I hate women," he complained. "Always wantin' to be waited on. Gee whizz!"

"I don't think you're very nice to your sister," Josie protested.

"I'm nice enough," Malcolm replied. "What's she ever done for me, I'd like to know, except tell on me whenever she got the chance?"

He stooped over and lifted the suitcases.

"What you got in these things—bricks?" he groaned.

Gloria followed him upstairs. After he had set down the suitcases, she held out a dollar bill.

"Would you like a dollar, Malcolm?" she asked.

He looked at her and at the dollar, and grabbed the dollar, inspected it, and stuffed it in his pocket.

"I don't mind doin' errands for you," he said, thawing. "Gees! Addie never gave me a nickel in her life."

Gloria turned the key in the lock after Malcolm was gone, and looked around the room. She opened her bag, took out a roll of bills, most of them yellow, and counted them—ten ten-dollar bills, two five-dollar bills, and six ones. She opened a drawer and looked in it and shut it. She went to the closet, opened the door, and peered around inside. She lifted an old shoe from the floor and pushed the yellow bills into the toe. Then she dropped the shoe on the floor again. The first question she asked when she got downstairs was:

"Can I have a key for a drawer in that bureau in our room?"

"Why, I guess so," Josie replied, surprised.

"I got to have some place to lock up my things," Gloria explained.

George entered, looking much healthier than when he went into the army. He always had been tall, and now he was well filled out, rather handsome, in an innocuous way, with dark hair and brown eyes, regular features and good teeth.

"I suppose that old guy's givin' you so much money you don't know what to do with it," George said.

Gloria looked at Josie.

"Now, Georgie," Josie chided gently, "you be good to your sister. Aren't you goin' to kiss her?"

"Why don't she kiss me, if she wants to?" George demanded. "Why should I do all the kissin'?"

Edward entered the living room. He was still thin, pale and hang-dog. Without any urging he went straight to Gloria and kissed her. She turned her head so that the salute fell on her cheek and not on her lips.

"That's a fine way," Edward complained. "You might think I hadn't been anywhere at all, let alone to France."

Adelaide awakened Gloria next morning.

"Wake up," she said. "I'm late now. Will you come on a party to-night with my friend and a friend of his? You'll never get anywhere hangin' around in this dump. Come on."

Gloria rubbed her eyes.

"What did you have to go and wake me up for?" she demanded.

"You sleep too much," Adelaide retorted, putting curvy legs

into step-ins. "I've got a man who's got money to burn. He's wild to meet you. Don't be a pussycat all your life. Get wise, Kid."

"I don't want to," Gloria said.

Adelaide slid into a dress.

"You give me a pain," she exclaimed. " 'I don't want to,' " she mimicked. "I give you a chance to have a good time and do somethin' with yourself; and that's all the thanks I get. Go to hell, will you?"

Gloria went riding with Cooper Patten every afternoon, except Sundays, for a month. Every Saturday, when he said good-by, he pressed a little roll of bills into Gloria's hand. When she was alone she counted the money. He always gave her one hundred dollars.

One Friday afternoon he took her out in the limousine, driving himself. Out in the country he stopped and opened a vacuum bottle.

"I feel like a little drink," he said. "You have one with me, Baby."

"I don't want to," Gloria said.

"I made this specially mild for a little girl," he assured her. "Just taste it and see how good it is."

He filled an aluminum cup and held it out to her. Then he poured a drink for himself.

"To the sweetest and most beautiful girl in the world," he said, touching his cup to hers.

Gloria watched him from big blue eyes, holding the cup indecisively.

"Come on, Baby," he urged. "Drink it. You'll like it."

He swallowed a mouthful.

"What are you afraid of?" he demanded. "Why, I made it just to please you. Don't you want to please me? Come on, Baby, don't be like that."

Doubtfully, blue eyes still on his, she raised the cup and swallowed. She made a wry face.

"I don't like it," she said, in a hopeless tone.

"Now, Gloria, don't act like that. Drink it. You'll like it."

She took another sip. Finally she finished it and he took the cup.

"Wasn't that good?" he asked.

She looked at him, face flushed, eyes bright.

"It feels warm down here," she said, smiling and placing her hand on her stomach. "But I didn't like the taste."

"Have just a little more," he said, pouring another drink.

After more persuasion she drank the second drink. She laughed.

"We had port wine after we were married," she confessed. "It made me feel funny."

"It makes you feel good, doesn't it?" Cooper Patten asked.

"It makes me feel funny," Gloria said, swaying slightly and brushing a curl from her forehead.

He put his arms around her. She lifted moist lips and eyes, pupils enlarged, to his. He pressed his mouth to hers. She relaxed against him. He released her gently. She leaned against him and sighed, running her hand gently up around his neck. He opened the door.

"What're you doing?" she asked, and laughed, hazily.

"I thought we'd sit in back for a few minutes," he said. "It's cozier there."

"Kiss me," she demanded, forward for the first time.

He kissed her. She stumbled and sagged against him, as she half fell, half was lifted into the back seat.

"I'm dizzy," she confessed.

He took her in his arms and kissed her. She pressed her warm lips to his, breathing hard. His hand touched her firm breast. She stirred uneasily, then relaxed. His hand had its way. He kissed her bared breast.

A half-hour later Cooper Patten stood beside the limousine holding Gloria, weeping and sick. He held her forehead with one hand, and supported her around the waist with his free arm.

"Oh, dear!" she moaned.

Then she retched.

"I'm so sick," she sighed, "so sick."

"You'll be all right," Cooper Patten comforted her. "You'll be all right in just a minute. Take it easy."

"Oh, dear! Oh, dear! I'm so sick."

She retched again, her stomach contracting spasmodically. Her face was pale under patches of rouge. Mascara ran from her eyes. Her curls stuck to her sweat-beaded forehead. She whimpered like a baby, or a puppy, in pain. She gasped:

"I wish I was dead."

"You'll be all right," Cooper Patten soothed. "You'll be all right, Baby. Take it easy."

Gloria moaned and retched again, without any results except froth. He wiped her mouth and chin with a handkerchief and dabbed at stains on her coat.

"Why did you do it? Why did you do it? Oh, dear!"

She began to weep, with a hopeless, lost quality, in the manner of one who mourns a world, and not an individual tragedy.

"I wanted to be good," she sobbed.

"Why, Gloria," Cooper Patten said, "you are good—as good as any one on earth. You are wonderful, my beautiful little sweetheart."

When Gloria reached home, she staggered up to bed. Josie heard her in the bathroom and, despite Martin Brady's protests, vocal and physical, Josie climbed the stairs.

"What is it, Baby?" she whispered, pushing open the bathroom door.

"I'm so sick," Gloria whimpered.

Josie finally got her to bed and to sleep. Next morning Josie called Dr. J. L. Pearson. He gave Gloria medicine, and ordered Josie to stay downstairs.

"A pretty little girl like you shouldn't be drinking," Dr. Pearson said.

Gloria gazed up at him with her big blue eyes, faintly blue underneath. Her face was solemn.

"I was awful sick, wasn't I?" she said.

"But you shouldn't drink, little girl," the doctor said seriously. "You are too young and too sweet and lovely. Why, you have your whole life ahead of you, to marry some fine young man, and have good healthy children. You should be exercising in the open air and going to school. Why, you're only a baby."

A limpid drop gathered in each blue eye. Gloria wiped her eyes with a handkerchief, without taking them from the doctor's face. She looked at him as if fascinated.

"You don't like the taste," he said.

She moved her head slowly from side to side on the pillow.

"It gags me," she said.

"Of course it does," he said soothingly. "It's nasty stuff. And now that prohibition has stopped the supply of good liquor you are likely to get poison. You're not going to drink any more, are you?"

Gloria looked at him, a faint trace of stubbornness in her expression.

"I don't know," she said.

Dr. Pearson sighed.

"Perhaps there's something troubling you," he said gently. "You know, patients tell doctors lots of things they wouldn't tell any one else in the world."

Gloria made no reply, merely watching him somberly.

"Well," the doctor said, arising, "if there is anything I can ever do to help you, Gloria, you come to me, won't you? Meanwhile, please don't drink. Why, you're much too sweet and beautiful a little girl to spoil your life and your looks with alcohol. And it makes you sick, besides. Good-by, Gloria."

"Good-by," Gloria replied in a small voice, with a ghost of a smile.

Josie called upstairs that afternoon:

"Gloria, Bessie Mayfield is on the telephone. She wants to talk to you."

"Tell her I'm sick," Gloria replied.

A few seconds later Josie's voice floated upstairs again.

"She says it's important. What will I tell her?"

"Oh, I'll come down," Gloria cried resignedly.

"Don't come if you don't feel well, Baby. I'll just tell her you can't."

"I might's well," Gloria grumbled.

Over her pink silk nighty she pulled a new pink brocaded velvet wrap with white feather trimming, pushed her feet into pink satin mules and, with one hand on her head, made her way downstairs.

Bessie wanted her to come over to the Mayfield apartment. Gloria said:

"Oh, I'm too sick. I feel terrible."

Bessie argued. Finally Gloria went.

When Gloria entered the apartment Bessie met Gloria at the door and kissed her. Two boys behind her jumped to their feet from chairs and stood waiting.

"Look who's here," Bessie cried. "The one and only Gloria. Gee! I'm glad you could come, Dolly," she added, kissing Gloria again. "Throw your hat and coat anywhere."

She turned to the two boys. One was a tall, slim lad with extremely pale blond hair and blue eyes, and the other was shorter and had dark-brown eyes and brown hair. Bessie took Gloria's hand.

"Frank Graves," she said, indicating the blond, "this is Gloria. Gloria, this is Stanley Lowe," she said, indicating the brunette.

Gloria gave each boy her hand, dropping her head slightly, blushing, and looking up at them under her lashes.

"Bessie told me you were pretty," Frank Graves said, holding Gloria's hand, "but she never told me how pretty. Where have you been all my life?"

Gloria smiled, showing white teeth.

"Yeah!" Stanley Lowe said, dark eyes on Gloria, "when Bessie gets tired of me I'm goin' to have her pick me out a girl."

"That would be a thrill," Bessie giggled, putting her

arm around Stanley's neck and kissing him. "I know just the kind I'd pick for you."

"I feel it in my bones that you and I 're going to get along," Frank Graves said to Gloria.

He took her hand and tugged it gently.

"Come on over and sit down," he pleaded, indicating the couch.

Gloria held back, smiling but stubborn. He laughed and pulled harder. Gloria put her hand to her forehead, her smile fading.

"Please don't, Mr. Graves," she said. "I feel terrible."

"Oh, I'm sorry," Frank Graves said, releasing the pressure of his pull, but retaining her other hand. "But don't call me Mr. Graves, Gloria. Call me Frank. What's the matter?" he added, in a tender tone.

"I've got an awful headache," Gloria replied, "and I feel sick. I wouldn't have come if I'd known anybody was going to be here. I didn't do my hair, or anything."

Bessie pushed Frank Graves's hand away, and kissed Gloria again, softly, smoothing the hair from Gloria's forehead.

"What's the matter, Baby?" she whispered. "Is it the curse?"

Gloria shook her head.

"I guess I had too many drinks," she replied. "I was awful sick. The doctor came this morning."

Bessie dropped Gloria's hand.

"The doctor!" she laughed. "There's only one doctor for what ails you, and that's a dose of the same medicine. Where are the cocktails, Stan? What're you doing—saving 'em? Come on, fill up the glasses."

Stanley Lowe lifted a big shaker from the floor by the couch, pumped it up and down two or three times, and began to pour drinks.

"I couldn't touch one," Gloria protested. "I couldn't hold it."

She made a wry face.

"Just thinking of it makes me sick," she said.

"These won't make you sick," Stanley said. "I made 'em myself."

"Just like he made the gin himself," Frank Graves grinned.

"I couldn't drink one," Gloria said, turning her head away, and putting her hands behind her back when Stanley held a glass towards her.

"Listen, Gloria," Bessie said, "honest, these aren't like most drinks. Stan makes 'em with lemons and oranges and some peels and some powdered sugar, and lots of ice. You wouldn't know there was any gin in 'em. Honest you wouldn't. Don't you like orange-lemonade?"

Gloria nodded, half-convinced.

"I would like some lemonade," she said. "I haven't eaten a thing, but just thinking of a drink makes me sick."

"Well, just you try this, Dolly," Bessie coaxed, taking the glass from Stanley. "Just take one little sip."

Gloria still hesitated.

"Honest," Bessie wheedled, "you taste it and see. Just taste it, and if I'm not telling the truth I'll never ask you to do anything else all my life. Try it. There."

She held the glass to Gloria's lips. Gloria put up a hand to steady it, and touched her mouth fearfully to the rim. She swallowed a little.

"There! Could you tell any gin was in that?"

Bessie relinquished the glass, leaving it in Gloria's hand. Gloria smiled.

"You couldn't, could you?" Bessie insisted.

"No," Gloria admitted. "It's just like lemons and oranges."

"Wait till you've had a couple and see how good you feel," Stanley Lowe said, raising his glass. "Chinchin. Down the hatch!"

Frank Graves tinkled his glass against Gloria's.

"Here's to the most beautiful girl in the world," he said. "Bottoms up."

160

"Where do I come in?" Bessie demanded, laughing. "What am I—a worn-out lollypop or something?"

"You're the most beautiful girl in the world," Stanley Lowe assured her gallantly, clinking his glass against hers. "So, all together now. Prosit!"

They drank, Gloria more slowly, until their glasses were emptied. Frank took some cigarettes from a small table and passed them.

"Have one?" he asked Gloria.

"I don't smoke," she said.

"Why don't you try it?" he suggested.

"I don't want to," she replied. "I don't like the taste."

"If she doesn't want to smoke don't urge her," Bessie said, skipping in a semi-circle and snapping her fingers. "Let's have some music. Start the phonograph, Stan."

"I'll be making another little drink," Frank Graves said. "How do you feel now?" he asked Gloria.

"All right," she said in her soft voice.

"Better?" he insisted.

"A little, I guess."

"Drink this," he suggested, handing her a fresh cocktail, "and you'll be all cured. I guarantee it. Gee, but you're a swell kid."

Gloria smiled, and sipped the fresh drink. The phonograph began to send out dance music. In a few minutes, with rugs up, they were dancing. Frank, holding Gloria close, bent his head and tried to kiss her. She turned her head away.

"No," she insisted. "Please don't."

When the music stopped Gloria snapped her fingers and did a little dance, and then laughed happily. Bessie smiled at her.

"Feel all right now, don't you, Dolly?"

"I feel wonderful," Gloria said.

Stanley pulled Bessie over on the sofa, and they lay with legs and arms entwined, kissing, and murmuring.

"Can't you people do something?" Bessie demanded suddenly. "Why don't you go out in the kitchen and make another drink?"

"Come on, Gloria," Frank said. "I guess we're in the way."

Frank caught up the cocktail shaker and preceded Gloria to the kitchen. He closed the door and took her in his arms. She struggled and pushed and turned her head.

"Don't," she said.

He persisted. She relaxed, head bent forward, silent. He kissed her cheek and a corner of her mouth, with no response from her.

"I'm wild about you, baby," he breathed. "Give me a kiss."

She kept her head down. He put a finger under her chin and tilted her head up. Her eyes were wet.

"Crying?" he exclaimed.

She looked at him, face sad, eyes set in stolid repugnance.

"Oh, I don't want to make you feel bad, Baby," he said. "I want you to like me. And you're going to like me."

He let her go.

"I'll never like you if you do that," Gloria assured him.

"I'll get you before I'm through," Frank Graves asserted confidently. "But I guess you're one of the girls that don't kiss the first time. Is that it?"

"Let's not talk about it," Gloria said. "Let's make some more cocktails."

A half-hour later Bessie yodeled from the living room. Frank Graves opened the kitchen door and disclosed Stanley Lowe, hair mussed and eyes red, in his shirt sleeves, grinning.

"All right to come in?" Stanley asked.

"Sure it's all right," Frank replied. "What did you think we were doing—baking a cake or something?"

"Get a drink for me—quick," Bessie called. "And we're all going to the Chicken Farm to dinner to-night. Wouldn't that give you a thrill?"

They went to the Chicken Farm in Stanley Lowe's touring car, Gloria and Frank Graves on the back seat. Frank kept his arm around Gloria. Stanley drove with one hand.

162

Mrs. Rigali, proprietress of the Chicken Farm, stout, with white strands showing in blue-black hair done up in old-fashioned style, with a bun in the back, coal black eyes, and the beginnings of a promising mustache on her upper lip, greeted them. They introduced Gloria.

"Such a pretty little girl," Mrs. Rigali said in a deep voice, smiling like an ogress at Gloria. "I hope she likes my little place and comes often."

They had chicken and spaghetti and red wine, and danced. Gloria, walking very carefully, sat down at the piano, and played.

"The kid's clever," Stanley said.

"I never saw her so peppy," Bessie confessed. "She's usually awful quiet, aren't you, Gloria?"

"This is my birthday," Gloria laughed, eyes unnaturally bright. "I don't want to go home till morning."

"Gosh, but you're beautiful," Frank said, leaning over the piano.

"That's the old oil," Gloria replied, smiling. "That's what they all say."

"But I mean it."

"That's what they all say."

Gloria went to the ladies' rest room. Mrs. Rigali followed her.

"Did you have a good time, Baby?" Mrs. Rigali asked, getting a fresh towel and laying out a new cake of soap.

Gloria swayed her hips and smiled hazily at the stout proprietress.

"You'd be surprised," she replied. "I'm having a won'erful time."

"I'd like to have you think of this place as your own, Baby," Mrs. Rigali said. "Come here any time, with men, or without them. You could make lots of money—such a pretty girl."

"That's the old oil," Gloria said, staring into her own eyes in the mirror and then applying lipstick with uncertain touch.

"I know plenty of men would be glad to buy you everything, darling," Mrs. Rigali said. "But don't you drink too much."

"Don't be an airedale," Gloria said, and began to laugh.

Mrs. Rigali smiled solicitously and somewhat uncertainly.

"Would you like a little black coffee, darling?" Mrs. Rigali asked.

"I'd like some wine," Gloria asserted. "I feel won'erful."

Gloria slept on the way home, unconscious of Frank Graves's kissings and pawings.

"We'd better take her to my house," Bessie said.

"Let's all go back to the Chicken Farm and get rooms," Frank Graves suggested.

"Why, you bum," Bessie cried. "What do you think I am?"

"Well, you and Gloria could sleep together; and Stan and I could sleep together. That would be all right, wouldn't it?"

"Yeah!" Bessie sneered. "I've heard that line before. Men are only after one thing; and they don't care whether a girl is drunk or sober, or wants 'em or doesn't. I never thought it of you."

"Oh, for Christ's sake!" Frank cried. "Jesus! I didn't suggest anything except—"

"Nothing except!" Bessie interrupted. "Well, don't bother any more. Nothing's going to happen to Gloria when she's out with me. She's my friend."

"Well, who's trying to have anything happen to her? God damn it, you're crazy."

"Hey!" Stanley exclaimed, turning around in the front seat. "Shut up, both of you. What're we going to do with Gloria?"

Gloria stirred and her eyes opened.

"I want to go home," she murmured.

"You'll go home with me, darling," Bessie said.

Gloria wobbled her head uncertainly from side to side.

"I want to go home," she insisted.

And Gloria finally had her own way. Frank led her up the front steps, opened the door with her key, shut it after her, and ran back and jumped into the automobile.

Hatty Pearson, plump, with brown hair and gray eyes, stepped into the dining room doorway after dinner, and reached up and smoothed Dr. Pearson's forehead with her hand.

"You know, Jimmy," she said, "you really should take a vacation. You're getting the worst lines, like an old man. You're tired out."

Dr. Pearson grinned, and slid an arm around his wife's stable waistline.

"I'll take one just as soon as I can," he promised.

"You've been telling me that for years," Hatty Pearson announced. "All I can say is that if you don't take a rest pretty soon you'll be sick or dead. No man can keep going day and night the way you do without paying the piper. And it seems to me you work the hardest for the dead beats."

Dr. Pearson slid his left hand between his wife and himself, and produced a good-sized gold watch from his waistcoat pocket.

"Eight o'clock," he said. "I've got to get to the office."

"Why can't you stay away from the office just one night?" Hatty Pearson demanded. "Why don't you stay home with your family and rest? The children hardly know you."

"Gosh! Hatty! There's no need of going all over that again, is there? I've got to work. It's my job."

"When you're dead these patients you're killing yourself for'll just go to another doctor, that's all," Hatty said. "Nobody's going to thank you for ruining your health."

Dr. Pearson walked through to the front hall, Hatty hanging to his arm. He stopped at the hatrack and picked up a soft, black felt hat and put it on. Then he grasped his medicine bag. He lifted his wife's full chin with his other hand and kissed her.

"Don't you worry about me, little girl," he said. "I'm all right."

"Worry!" Hatty exclaimed. "You're the worrier. Your going it day and night is bad enough, but when you aren't working, you're worrying. And some of the people you worry about—that Boyd girl for instance!"

Dr. Pearson patted her cheek and kissed her again.

"Everybody isn't well balanced like you, Hatty," he said. "Gloria Boyd is a pitiful case. She's found an escape in alcohol. It's just one of many tragedies of the same kind, but I never can get used to them. And she's such a sweet and really beautiful child. It's a damned shame."

"What she needs is a good spanking," Hatty Pearson exclaimed. "If I'd had her I can tell you she'd have been different."

"Maybe she would," Dr. Pearson admitted, "but you didn't have her. She's headed for misery, I'm afraid."

"Well, people have to have character and moral standards," Hatty said. "And it's too bad if you have to worry about those who haven't."

"A good many people feel as you do, I guess," Dr. Pearson said, "but I can't help but feel that there's more to it. For instance, other girls might drink a little, or even more than was good for them on occasion, and still have pretty good chances of living a fairly normal life. But this girl is pathological; she's in a fair way to being an alcoholic: she wants to run away back out of the real world to the cradle, where there are no troubles and no responsibilities. And she's found the way, by drinking."

"From what I hear of her she should be in a reform school," Hatty said.

Dr. Pearson smiled and kissed her again, as he opened the door.

"Now you're just talking, Hatty," he said. "You'd be the first one to get sentimental over her. I'm telling you she's the most lovable little thing you ever saw—just had a raw deal from birth, almost. Well, I've got to go. See you later."

"What time will you be home?" Hatty asked, holding the door open, and looking out. "Can't you get home early tonight?"

"I'll try," he promised.

"You'll try," Hatty said, "but you'll probably stop in at the club about midnight, or sit around in Grayson's drug store."

"I'll be home as early as I can," Dr. Pearson called back from the front walk. "I've got a few calls to make after office hours. By-by."

Hatty Pearson threw him a kiss from her fingertips and closed the door. She leaned against it for a moment in a gesture of despair. Then she straightened up and, lifting the front of her skirts in her left hand, put her right hand on the banister and ran upstairs.

Howard, thirteen, the oldest, met her in the hall.

"I'm stuck with some of this darned old algebra, Ma," he said. "Will you help me?"

"I'll see what I can do," Hatty replied. "But first, I've got to get your brother and sister to bed."

Later, when she was working with Howard on his algebra, Hatty said:

"Howard, you've got the most wonderful father in the world, but when you grow up I hope you'll have learned a lesson from him, and not give all of your time caring for other people. Always remember your own family is worth some attention."

"Aw, don't cry, Ma," Howard said.

"I'm not crying," Hatty replied, dabbing hastily at her eyes with her hand and suddenly hugging Howard. "Your father is one of the finest and noblest men that ever lived," she continued, "and I adore him, but he isn't much help around the house."

She smiled wryly at Howard.

Dr. Pearson attended Madame Cele and Lord Frederick when occasion required. He had won Madame Cele's heart by setting her French poodle's leg one night, after it had been run over by a motorcycle.

"I didn't think you'd be willing to doctor a dog," Madame Cele said.

Dr. Pearson grinned.

"I'll take a chance on anybody that's sick," he replied. "I operated on a rooster once and sat up half the night with him."

"You did!" Madame Cele cried, clasping her hands. "That is too wonderful!"

"The operation was a success," Dr. Pearson continued, as he bound the splint on the injured leg, "but the patient died. He was a prize rooster that belonged to Professor Baldwin, in Polyclinic."

"Oh, that was too bad."

"We can't save everybody," Dr. Pearson said cheerfully, "but this fellow here's going to be as right as a trivet. Look at his eyes. He knows I'm trying to help him. Look at him."

"Oh, Pierre knows," Madame Cele nodded. "You know the doctor is doing good for you, don't you, Pierre?"

Pierre wiggled his tail, shaved except for a tuft at the end, and lapped at the doctor's hand with a red tongue.

Dr. Pearson liked Madame Cele. He ate pickled herrings and drank a glass of beer with her when he called, and always had a little chat with Lord Frederick.

"As nearly as I can figure it out," Dr. Pearson told Hatty, "Lord Frederick comes of some pretty high-up family in Austria, and used to be pretty sweet on the Madame. But he started losing his mind and was sent to a sanitarium. The Madame got him out somehow, and now he lives with her, perfectly happy."

"Exactly what is the matter with him?" Hatty asked. "I've always wondered."

"Well," Dr. Pearson said reflectively, "I'm no psychiatrist, but I'd say he has a touch of dementia praecox, a good solid streak of paranoia, and some attributes of a manic-depressive."

"Why, Jimmy! With all that he must be dangerous."

Dr. Pearson shook his head gently.

"I don't think so," he said mildly. "And I understand that's the concensus of opinion of the experts. He's harmless enough. But can't he tell some tall ones? Oh, boy!"

Gloria Boyd dropped in at Madame Cele's rather frequently. Madame Cele loved to drink, and she and Gloria would drink until Madame Cele lifted up her skirts and danced, while Gloria played the old music box. That was in the afternoons. Often Gloria fell asleep and had to be waked up in order to get home in time for dinner.

Her nights were busy ones. Bessie Mayfield and Frank Graves and Stanley Lowe and she went to roadhouses and to the Chicken Farm, except on Wednesdays and Saturdays. Then Gloria was with Cooper Patten.

Early one Thursday morning Gloria said good-by to Cooper Patten at the front door and started upstairs. Just as she reached the top the front doorbell rang. She turned around, swaying a little, and put a foot on the second tread. Then she withdrew it and stood, staring down into the dim front hall.

The doorbell rang again. It could not be Cooper Patten because the sound of shifting gears in his roadster had come immediately. Gloria hurried down the hall to the front room, once Julius Fleeter's, where Uncle Edward now slept, and rapped on the door.

"What is it?" Edward asked.

Gloria pushed open the door, went to the window and looked out.

"Aw Cheese!" Edward whined. "This is a fine time of night to be runnin' aroun' wakin' everybody up."

"Somebody was ringing the front doorbell," Gloria said.

She was trembling. Her eyes were dark with fear.

"Well, what's the harm of that?" Edward demanded. "It was prob'ly Patten. That's who you're out with, wasn't it?"

"It wasn't him," Gloria said nervously. "I heard his car when he drove away. Please, Uncle Ed, look down and see if you see anybody."

"It's your imagination, I guess," Edward said, rubbing his eyes.

But he got out of bed and shambled to the window. It was September, a cool, pleasant morning.

"I don't see nobody," he reported. "I guess you on'y imagined it, Gloria. Give me a kiss and go to bed."

He started to put his arm around her neck. She pushed him so vigorously that he fell back on the bed; she ran to the door.

"You wait till I do somethin' for you again, you little bum," Edward cried. "You go chasin' an' think you can pull that stuff around here. This is a hell of a house."

George came to the door of his room.

"For Christ's sake!" he exclaimed roughly. "You God damn' little bitch—get the hell to bed. What is this—a whore house?"

"Shut up!" Gloria screamed back at him and ran into her room and slammed the door and turned the key in the lock.

"What's the matter?" Adelaide asked drowsily. "My God! Is there a fire, or somethin'?"

Gloria told her about the doorbell.

"It was prob'ly nothin'," Adelaide said. "Hurry up and get to bed, will you?"

Two nights later, when Gloria returned home with Bessie, Frank and Stanley, the doorbell rang again, this time just as she had reached the door of the bedroom. She returned, trembling, to the head of the stairs and peered down. Martin Brady, in yellow and blue pajamas, appeared in the downstairs hall.

"Don't go," Gloria called in a tremulous stage whisper.

Martin opened the door and looked out. He stepped outside on the porch and peered around. Then he moved inside again and shut the door. He spied Gloria.

"Who was that?" he demanded in a husky undertone.

"I don't know," she whispered back. "It's like the other night I told you about."

"Humm-m!" he said, rubbing a hand through tousled light air and smothering a yawn. "Somebody might be playin' a joke."

He scratched his left arm with his right hand, looking back reflectively at the closed door.

"But it's damn' funny," he added. "It looks like it might be somebody that waited till whoever came home with you was gone an' then rang the bell quick, hopin' you'd be right there and open the door."

"I'm scared," Gloria said.

Martin Brady yawned again.

"Hell!" he exclaimed. "There's nothin' to be scared about now that you're in the house. Go to bed. We'll talk it over in the mornin'."

Adelaide returned while Gloria was undressing.

"Did you see any one out in front?" Gloria asked.

"No," Adelaide replied. "Did you want me to?"

Gloria told her about the bell.

"I guess a kidnapper must be on your trail," Adelaide said.

"Don't talk like that," Gloria pleaded. "I'm scared."

She went to the door, and turned the key. Then she went to the east window. The room was on the southeast corner, with one window facing the east, and another facing the south.

"Could anybody climb up here?" she asked, looking out.

Adelaide joined her. The roof of the back porch was just below the window.

"I suppose it's possible," Adelaide admitted, "but I guess nobody's goin' to try it. What're you doin'?" she added, raising her voice.

"I'm going to close the window and lock it," Gloria said. "I'm afraid."

"We need the window open for fresh air," Adelaide said. "Anyhow, the screen is just as good as the glass."

"I'd feel better if it was closed."

"All right, Baby," Adelaide grumbled. "Go ahead and close that one. But, believe me, you're goin' to leave the other one open."

"I don't care about that," Gloria said, shutting the east window and pulling the catch.

In the night, Gloria sat straight up in bed and screamed. Adelaide raised on her elbow.

"Huh?" she mumbled.

Gloria was shaking, eyes wide. She began to weep.

"I'm afraid," she whispered. "I saw some one at the window."

Adelaide rolled back the covers and jumped out of bed.

"My God, but you're a pest," she said.

She walked to the window and pressed her nose against the pane. Gloria watched her, hands pressed to her breasts.

"There's nobody there," Adelaide reported. "I can see the roof just as plain."

Adelaide went out into the hall to the bathroom. When she returned Gloria still was sitting up, bed clothes clasped around her, looking at the window.

"Will you look again, Addie?"

Adelaide made a face, but she went to the window.

"Not a thing in sight," she said. "Now, Baby, go to sleep."

Gloria cuddled up against Adelaide, putting one of her legs over Adelaide's, and her arm around Adelaide's shoulder.

"Addie," Gloria whispered.

"What?" Adelaide asked sleepily.

"Do you know who I thought I saw at the window?"

"No," Adelaide replied. "Who?"

"I'm afraid," Gloria sighed.

"Who did you think you saw, Baby?"

"Uncle Julius," Gloria said in an awed whisper. "I'm so frightened."

Adelaide laughed comfortingly.

"If it's Uncle Julius what could he do?" she demanded. "I wouldn't be afraid of him. Go to sleep, Baby."

Gloria drew a long, shuddering breath.

"I could never sleep alone," she said.

Gloria was walking swiftly towards Madame Cele's in a cold rain, slanting in from the bay on a southeasterly blow.

She never carried an umbrella or wore rubbers. She had the collar of a gray mixed tweed coat turned up.

"Ah, there, where d'ye think y're goin'?" asked Mike Duff.

She started, and looked up.

"Oh, you scared me, Mr. Duff. I was just running around to Madame Cele's. This is such a gloomy day."

"All weather should be alike to such a pretty little girrl," Mike observed. "What's this I hear about some wan ringin' th' bell, and thryin' th' winders at your place?"

Gloria stopped and raised frightened eyes to his.

"Who told you about it?" she asked.

"Sure, Mr. Brady, your stepfather, told me on'y a few minutes back," Mike said. "An' I told him for you not to worry any more at all, at all. I'll slip the worrd to me pal, Pat Deever, who's got the night shift, an' he'll keep an eye on th' house—an' mebbe I won't be far away."

"I wish he hadn't said anything," Gloria said.

"Sure, an' why not?" Mike Duff inquired, surprised. "I'll walk along wit' you a little ways. Sure, if some wan's tryin' some funny bus'ness, who sh'd know about it except us?"

Gloria was silent for a moment, then she turned her head around and up, cheeks rosy and moist from the rain, raindrops glistening on her hair. Her eyes were like pansies, soft and appealing.

"I don't care if you know about it, Mr. Duff," she explained, "but I'd be afraid to have the police force around asking questions."

Mike Duff laughed. He adjusted the neck of his rubber coat, nightstick dangling from strap.

"Now don't you be worryin', Baby," he said. "Nobody's goin' to be ast anythin'. But if your doorbell rings afther this, you'll know who rang it."

Madame Cele made her own beer and was proud of it. It was not unusual for Croquet to drop in afternoons, and other persons, of different ages and sexes, also gathered there to drink beer and talk.

Margaret Blane, gray hair smoothed back from a dark, aquiline face, with big, dark, feverish eyes, walked with difficulty, using a rubber-soled stick. Maggie Blane once had been one of the greatest of the chest singers in vaudeville. In her day she had stood them up in the aisles, and sent audiences into hysterias of adulation. Now she limped about on her stick, burning eyes of a witch watching fellow human beings as if she knew a dark secret she wasn't going to tell. She drank enormous quantities of everything—beer, whisky, gin, brandy —anything. When she was comfortably tight, she sang for her friends at Madame Cele's.

"Ah, Maggie," said old Vernon Leighton, who once played heavies and had toured with Sir Henry Irving, "there's no one left with a voice that stirs the old soul like yours. Why, you're just as good as you ever were."

Margaret Blane fixed old Vernon with her dark eyes, swimming in moisture and set in puffy, blue caverns. She jerked her head back.

"You'll never change, Vernon," she said in her hoarse, deep, tired voice. "Always blarneyin'."

Frank X. McCabe, a bookmaker's runner, always pickled in alcohol, whom every one called Mack, was Margaret's shadow.

"You used to tear the heart out of me, Maggie," he said, "an' you never knew it. But there was lots of us in those days."

Margaret sounded her rare laugh, which sounded like a croak.

"You wouldn't believe it," Mack told Gloria, "but Maggie Blane is the only girl I ever loved. She's why I never married. I used to stand outside of stage doors just to see her come out —and she never saw me."

"Ahh!" Margaret Blane exclaimed, with a shake of her head.

Mack, gray-white hair combed in old-fashioned bristling pompadour, dark eyes shining feverishly in clean-shaven, mottled cheeks, beak of a nose, red, patted Margaret's sinewy hand with his own shaky, veined hand.

"That's the truth, Maggie," he said fondly, his dark, sentimental gaze on her. "Maggie's me fairy princess," he announced. "Ain't you, Maggie?"

Margaret Blane laughed again, no mirth in it. She stared at Gloria, took her roughly in calloused old fingers by the tender chin, and peered into the shrinking face. Margaret shook her head and sighed.

"Don't scare the little girl, Maggie," Mack said. "She doesn't mean anything," he told Gloria.

Margaret Blane dropped Gloria's chin and wagged her head.

"She has a good chin," she said, "but she doesn't use it—just a plaything."

She frowned fiercely at Gloria.

"Don't be a doll," she rasped. "Don't let the men paw you. Be hard."

She looked up at Mack, fumbling with her rubber-ferruled cane.

"She's soft—soft," Margaret sighed.

Chase Morgan, an artist, walked over.

"I'd like to paint you, Baby," he said to Gloria.

Margaret Blane tossed her head.

"I know you artists," she said. "Keep away from 'em, Baby," she advised. "They aren't satisfied till they get your clothes off—the altogether they call it."

Chase Morgan was a big, handsome chap, about forty, crisp black curling hair touched with gray and slightly worn at the temples; blue eyes, roman nose, mouth and chin. He wore beautifully tailored clothes carelessly; his cravat was likely as not to be under his left ear instead of in the center of the attached collar of his soft blue shirt. He walked with an air—even if it might be in heavy boots, stuck with muck and chicken feathers. He had a place down on Long Island, where he kept fighting cocks and dogs and a horse or two.

He could drink all afternoon and evening and still maintain a perfect equilibrium. He talked on everything from Schopenhauer to shooting big game in Africa. He had been every-where—knew everybody.

He laughed at Margaret Blane's warning.

"The only reason I ever knew for a woman to hide her figure," he observed, "was because there was something the matter with it. If there's anything more beautiful in the world than a beautiful young girl's beautiful shape I'd like to see it."

"I told you," Margaret Blane said.

"Well, come to my studio and I'll paint your face," Chase Morgan compromised easily. "It's a face I could paint all year, Baby."

Gloria smiled, fascinated but timorous.

"I've had people stop me on the street and ask me to be painted or photographed," she confessed. "But I wouldn't do it."

"I should say not," Margaret Blane said. "You'd be a fool if you did."

"It's the old army game," Mack said.

Chase Morgan dropped his hand lightly on Gloria's black curls, ruffled them gently. She twitched away her head.

"You come to the studio," he said, "and I'll paint you a picture. Bring Maggie and Mack with you, if you want."

He sauntered off, head up, jaunty.

"He used to be a great lady killer," Mack whispered, look-ing after him.

"He's still a handsome man," Margaret said.

"He's too fat," Gloria asserted. "I only like big men, but I don't like them too fat."

Chapter 12

GLORIA WAKED up, screaming. It was dark in the room. There were two shaded windows on her left and none on her right, as in her own room. She screamed again.

Frank Graves sat up in bed beside her and put a soothing arm around her.

"It's all right, Baby," he assured her. "Don't make a noise. You're all right."

"Where am I?" Gloria gasped.

"You're at the Chicken Farm," Frank Graves said. "You got awful tight and passed out, and it was pouring rain, so we fixed it up to stay here."

"Where is Bessie?" Gloria cried, pushing Frank away.

"Here I am, Dolly," Bessie said from a doorway. "What's the matter, Dolly?"

"I don't want to stay," Gloria said. "I want to go home."

She got out of bed. She was wearing brassière and step-ins. She wavered on her feet. Bessie, overcoat over bare flesh, bobbed hair untidy, went to her.

"Where're my clothes?" Gloria asked dazedly. "I want to go home."

"You don't want to go home, darling," Bessie soothed. "It's raining. Listen!"

Wind howled around the eaves. The shades flapped. Water cascaded against glass and wood. A burst of lightning lighted the room dimly for an instant.

"Lightnin' in December!" Stanley Lowe observed from the door. "Can you beat it?"

Gloria cowered against Bessie. Frank Graves, in his athletic underwear, got out of bed and joined the others. He put his hand on Gloria's arm. She pulled violently away.

"You leave me alone," she cried.

"Come on, Baby," Frank said. "Don't be like that. Nobody's going to hurt you."

He tried to put his arm around her.

"Get away, you bastard," Gloria cried.

"In a minute I'll give you a good spanking," Frank promised.

Bessie pushed Frank away.

"Stan, take Frank in the other room a minute," she said. "I never heard you talk like that before, Baby," she said.

"I don't care, he is a bastard. Everybody's a bastard."

Gloria began to weep.

"I want to go home, Bessie," she pleaded.

"You can't go home so well now, Dolly," Bessie said. "It's really an awful storm. You can say you were at my house."

Finally Bessie and Gloria went to bed together, and Frank and Stanley, grumbling, doubled up. In the morning, Bessie said:

"Dolly, I never saw any one twitch and moan like you do in your sleep. It's awful."

"I wake up every night thinking I see some one climbing in the window," Gloria confessed. "It's an awful nightmare. A big, black man is after me."

On the ride home, Frank Graves said to Gloria:

"A lot of credit I got for leaving you alone."

"It's lucky you did," Gloria said.

"Wait till next time," Frank promised. "I'm wild about you, and you're going to be all mine, and nobody else's."

When Gloria reached home, Josie emerged from the kitchen to meet her.

"I've been so worried, Baby," Josie said.

"I was at Bessie Mayfield's," Gloria explained. "It was raining so hard she thought I'd better stay there for the night."

"You might've telephoned," Josie said. "I didn't sleep a wink."

Gloria waked up the next night, her scream still ringing in the room.

"For Christ's sake," Adelaide said, "shut up."

"I want to go home," Gloria said, staring around, bewildered.

Adelaide laughed harshly.

"You want to go home," she repeated. "Well, you're home now, in your own bed. What d'you know about that? Go to sleep."

Next morning, Adelaide said:

"It's no use, Gloria. I can't sleep with you any more. It's driving me nuts. You groan and jump around in your sleep, and this new stunt of waking up and yelling you want to go home is too much. I got to have my rest."

"I can't sleep alone," Gloria said. "I'll try to be quiet."

Adelaide, putting dark make-up around her dark eyes, in startling contrast to her yellow hair, made lighter with washes, shrugged her shoulders and made a grimace.

"I guess you won't find it's very hard to find some one to sleep with you," she said callously. "I've got some one, and he's been trying to get me to move over to Manhattan with him for a long time. I guess I'll go. This is a hell of a dump anyway. Uncle Ed and George and Malcolm always tryin' to borrow money. My God! The names they call me."

Adelaide went into the hall. George was waiting.

"Addie," he said, "lend me ten dollars, will you?"

"You go to hell," Adelaide replied.

"I got to have ten dollars," George persisted. "You've got plenty. Don't be a tightwad all your life."

"Don't be a beggar all your life," Adelaide retorted. "I'd be ashamed. A big bum like you tryin' to get money out of his sisters."

"Why you God damn' lousy whore," George shouted. "You street-walking bitch!"

He hit her in the jaw. She screamed. Gloria ran into the hall. George hit Adelaide again.

"You leave Addie alone," Gloria cried.

Adelaide, screaming, kicked at George's groin.

"Oh, you would, would you?" he snarled, grabbing her foot and twisting it.

Adelaide screamed frantically, and as George's other hand swung near her mouth, she sank her teeth in it. George let go her foot and yelled:

"Ouch! Jesus! Stop that!"

Josie hurried up the stairs. Her son Frank called after her: "Don't go up the stairs, Ma. You know what the doctor said."

Josie arrived at the landing, her face contorted with pain, hand pressed against her heart.

"Stop!" Gloria cried. "Mama's got an attack. Where's her medicine?"

Adelaide released George's hand, which he promptly raised and examined, growling.

"Now look what you've done, George!" Gloria said.

George glared at her.

"And you're just the same," he rasped. "A God damn' little no-good whore, comin' home all hours, and stayin' out whenever you want to, and gettin' breakfast in bed and à la carte service. If Ma was worth anythin' she wouldn't stand for either of you. A fine pair of sisters for a guy to have! Jesus Christ!"

Frank came running upstairs, breathless.

"Here's Mama's medicine," he panted.

"George!" Josie choked, rolling her head. "George!"

Her face was drawn and terrible. She was fighting for breath and against the agony in her chest. Gloria, with trembling fingers, uncorked the little bottle, and shook out some pills. Josie took one after another, collapsed against the wall.

"We'd better get her into bed," Adelaide said.

"I'm—all—right," Josie said. "Leave me alone for a minute."

After Josie was helped downstairs to her own bed, where she insisted on being taken, Gloria handed George a twenty-dollar bill.

"I'd rather give you money," Gloria said, "than have Mama upset."

"You're a good kid," George replied, stuffing the bill in his trouser pocket. "But Addie's a hardboiled bum. Keep away from her."

Adelaide returned that same afternoon and took all her clothing away in a taxicab. Josie, in bed, called:

"Is that you, Addie? What you doin'?"

"Moving out of this dump," Adelaide replied harshly. "I've got a room in New York."

Josie sat up in bed, face working, tears in her eyes.

"You aren't really goin' to leave me, are you, Addie?"

"Sure, I am," Adelaide replied. "And everybody'll be better off."

"Georgie doesn't mean what he says," Josie exclaimed.

"Oh, no," Adelaide sneered.

"I wish you wouldn't go."

"There's no need of beefin', Ma. I'm goin'. I'm sick of everything around here."

Josie struggled to a sitting posture.

"You'll kiss your mother, won't you, Addie?"

"Sure," Addie said, and dropped a hasty peck on Josie's mouth. "You might think I was sailing for Europe. My God!"

"I don't like to see my children leave their home," Josie said. "I always tried to keep a home."

Addie tossed her head impatiently.

"I'll be seeing you, Ma," she said. "I hope you feel better."

She was gone.

Gloria went, half-shamed, to Josie's side, and touched Josie's forehead with her fingertips. Gloria bent down and put her soft cheek against Josie's.

"You love me, don't you, Baby?" Josie murmured, hugging Gloria.

Gloria pressed hard against her mother, and whimpered. Josie drew her onto the bed, and they lay in one another's arms, cheeks wet with tears.

"I love you, Mama," Gloria whispered.

"Mama's baby doll," Josie murmured. "Mama's baby doll."

When Gloria went to bed she locked her door and fastened the catch on the east window over the ell. During the night she awakened, sitting up in bed. She felt vainly for Adelaide. Then she lay, eyes fixed in the dark, tense, sleepless.

Philip Kellar, scion of the perfumery Kellars, son of Radna B. Kellar, met Gloria at a dance in Rapp's Inn. He was twenty, robust, red-headed, blue-eyed; a hard-drinking, girl-chasing lad, who had been expelled from Yale for a long series of escapades which culminated in a motor accident at New Milford, in which a girl was seriously injured.

Gloria went riding with Philip Kellar, and drank and danced with him and his crowd. Philip Kellar said incessantly:

"This is my girl. Hands off. I'm going to marry her."

Frank Graves hung about the Boyd home like a shadow, and when Gloria and Philip Kellar left a restaurant or roadhouse together, Frank always was visible.

"I'll kill you and kill myself," Frank told Gloria finally. "Nobody else can have you."

Another time, Frank tore a wrist watch from Gloria's arm, and threw it into the water at Brighton Beach.

"You can't wear anything Phil Kellar gives you," he cried. Frank pinched her until she was black and blue.

"You must be crazy to stand for anything like that," Bessie Mayfield told Gloria. "I wouldn't."

"I'm afraid," Gloria confessed.

Bessie laughed.

"People who are always threatening never do anything," she counseled. "He'll think a long time before he shoots you or himself. Believe me."

Philip Kellar was cross-examined about Gloria by old Radna

B. Kellar, a lance of a man, sixty-five, but appearing not more than forty, with no white showing in his sandy hair.

"We will have her at the house for dinner," old Radna B. said.

Gloria tried in every way to avoid going to the Kellars' for dinner, but Philip bullied her into it. She finally went, a timid little figure in the big hall, in the great dining room. Old Radna B., and Mrs. Kellar, white-haired, with dark kindly eyes, and a sweet face, were charming to her, but condescending.

"What is your father's business, Miss Boyd?" Radna B. asked kindly.

Gloria stirred restlessly.

"I haven't any father," Gloria replied in a still voice.

Philip looked encouragingly at Gloria across the shining table.

"What are you studying in school, Miss Boyd?" Mrs. Kellar asked.

"I don't go to school," Gloria confessed.

"Boyd," Mrs. Kellar said. "You're not by chance one of the Irvington Boyds?"

Gloria flushed and toyed with silverware, as more questions of family were asked.

When she and Philip were in his sport roadster on their way home, Gloria said:

"Why does everybody have to ask so many questions about me?"

"Well," Philip replied coaxingly, slipping his free arm around her waist, "you know how it is with those old dodos. They're always finding out from people they meet if they have any friends in common."

"It's nobody's business," Gloria exclaimed.

"Don't let it worry you, Baby," Philip soothed. "What the hell do you and I care about that stuff?"

Gloria pulled herself away from him impatiently.

"It makes me sick," she cried, nervously, her lips trembling.

"They just kept asking questions. I never felt so bad in my life."

"Well, it's natural for 'em to want to know something about their daughter-in-law," Philip Kellar said.

"I'd never marry you," Gloria asserted.

She began to weep.

Philip Kellar stopped his car and hugged her. She pushed him away, made it impossible for him to enfold her in his arms.

"Leave me alone," she sobbed. "You should never have taken me there in the first place. Me sitting there, with your father and mother looking at me and trying to find out all about me."

"Say, Baby," Philip exclaimed. "Don't blame me for what those old dodos do. I don't give a damn about your family or whether you've got a father. I don't even give a damn about Cooper Patten, as long as you give him up, now that you 'n' I 're going to get married. My little wife!"

He tried to hug her again.

"I'm not going to give up Cooper," Gloria cried. "So there."

Philip's face reddened.

"If you don't give up that old chaser you'll never see me any more," he promised.

"I don't ever want to see you any more," Gloria said. "Let me out."

"Aw, Baby, don't talk like that. I love you. Gee! I'm crazy about you. You know that. We can get married, and everything 'll be all right."

"I want to get out," Gloria insisted. "I'll go home on a car."

Philip Kellar drove Gloria home, but despite his pleas she never went out again with him.

A month after Adelaide went to live in Manhattan, she persuaded Gloria to visit her. Adelaide had a furnished living

184

room and bedroom in an apartment hotel. Photographs of a dark, handsome, clean-shaven man about thirty decorated the bedroom.

"That's him," Adelaide said, picking up a photograph from a table and kissing it. "He's away on a trip. We're going out with two swell boys to-night. Let's have a drink."

They drank gin. They went out with the two boys and danced. Gloria had difficulty in getting rid of her escort. Adelaide said:

"What do you expect the first time she goes out with you? She isn't that kind of a girl."

Adelaide and her boy friend slept in the bedroom. Gloria slept on the sofa in the living room. When the doorbell rang the next afternoon, Adelaide, with nothing on, walked out of the bathroom to answer it.

"Don't walk around like that, Addie," Gloria protested.

"Oh, shut up," Adelaide replied pleasantly. "It's nothing but a messenger boy," she added to Gloria over her shoulder. "Jack sends me a telegram every day."

To the messenger boy, she said:

"Wait a minute."

To Gloria she called:

"Got a quarter, Gloria, for the boy?"

Gloria gave her a quarter. Adelaide handed it to the boy, and closed the door.

"I should think you'd be ashamed," Gloria said.

"Now don't start that stuff," Adelaide said sharply, opening the telegram. "Jack sends me love and a thousand kisses," Adelaide said. "Gee! He's the only man I ever could love."

"Hey, Kid, come on back to bed," the young man called from the bedroom.

"Be right there, Andy," Adelaide replied.

"I wouldn't even let you see me with my clothes off," Gloria said. "It isn't right to go walking around like that."

"Oh, go to hell, will you?" Addie snapped. "If you don't like it here, get out."

"I'm going," Gloria said.

And she went, while Adelaide was screaming:

"Hold your horses, Andy, I'll be there in a minute."

Frank Graves was waiting outside when Gloria returned home.

"Where were you?" he demanded.

"None of your business," Gloria replied, trying to walk around him to get into the house.

Frank clenched and unclenched his hands. His face was pale and his eyes were furious.

"If I had you somewhere I'd choke you to death," he said in a hoarse voice. "You were out with some man."

"I was not," Gloria asserted, pale.

"I watched the house till two o'clock this morning, and I have been here since nine o'clock," he said. "And you weren't home last night. You better tell me where you were, or you'll be sorry."

"Oh, I was only over visiting my sister," Gloria said. "Let me pass."

"That bum!" Frank Graves exploded. "She sleeps with any guy that's handy. She's a bum."

"Don't talk that way about my sister."

"I'm not going to have you going around with her. She's a floosy."

Gloria ran around Frank and up the steps. His manner changed from wrath to pleading.

"Aw, Gloria," he begged, "let me come in, will you? Will you go out with me to-night?"

"I don't ever want to see you again," Gloria said, and went in and slammed the door.

Gloria sat up in bed a week later, her own shriek still ringing in her ears. A vague figure moved in the darkness. Gloria screamed:

"Mama!"

A man's hand dropped over her mouth. A scent of violet was in the air.

"Shh!" Julius Fleeter whispered. "Keep still, Gloria."

Gloria sat, silent, bony hand pressing on her lips, rough cloth of coat sleeve rasping her cheek. She moaned; a long shiver shook her body.

"I've come for you," Julius Fleeter whispered hoarsely. "Get hold of yourself and get dressed."

Her blue eyes, terrified, stared into his close-set gray ones, inches away.

"I couldn't let anybody else have you, Baby," he said. "You're mine, or nobody's. We'll get your clothes."

He eased the pressure on her mouth, and, as if it had been dammed up by his hand, a high pitched wail burst forth, to be smothered instantly as he clamped his hand over her mouth more harshly.

"Gloria," he whispered, "keep still! It's your Uncle Julius. Everything will be all right if you just do what I say. If you don't you'll be sorry. I'm desperate. I thought I could give you up, but I can't. Now, are you going to mind me?"

He shook her and glared into her eyes.

"Are you?"

Gloria stared back at him, a picture of fright.

"I'll give you one more chance," Julius Fleeter whispered. "Remember now. I'm desperate. I mean what I say. One more chance!"

He took his hand from her lips. She made no sound. He put his arms around her and crushed her soft body to him. He kissed her hair and eyes and unresponsive mouth. She smelled sweet and young in the dimness.

Martin Brady was in Baltimore. Josie Boyd, sleeping with Ernest downstairs in the front room, awakened at Gloria's first cry. Josie sat up in bed, listening. She slowly clambered over Ernest, on the outside of the bed, to the floor. Ernest moved, opened his eyes.

"What is it, Ma?" he asked.

"I thought I heard Gloria scream," Josie said.

"Aw, she's always screamin'," Ernest said. "Come back to bed, Ma. You know what the doctor said."

"I'm all right," Josie replied. "You stay there, Ernie. I'll just listen in the hall a minute. I'm so worried about that poor baby."

Josie gathered her nightgown about her and went through the door, purposely left ajar, into the front hall. Gloria's second cry, so quickly choked, reached her there. She started upstairs, hurrying in bare feet.

"Ma!" Ernie called. "Ma! Don't you go upstairs now. Remember what the doctor told you."

Josie, half-way up, sagged against the banister, hand on her heart. She gasped with pain. Her medicine was downstairs on the table beside her bed. She took another step upward, swayed, and stopped; and another step. There she hung on the banister, fighting for breath.

She mounted another step. Each step was torture. Finally she leaned against the lintel outside Gloria's door. She opened her mouth to call, but only groaned through blue lips. She twisted the handle of the door and, doubled over grotesquely, pushed the door open.

An electric bulb burning low under a yellow silk shade on the dresser revealed Julius Fleeter's startled face, Gloria's frightened eyes. Gloria's mouth opened and she screamed piercingly.

Josie's eyes, dark with pain, focused on Julius Fleeter. Her face was strained and unnatural.

Ernest called from downstairs.

"What's the matter, Ma? I'm coming."

The voices of George and Malcolm rose from their rooms. Footsteps sounded. The house was awakened.

"For Christ's sake!" George shouted.

Josie slumped to the floor, her breath rattling dryly in her throat. Gloria kept on screaming. Julius grabbed her arms savagely.

"You won't dare say I was here," he snarled.

He pushed her aside and she fell on the bed. He stepped to the east window and went through it to the porch roof. He closed the window after him, just as Ernie ran in, followed by George.

Ernest plumped down beside Josie.

"Mama!" he cried. "Here's your medicine. I brought it."

"What the hell did she have to climb those stairs for?" said George. "The damn' fool."

He turned to Gloria.

"A fine bum you turned out to be, wakin'—"

Ernest screamed.

"Look at Mama, George," he said.

George and Malcolm, just arrived, stooped over Josie. George gulped.

"She's dead," he said in a still voice.

Malcolm and Ernest began to wail. Gloria fell on the floor on her knees.

"Mama," she sobbed. "Mama!"

"Somebody ought to call the doctor," Uncle Edward said from the doorway. "Come on, George, help me lift her on the bed."

Chapter 13

Ma Brennan wiped her old eyes with a coarse linen handkerchief.

"I don't understand how you can talk to your old grandmother like that," she said to Gloria. "After all I've done for you."

"Reading my letters and listening to my telephone calls and keeping track of me and whispering with Cooper about it— that's what you've been doing," Gloria charged. "Telling him about the boys I go out with."

"I haven't, Gloria."

"Don't lie about it, Gran'ma. Didn't I catch you?"

Ma Brennan sniffled.

"Well, everythin' I did was for your own best good," she said. "I've cried my eyes out over you, and prayed for you, and worked my old hands off for you."

Gloria's young face was hard.

"You're like all the rest," she said. "Hanging around Cooper because you think you'll get something out of it. Well, this is the time you get fooled. I couldn't live with you any more. You want to be his friend. All right then."

"But Mr. Patten wants you to do what's right," Ma Brennan exclaimed. "He's always thinkin' about you and what's best for you. I was just hopin' to save you from yourself."

Gloria began to weep hysterically.

"After my mother died, I thought you'd be for me," she said, "but you never were. You're always siding with Cooper."

"But, Baby, he on'y wants you to be good."

Gloria laughed.

"You know what he wants. He promised me I could study art, didn't he? He told me he would help me marry a banker, didn't he? A lot of help he's been. He only wants one thing, and you know it, only you're too deceitful to admit it."

"Why, Gloria, you don't realize what you're sayin'! You've been drinkin' again."

Gloria stamped her foot and threw her bag violently on a chair in the living room of the apartment Cooper Patten had taken for her after the death of her mother the year before.

"If I've been drinking who started me drinking?" she cried. "If I keep on drinking why do I keep on? I couldn't stand that old fossil unless I did drink. I couldn't stand you unless I drank. I couldn't stand myself, either. I wish I was dead. I wish you'd go, Gran'ma. You go back to Camden. I couldn't stand having you around here any more."

"After all I've prayed for you."

Ma Brennan shook her old blonde-white head sadly.

"It isn't as if I hadn't suffered with a young one like you, dreamin' and yellin' in your sleep, and even scratchin' me. An' all the mornin's I've nursed you."

Ma Brennan dabbed the handkerchief to her eyes again. The doorbell rang. Ma Brennan looked up.

"That should be Mr. Patten now," she said. "Maybe he can talk to you."

"He won't talk to me," Gloria announced, snatching up her bag again. "I told him you had to go to-day, and you're going. If you don't go, I'll go. You thought you could get on the right side of him. Well, you'll see who it is he wants."

Gloria caught a sobbing breath. Ma Brennan pushed a button which slipped the catch on the front door, three flights down.

"My whole family is only after his money," Gloria said. "You, too. Yes, you are, too. George just got fifty dollars. Malcolm is always hanging around. Uncle Edward borrows money from Cooper. What did they ever do for me?"

"I can't talk with you when you're like this, Gloria," Ma Brennan said. "You aren't responsible. That's all I can say."

"I don't care what you say, Gran'ma," Gloria replied. "You were pretending to be my friend, and all the time you were telling Cooper everything about me. I'm glad I found out."

Cooper Patten entered.

"Hello, Baby," he said. "Hello, Mrs. Brennan."

He glanced quickly from one to the other.

"What's the trouble?" he demanded, looking at Gloria.

"She's in another of her tantrums, Mr. Patten," Ma Brennan exclaimed. "I'm just about wore out tryin' to do for her."

"Why, Baby," Cooper Patten said soothingly, stepping towards Gloria.

Gloria jerked her shoulder from his hand.

"Don't pretend, Cooper," she said. "I told you on the 'phone about it. You and Gran'ma 've been talking about me, and she's been telling you about me. Either she goes, or I go, one or the other."

Cooper Patten laid his hat down, the lid over the eye towards Ma Brennan drooped in one of his impressive winks.

"Let's talk this over," he said persuasively. "Your grandmother certainly hasn't done anything she didn't think was for your own good, Baby."

"I'm not going to talk about it any more," Gloria replied. "I'm going out now, and if she's here when I come home I'll go away again and never come back. I never want to see her again."

Cooper Patten looked quickly at Ma Brennan and rose, raising pleading hands to Gloria.

"If you'll wait just a minute, Baby, be calm for just a second, I'm sure we can straighten everything out."

Gloria pulled herself away from his hands and yanked the door open.

"I mean what I say," she cried. "I'm going."

"Wait a minute," Cooper Patten called, starting after her.

The door slammed in his face, and Gloria's foot-beats

sounded a moment in the hall, and then gradually died out as she ran downstairs.

Cooper Patten turned to Ma Brennan and extended his hands palm upwards in a gesture of helplessness. Ma Brennan sniffled.

"An' I on'y did what I thought was best," she said. "You know that, Mr. Patten."

"Of course, you did," Cooper Patten said. "But I guess we should have been more careful."

"I wanted to help you," Ma Brennan said. "Your money was payin' for everythin'. It on'y seemed right."

"It was right," Cooper Patten said. "And you know I'll never forget your help. But it's got her pretty well stirred up."

"If I was you I'd put my foot down with that girl," Ma Brennan asserted. "She's goin' completely wild."

Cooper Patten put his hands behind his back and walked to a front window facing the street. He looked down through the white lace curtains. Sound of a motor starting came from the street below.

"She'll kill herself in that auto some day," Ma Brennan said. "You mark my words."

Cooper Patten turned back from the window, took a cigarette from a case and lighted it. He blew out a cloud of smoke.

"I'm sorry about this," he said.

Ma Brennan looked at him.

"She can't live here alone," she said. "It ain't respectable."

Cooper Patten sighed.

"It complicates matters," he admitted. "But there it is. We can't get away from it."

"You mean I've got to go, Mr. Patten?" Ma Brennan cried. "You're goin' to let that willful girl have her own way?"

"I guess we'd better for the present anyway," Cooper Patten said placatingly. "I'll fix it right with you. You get your things packed. After that, we'll see how things shape up."

Ma Brennan put her hands to her throat and went through motions of choking.

"Don't worry now, Mrs. Brennan," Cooper Patten exclaimed hastily. "I know it's a shock. But everything'll come out all right. Leave it to me. You won't regret it."

"This wouldn't 've happened if I hadn't been watchin' out for your interests," Ma Brennan cried tearfully.

"I'll never forget it," Cooper Patten replied. "But the best thing to do right now is take things easy."

When Gloria Boyd returned to the flat that night with Bessie Mayfield, Ma Brennan was gone.

"I couldn't sleep alone," Gloria repeated to Bessie. "I'd be afraid. Will you have a drink?"

"Got some Scotch?" Bessie asked.

While they sat talking over their Scotch and mineral water, the telephone bell rang. Gloria set her glass on the floor, and went into the bedroom to answer it.

"The 'phone rings all night," she complained, "unless I plug it."

Frank Graves, on the wire, wanted to come up. Gloria told him that Bessie was there and he couldn't. They had a long argument. At last Gloria hung up the receiver and returned to the living room.

"What do you fool with Frank for, Dolly?" Bessie asked. "He's crazy."

"I try to keep away," Gloria said, "but he's always after me. He stands outside all night in the rain."

She laughed nervously and took a long drink of Scotch.

"Just tell him to go to hell," Bessie advised.

"He says he'll kill me and himself," Gloria said. "He tore a pair of new stockings last week because he thought another boy had given them to me."

"I wouldn't stand for it," Bessie asserted.

The telephone bell rang.

"There goes the telephone again, Dolly. Why don't you plug it?"

Gloria went to the telephone again. After they were in bed she answered two more calls before she went to sleep, and waked up to answer, drowsily, two or three more.

"I'd go crazy myself in this place," Bessie complained. "No wonder you have the jumps."

"It's just boys that want to know if they can come up, or if I'll go out with them," Gloria said.

"Does Chase Morgan call up?"

Gloria shook her head.

"I think he's sweet though," she confessed. "He's regular."

"He's a man," Bessie agreed.

"I've slept at his studio a couple of times," Gloria said. "You know that time I had a fight with my sister; and after that, once, when Ethel took me to see that silk man and he tried to keep me in his apartment, and Ethel hit him with her mesh bag. I told you about it."

"I could have a case on Chase Morgan myself," Bessie said. "I think he's grand."

"He's always wanting to paint my picture," Gloria said.

"Well, why don't you let him?"

"I don't know," Gloria replied. "I feel kind of funny about it."

"You're crazy, Dolly. I'd love to have my picture painted. It would be a thrill."

"Maybe I will some time. Only I think pictures should make you look better than you really are."

"Doesn't Chase ever get fresh?" Bessie asked.

Gloria shook her head.

"He just leaves me alone," she explained. "And there's a colored maid comes in at noon and I get my coffee and orange juice."

Bessie laughed.

"I'll bet it bothers you because he doesn't get fresh," she asserted. "You know, I think you're kind of stuck on him at that."

"I am not," Gloria protested.

Bessie smoothed down Gloria's curls.

"Does that good-looking boy that lives across the street—what's his name—that poses for collar ads, come over to see you any more?"

Gloria made a face.

"Once in a while," she said. "He wants to borrow money or the car."

"He's awfully good looking. I could have a case on him myself."

"He's too young," Gloria replied loftily. "I only like men. I like men that are tall, with gray hair. I think they're cute."

"Do you like Wallie Reed?"

"I think he's nice," Gloria replied.

In the morning Bessie went into the kitchen and made coffee. She poured coffee, black, into two cups and then added whisky.

"Come on, Dolly, get your bottle," she called.

Gloria emerged from the bathroom, holding a hand to her forehead.

"I feel sick," she complained. "I always feel sick in the morning—like throwing up. And my head aches."

Bessie handed her one of the cups.

"Take this, Dolly," she said. "Where do you keep your aspirin?"

"I don't want any."

Bessie found the aspirin and persuaded Gloria to take two tablets. Fifteen minutes later Gloria took a shower bath. She did a little dance step in brassière and step-ins.

"Let's go places and do things," she said.

"Feeling better, aren't you, Dolly?"

Gloria smiled and nodded.

"You have a wonderful shape, Dolly," Bessie said, appreciatively. "I wish I knew how to make my breasts fuller. I'm so flat there."

"Men look at me there," Gloria said. "It makes me feel ashamed. That's why I used to wear tight brazeers, but Chase

196

Morgan told me I'd break down the muscles. I don't know, though. Do you think I look too big there?"

Gloria posed in front of the full-length mirror set in the bedroom side of the bathroom door, looking at herself—black curls, pink cheeks, big blue eyes, slim rounded figure in scanty pink silk.

"You're just right," Bessie said heartily. "Don't be silly. I wish I'd be bothered by men looking at me like that. The rest of me is all right, but I guess there was a shortage on breasts when I was being put together. I heard that it means your ovaries are undeveloped too. Did you ever hear that?"

"No," Gloria replied.

"But some men like a girl to be flat," Bessie laughed. "I don't seem to have to worry, anyway. I guess I'll call up Stan. Will I fix you another drink first?"

"I'll have one if you will," Gloria said.

"There's a good picture at the Bijou," Bessie said.

"I'd rather go to Costigan's and drink some beer this afternoon," Gloria said.

Gloria Boyd, Bessie Mayfield, and Stanley Lowe, Stanley driving, arrived at the Chicken Farm at ten o'clock. They had stopped at several other speak-easies during the day. Gloria and Bessie were arm-in-arm, whispering and giggling. Mrs. Rigali met them at the front door.

"There's a man here that admires you very much, Miss Boyd," Mrs. Rigali said. "I'll introduce you."

She leaned over and whispered in Gloria's ear.

"He's a big bootlegger—lots of money."

"I don't want to meet anybody," Gloria said. "I just want to drink—huh, Bessie?"

"We don't want to meet anybody," Bessie agreed.

And she and Gloria burst into laughter, as if they had a humorous secret between them. Mrs. Rigali smiled indulgently.

"You are havin' a good time," she said. "Me—I like to see young people have a good time. I will give you a good table."

"We want some of your spaghetti—with the meat sauce, and

plenty of tomato in it," Stanley Lowe said. "And a barrel of red ink."

Mrs. Rigali nodded.

"Those spaghettis I make myself," she boasted. "I eat them myself."

Gloria and Bessie, Bessie taking the man's rôle, danced together across the floor to a table near the four-piece orchestra. The long room, seating about two hundred, was comfortably thronged.

"I want a highball first," Gloria said. "Scotch."

"I'll have one too," Bessie announced.

They both laughed again.

"Why don't you wait till you've had something to eat?" Stanley asked. "You've both been drinking all day. Let's wait for the spaghet'."

Bessie shook her head.

"We want highballs first," she insisted. "Don't we, Dolly?"

Gloria looked at Stanley and smiled, eyes hazy.

"We want highballs," she repeated.

"Three highballs?" Mrs. Rigali inquired, looking at Stanley.

"I suppose so," he agreed unenthusiastically. "What they do with the booze, I don't know. They must have hollow legs."

A waiter, black-haired, dark-eyed, sullen, took the order.

"I want you to give these people the best service, Tony," Mrs. Rigali directed.

Tony nodded and hurried away.

Gloria, Bessie and Stanley were drinking their highballs when Mrs. Rigali appeared at their table again, this time with a man in tow. He was of medium height, immaculately dressed, with sleek brown hair, inscrutable brown eyes, a hard mouth, a scar lifting the left corner of it. His shoulders, running straight from his neck to the tops of his arms, were the sort that one sees among professional wrestlers and boxers. A big solitaire diamond glistened on the ring finger of his hairy left hand.

"This is my friend, Mr. Perone," Mrs. Rigali said. "Paul Perone. This is Miss Boyd, Mr. Perone, and Miss Mayfield, and Mr. Lowe, Mr. Perone."

Gloria gazed at Paul Perone over the top of her highball glass, smiling uncertainly. Bessie Mayfield said:

"How do you do, Mr. Perone?"

Stanley arose from the table, shook hands with the new acquaintance, and said:

"Mr. Perone."

Paul Perone said, looking at Gloria:

"I been askin' Mrs. Rigali to interdooce me to this little lady. She's the prettiest skirt I seen in a year."

Gloria and Bessie giggled.

"I'll buy a little drink," Paul Perone said. "Waiter!" he added, not raising his voice.

"Yessir," said three waiters in unison, materializing at his elbow.

"Champagne for this table," Paul Perone said.

"I'd rather have Scotch," Bessie Mayfield objected.

"I'd rather have Scotch, too," Gloria agreed.

"Make it Scotch," Paul Perone said. "And make it snappy."

"Yes, sir," the waiters said.

A chair had been arranged for Paul Perone's convenience. He pushed it away, a harmless enough gesture, but one which he executed with a muscular vigor that seemed to indicate he didn't care whether the chair were wrecked or not. He might have killed a man no less callously.

"Let's me and you step a little," he suggested to Gloria, opaque brown eyes boring into her blue ones.

Gloria smiled dully and glanced at Bessie Mayfield. Bessie giggled again and nudged Gloria.

"Go on, Dolly, and dance," Bessie urged.

Gloria waited long enough to take another sip of her highball, and rose. Paul Perone encircled her with his right arm and they started.

"You're some stepper, Baby," Paul Perone said.

Gloria gave him a flash of blue eyes and dropped them again.

"I love dancing," she said.

"They's a lot of dames on'y think they can dance," Paul Perone observed. "You can dance."

Paul Perone could dance too. He moved his feet lightly in intricate patterns, his body of a boxer swaying airily. Gloria was just a little uncertain, but she rested secure and easy against his arm, solidly muscular.

They returned to the table. Gloria was flushed, eyes bright. Paul Perone showed no more signs of exertion than if he had been sitting under an electric fan all evening.

"He's a wonderful dancer," Gloria whispered to Bessie, slipping into her chair.

Gloria looked across at Paul Perone.

"Try a dance with Bessie," she advised.

Paul Perone made a grimace that might pass for a smile.

"I on'y dance with one partner when I got the right partner, Baby," he said.

"How about dancing with me, Bessie?" Stanley asked, rising.

Stanley and Bessie danced; and Paul and Gloria danced again. After that Paul and Gloria were on the floor almost continuously, Gloria laughing excitedly. Stanley whispered to Gloria once, when Paul rose to talk with three men at the door:

"I'd be careful of that bird, Baby. He looks like a gunman to me."

"You're goin' to have di'monds, Baby," Paul Perone told Gloria. "Di'monds, and one of them foreign cars with a chauffeur."

"That's the oil," Gloria said.

"That's on the level," Paul Perone asserted somberly.

"You must've been taking hop," Gloria said.

Paul Perone's eyes, open-lidded, rested on hers. They gave

the curious effect of never blinking, two shining brown holes in a mask.

Bessie Mayfield caught her breath audibly and nudged Stanley Lowe.

"Look," she whispered. "There's Frank."

Stanley turned suddenly in his chair.

"Over by the door," Bessie explained, excitement thrilling her voice. "See him? He's looking for Gloria, I'll bet."

"I hope he doesn't try to start something," Stanley said. "This Perone guy looks bad to me."

"He's crazy," Bessie said. "There!" she cried, raising her voice. "He's just seen them dancing. Doesn't he look crazy, Stan? I wish we were out of here. He'll make a scene. You wait and see."

"I see him," Stanley said. "Wait here. I'll see if I can steer him away."

Stanley rose. Bessie dug her fingers into Stanley's forearm.

"My God!" she breathed. "Well," she added, "he had it comin' to him."

Frank Graves stepped out on the dance floor. He bumped into a pair of dancers, and then into another pair.

"Watch where you're goin'," a hoarse voice bawled.

"Where the hell do you think you are?" another voice demanded.

Gloria saw Frank approaching past Paul Perone's shoulder. Her hand in Perone's trembled. She stopped dancing suddenly.

"Oh, dear!" she breathed.

"What's th' matter, Baby?" Paul Perone asked.

At the same moment Frank Graves pushed Paul Perone aside, and took Gloria's arm roughly. She screamed.

"Don't, Frank," she pleaded. "You hurt."

"I'll hurt you worse," Frank said hoarsely. "I've been looking everywhere for you. Where did you dig up this pimp?"

He jerked his head contemptuously at Paul Perone, four inches shorter and smaller-looking in every way. Paul Perone was straightening his coat collar, pulled away from his neck by Frank's violence. Paul Perone's eyes were on Frank Graves's face. Paul moved them to Gloria.

"Who is this guy?" Paul asked. "Your husban'?"

Gloria, shaking nervously, tried to free herself from Frank's grasp.

"No, he isn't," she said. "He's always following me."

"Oh," Paul Perone said, and shifted his gaze to Frank again.

"Please, Frank, don't," Gloria pleaded. "Everybody is looking at you. Let me go."

"You heard the lady," Paul Perone said. "Let her go."

"You keep your nose out of this," Frank Graves said, dropping Gloria's arm and turning savagely on Perone.

Frank thrust savagely at Perone with his left arm.

Crack! Paul Perone's fist smacked solidly on Frank's jaw, and Frank staggered back, face dazed, hand involuntarily raised to damaged chin. Paul Perone's brown eyes stared without expression at Frank. Gloria, stifling a sob, began to walk off the dance floor.

A woman screamed. A young man, medium height, dark complexion, blue suit, hit Frank on the jaw from behind. More women screamed. Mrs. Rigali, in rustling black dress, panting, her face distorted with fear, was hurrying towards the group. The music stopped. Paul Perone stood quietly, waiting with still brown eyes. A second young man, medium height, dark complexion, turned to the orchestra.

"Play, you bastards," he said. "Play loud."

The orchestra began to play raggedly.

"Louder," said the second young man.

"Stop!" Mrs. Rigali panted. "Don't! Not here!"

Music blared harshly. Frank Graves, recovering himself, started for Paul Perone, standing quietly, just looking. A revolver spat twice, and twice more, behind him. Frank Graves's face went blank, he took one stumbling step, hesitated, and smashed to the floor.

"Now you've done it!" Mrs. Rigali screamed. "Oh, my God!"

"Why, somebody shot the guy," Paul Perone said, looking around as if surprised.

The dancers ran towards the door in a milling throng. A woman fell to her knees. A man tripped over her. Women screamed; men swore. The orchestra made weird noises.

Stanley Lowe grabbed Gloria. Bessie was running ahead. Gloria was sobbing.

"Oh, dear!" Gloria moaned. "Oh, dear!"

"Quick now!" Stanley said. "Here's the car." Bessie jumped in. He bundled Gloria in. All around self-starters were whirring, motors coughing. Stanley's hand trembled as he fumbled with the key to the ignition.

"Hurry, Stan," Bessie cried. "My God!"

The key slid in, Stanley stepped on the starter. Another car ground against their mudguard. Stanley backed and turned, jerking from one speed to another.

"Hurry," Bessie repeated.

Stanley swung out into the road, almost turned towards Brooklyn, but at the last minute twisted the wheel violently and headed down the Island.

"Where you going?" Bessie demanded.

"I'm going to duck around back ways," Stanley said. "The police'll be on the job in a minute."

A siren wailed back of them.

"There's one now," Stanley said, turning again into a side road. "If a cop asks us any questions, we've been down to Gruber's. We were there earlier anyway."

"Is Frank dead?" Gloria asked.

"I guess he is," Stanley replied.

"He was always looking for trouble," Bessie said. "I don't think he was in his right mind."

"They shot him in the back," Stanley said. "A lot of dirty murderers. But what could you do?"

"It wasn't Paul whatever-his-name-is," Bessie cried excitedly. "I was watching him when the shots were fired, and he was just standing there."

"He had his gang," Stanley said. "But take a tip from me right now. You didn't see anything, and you don't know anything. You'll save yourself a lot of trouble."

"Will they arrest us?" Gloria asked.

Stanley turned into another road and settled back more comfortably in the seat, Bessie beside him, and Gloria on the outside.

"I feel better now," he observed. "Light me a cigarette, will you, Bessie?"

"Gee, that was quick for Frank, wasn't it?" Bessie said.

She lighted a cigarette and poked it between Stanley's lips.

"Will they arrest us?" Gloria asked again.

Stanley laughed nervously.

"Gosh, Baby," he said, "I don't know what'll happen. Of course they can't do anything to any of us anyway, but they could make it damned uncomfortable for a while—witnesses and third degrees and everything."

"Oh, dear," Gloria exclaimed faintly. "I'm frightened."

"You got to keep a stiff upper lip," Stanley warned. "Chances are nobody that was there is going to tell any more than they can help. The way I figure, we've all got a good chance of keeping out of it. Mrs. Rigali isn't going to tell anything and the waiters aren't, either. If I was a waiter I wouldn't want to be telling anything about Paul Perone."

"I was afraid of that man," Bessie said excitedly. "Didn't I say there'd be trouble? Didn't I?"

"I'm sorry for Frank's old man," Stanley said. "Frank has given his old man plenty of trouble. And now this. His old man is a grand old guy."

"Frank was a pest," Bessie said. "But I wouldn't have wanted to see him murdered like that."

"I don't know what was the matter with him," Stanley said. "I knew Frank ever since we were kids. He always was a jealous feller—always talking about killing some dame or committing suicide."

"He's been scaring Dolly out of her wits," Bessie said. "His mother's dead, isn't she?"

"In a sanitarium," Stanley replied. "She'll never know what happened. It's the old man I'm sorry for. He's a prince."

"Just goes to show you what's the use of being good," Bessie observed. "It seems to me the good people are always suffering."

"Well, what're we going to do?" Stanley demanded. "We can't drive around all night. Want to go home now, Gloria?"

Gloria shuddered.

"I couldn't," she said.

"Well, why don't you go to Bessie's?" Stanley suggested.

"Don't you think it would be better if we didn't stay together to-night?" Bessie said. "Anyway, the old lady is on the warpath. I don't feel like battling with her."

"Gloria's got to sleep somewhere," Stanley said.

"Why don't you call up Chase Morgan, Dolly?" Bessie said. "Nobody'd think of looking for you there, would they?"

"I don't know if he's in," Gloria replied doubtfully, drawing a quivering breath.

"He told you to go there any time, didn't he?" Bessie asked. "If I were you I'd go right in."

"I was wondering about the car," Stanley interrupted. "The license number. If the police heard Gloria was mixed up in the shooting they'd look up her license number, wouldn't they?"

"Let's leave the car somewhere," Bessie exclaimed. "Maybe they're looking for it now."

Three frightened faces peered into the darkness on each side and behind. Lights of an automobile were approaching from behind.

"That might be the police," Bessie said.

"Stop that," Stanley protested. "You'll give us all the willies."

"Every car I see now will be the police," Bessie said. "I keep thinking I see men hiding behind trees and in dark corners."

"Oh, shut up, Bessie," Stanley growled. "I have all I can do to keep from giving her all the gas she can take, as it is. I was only considering every possibility."

"I was never so scared in my life," Bessie said.

"I suppose we had better leave the car somewhere," Gloria said in a weak voice. "I don't want to be arrested."

"I'm sorry I said anything about it," Stanley said.

"We can park it and lock it and take a cab," Bessie said. "Dolly has done that often enough, haven't you, Dolly?"

Bessie laughed hysterically.

"She's parked it and forgotten all about it till next day, and it's always been there."

"It's insured anyway, isn't it?" Stanley asked. "Do you want to telephone?" he added. "There's a drug store over there."

"Where are we?" Bessie asked.

"Jackson Heights, I guess," Stanley said. "I don't know just how we got here, but that's what it looks like."

Gloria hesitated.

"Will you come with me?" she asked Bessie. "Come on."

"All right," Bessie agreed. "I'll telephone Mother too, and we'll know if the police have been there."

"I'm awfully shaky," Gloria said. "I'm all wet."

Bessie laughed nervously.

"We're a couple of fools," she said. "I keep forgetting we haven't killed anybody. The way I feel you'd think I did it."

"Me too," Gloria confessed.

"Have you got change, Dolly?"

"Wait till I look."

Gloria fumbled in her bag.

"No," she said. "Get this changed, will you, Bessie?"

Bessie took the five-dollar bill Gloria handed her.

"Let's get a coca-cola or something," she suggested. "I need some cigarettes."

Chase Morgan answered the telephone.

"Hello, Baby," he said. "What's the matter? Your voice sounds funny."

"I'm nervous," Gloria replied. "I was wondering if it would be all right for me to come up there to-night? I don't want to go home."

"Sure thing, Baby," Chase Morgan said heartily. "Didn't I tell you you don't have to ask—key is always in the window—you know the place."

"But you're going to be there?" Gloria asked anxiously.

"Of course I am. How long before you'll be here?"

"I don't know—maybe half an hour."

"All right. I'll be waiting for you."

Gloria had to wait for Bessie to finish her call. Bessie smiled through the glass in the door, opened the door a trifle, put her hand over the transmitter, and whispered:

"Mother doesn't know anything—it's all right."

Gloria smiled tremulously. A moment later Bessie hung up the receiver and stepped from the booth.

"Cooper called up a little while ago, asking for you," she reported. "I told Mother I hadn't seen you."

Chapter 14

CHASE MORGAN walked into the living room of his house in Northington, Long Island. He wore a blue flannel shirt, open at the throat, with sleeves rolled up over muscular arms, and corduroy breeches tucked into big felt shoes.

"Hey, Baby!" he called.

"Here I am," Gloria replied, appearing from the dining room. She was wearing one of Chase Morgan's bathrobes, pinned together, sleeves rolled up to the elbows. A towel was bound around her forehead. She held a scrubbing rag in her hand. Chase Morgan grinned, showing solid teeth.

"A workin' woman," he said.

An Irish setter bitch wandered in from the hall, plumed tail waving lazily, soft brown eyes beseeching affection, red tongue curling from grinning mouth. Chase dropped his hand on the setter's neck and scratched.

"Good girl," he told her.

"I've been cleaning," Gloria said, wiping perspiration from her forehead with her bare forearm.

"Seems to me you're always cleaning," Chase said. "What're Sam and Sarah supposed to do—cheer while you work?"

"I like to clean," Gloria said.

"You're a sweet kid," Chase Morgan announced, elevating her chin with a finger and kissing her. "Most all over the shakes too, huh?"

Gloria nodded. Her hair was twisted up from her neck. She looked like a little girl playing at being grown up.

"Come and see how clean the bathroom is," she invited. "I'll bet it never was so clean before."

He tramped across the heavy rug into the library and stood in the door of the downstairs bathroom. Gloria looked at him expectantly, blue eyes shining.

"By God, it's wonderful," Chase Morgan boomed.

He slid a hand under each armpit and lifted her up high in air and kissed her again.

"Who'd 've ever thought you were a natural born house-keeper?" he asked.

"My Mother used to cook and take care of all of us," Gloria said. "This is nothing. I love to do it."

She cocked her head to one side and admired her handi-work.

"You didn't look behind the tub," she said. "I never leave a speck anywhere when I clean."

"You're a wonder," Chase Morgan said. "I love you more every day. How long is it since you've had a drink now, Baby?"

Gloria screwed up her face in an expression of intense thought.

"Seven days," she replied. "I used to have to drink, I guess, to stand Cooper."

"Well, well, well," Chase Morgan exclaimed. "Who'd ever thought it?"

He sat down in a green, wing-back chair near the window. She climbed on his lap, the bathrobe falling away from a slim leg. He bent over and kissed her knee. She slid her arm around his neck and held up her face, lips puckered. He kissed her mouth.

"I could cook, too," Gloria said.

"Cook if you want to," Chase Morgan said. "But I'd suggest leaving that end of it to Sarah. Why don't you get some clothes on and come outside? It's a gorgeous day. I've just been running the dogs."

"I will in a little while," Gloria said, keeping her arm around his neck. "I had to wash out my things and now I've got to iron. I've only got one pair of stockings left of those you got for me."

"We'll have to get some more," he said.

He took her arm from around his neck and held her away from him, looking down into her face.

"Look here, Baby," he said, suddenly serious. "What're you going to do anyway? Here I am getting more stuck on you every day, and I don't even know what's going on behind that beautiful face of yours."

She tried to hide her face from him by bending it down, but he forced her chin up with gentle pressure of big hands.

"You know what I told you," he said. "If you're going to live with me you've got to shake every one of the fleet of sharks and harpies you've been running with. You've got to make up your mind."

Gloria smiled nervously.

"I'd never share any woman with anybody," Chase Morgan said. "I'm not moral, God damn it, but I have my limits. I won't do it."

Tears gathered in Gloria's eyes. She felt in his shirt pocket. He twisted in the chair and pulled a handkerchief from his trousers pocket. She applied the linen to her eyes, trying to smile.

"Here!" Chase Morgan exclaimed gruffly. "Here! This'll never do. You're probably the most abused little kid in the world—everybody taking advantage of you since you were in the cradle. Look at the way you go mopping and dusting around this dump and running with the dogs and playing with the puppies."

Gloria blew her nose and wiped her leaking eyes again. Chase Morgan kissed her neck. She snuggled against him, silent.

"You've been a little hell raiser," he resumed in a judicial tone. "But it hasn't been your fault. Nobody could blame you —God or man."

"It wasn't my fault I was bad," Gloria whispered. "Was it?"

"You never were bad, Baby," Chase Morgan assured her. "You got a stinking, rotten deal. Why, you're nothing but a baby now."

He kissed her again. She smiled wistfully at him.

"But you've got to make up your mind," he said abruptly. "If you're going to stay with me you've got to cut loose from everybody."

"There's a lawyer always asking me to marry him," Gloria said shyly.

Chase Morgan frowned and shook her gently.

"You stop that, Baby," he ordered. "I've no doubt plenty of men have told you they wanted to marry you—only, I suppose a lot of 'em couldn't because they already had wives."

"Some of them," Gloria admitted.

"Gosh! I'm stuck on you, Baby," Chase Morgan exclaimed, hugging her closely to him and kissing her face. "You're the most beautiful little girl in the world—and as sweet as pie."

He rose abruptly, holding her in his arms. He turned and plumped her down in the chair.

"You've got to make up your mind for yourself," he told her. "I'm going in to the studio this noon. I've got a lot of work to do."

"Can't I go?" she asked.

He shook his head.

"Not to-day," he said. "But everything is all right now. I've told you that. The police aren't after you. They don't know who killed that chap. It's a good job I got your car and drove it out here, isn't it?"

She nodded.

"Well, I'm going to get shaved and dressed."

He turned and walked into the hall. In a moment his feet sounded on the stairs.

When Chase Morgan returned that night, Gloria was gone. He ate dinner alone, drinking ale. After dinner he began to drink Scotch highballs. At midnight he went to bed. But he couldn't sleep.

At three o'clock an automobile stopped outside the house and a horn began tooting madly. A score of dogs howled. He went to the window. Gloria called:

"Let me in."

He ran downstairs in his pajamas and opened the front door. Gloria and Bessie Mayfield, giggling, were pulling boxes and bags, picture frames, and pillows from Gloria's automobile.

"Hello, Chase," Bessie called, waving her hand. "Gloria's moving."

"I sent two trunks by express," Gloria explained. "We piled everything else in the car."

"You should've heard what she told Cooper," Bessie laughed.

"He said I was crazy," Gloria giggled.

"She told him she never wanted to see him again—that he made her sick," Bessie said.

"And he cried," Gloria said. "Didn't he, Bessie?"

"He was crying," Bessie agreed. "I'm dying for a drink, Morgan. Get us a drink, will you?"

"I want a drink too," Gloria said.

"Have you been drinking again?" Chase Morgan demanded.

"She just had one or two," Bessie explained. "How do you think she could stand all that excitement without it?"

"Can you wait till we get these things inside?" Chase Morgan wanted to know.

"If you hurry," Bessie giggled. "Oh, dear! This is a thrill. Cooper said he had just signed a new lease for the apartment."

Bessie bent over, laughing.

"I was kind of sorry for him," Gloria said suddenly.

"Sorry for him!" Chase Morgan snorted. "He ought to be horsewhipped."

· Sam and Sarah, colored, cook-housekeeper, gardener-chauffeur combination, appeared, smiling.

"You get some highballs, Sarah," Chase Morgan ordered, "and Sam, you lug this stuff upstairs."

Gloria, Bessie and Chase sat in the library, drinking highballs, Gloria on Chase Morgan's lap.

"Isn't it nice here, Bessie?" Gloria asked, contentedly.

"Swell," Bessie replied, looking around again at the books in fine bindings, at the prints, at the lamps with jade ornaments. Through the opened door she had a glimpse of the living room, where were water colors and a big oil painting of Chase Morgan in Elizabethan costume.

"And there's a duck pond out back and ducks in it, and about twenty dogs, and nine puppies, and fighting chickens," Gloria said. "Wait till you see upstairs. It's awful cute— Colonial."

"There's nothing the matter with your head, Dolly," Bessie said.

Gloria stretched her neck and kissed Chase Morgan.

"This is my baby," she announced. "I didn't come over here for the furniture or the dogs, did I, Chase?"

Chase Morgan grinned.

"God! I don't know," he said.

"You take that back," Gloria demanded. "Take it back."

"I take it back," he said.

When Gloria and Bessie were undressing upstairs, both a bit tight, Bessie said:

"You mean to say he never did anything?"

"Honest he didn't," Gloria replied.

"I couldn't live like that," Bessie said. "What's the matter with him?"

"I guess it was because he thought there was somebody else," Gloria said. "He sat up with me all night the first night, and after that he slept beside me. I was awful nervous, and waking up and screaming. But he didn't touch me."

"Maybe there's something the matter with him. Perhaps he's too old."

"No, there isn't," Gloria said, pulling on blue pajamas.

Her eyes were bright.

"I'm going in there to-night," she said, lowering her voice to a conspirator's whisper.

Bessie giggled, and lowered her voice too.

"Take it away from him, Dolly," she said.

Gloria tiptoed down the hall and pushed open the door into Chase Morgan's room.

"Who's there?" he asked.

"It's me," Gloria whispered, sliding across the floor towards the bed.

"What do you want, Baby?"

"You," she whispered.

"You little divil," he said. "Get back to bed."

Her pajamas dropped to the floor and she rolled into bed. He put out his hand and touched her bare breast.

"Let me get covered up," she said.

She put her arms around his neck, and pressed her lips to his.

"I love you, Chase," she breathed. "You're the most wonderful man in the world."

He kissed her. She lay quietly, blue eyes shining up at him from her still face on the pillow.

Four months later Gloria Boyd was alone in the house when the front doorbell rang. She went humming to the door and opened it. George Boyd grinned down at her. She started back.

"Glad to see me, ain't you?" George said.

"What did you come out here for?" Gloria asked.

"Money," George said. "Mazuma. I'm busted. Why in hell should I starve when you're livin' like a queen?"

He pushed into the hall.

"I haven't any money, George," Gloria said, looking at him from frightened eyes.

"Well, you'll find some or somethin' I can hock till you can get some," George said roughly. "What's the use of havin' floosies in the fambly unless you get somethin' out of 'em?"

214

"I haven't any money," Gloria protested. "You get out of here."

George looked around the hall, into the dining room on one side and the living room and library on the other.

"A swell dump, all right," he nodded. "Pretty soft for you."

"You get out of here!" Gloria said. "If you don't I'll scream."

"Go ahead and scream," George said. "The dingies have gone. Don't you think I know?"

"You get out of here, George," Gloria panted.

She wrung her hands helplessly.

"You ought to be ashamed," she said.

George laughed.

"*I* oughta be ashamed," he repeated, accenting the pronoun. "That's a hot one!"

He suddenly grabbed Gloria's wrist. His voice changed to a snarl.

"Cut out that stuff," he warned. "Dough is what I want. And I'm goin' to get it. How'd this guy here like to hear about Uncle Julius and the baby you had and Cooper Patten and everythin'? He'd like that, wouldn't he? How'd he like to hear about Addie?"

He backed Gloria against the wall.

"Huh!" he grunted.

Gloria dug both hands into her head, in a gesture characteristic of Ma Brennan. She looked wildly at her brother. Her lungs labored with spasmodic breaths. Her face was distorted as if she were about to weep, but she remained silent.

"Come on," George exclaimed, slapping her sharply on the cheek. "Come on, you little tramp. Get your pocketbook."

Tears ran down Gloria's cheeks. But she didn't move. She just stood, tense, staring at him. He slapped her again, harder. His voice raised in rage.

"I'll take no foolin', Gloria. I'm desperate. I always hated your guts anyway."

He slapped her again. She slipped to the floor, moaning.

215

"I'll give you one more chance," he said, breathing heavily.

She remained mute. He kicked her in the hip. She whimpered. He kneeled down and put his hands around her throat.

"I'll choke it outa you," he said, squeezing his hands together.

Chase Morgan ran up the steps and into the hall, footfalls muffled by rubber-soled shoes. He hit George a terrific blow in the head and jumped on him. Gloria staggered to her knees.

"No," she gasped.

Chase Morgan picked up the lax body and threw it down as if it were a sack. His face was congested with rage.

"Don't," she wailed, catching at his hand. "Please. It's my brother. You'll kill him."

Chase Morgan suddenly straightened, letting George lie, unconscious. He brushed a hand over his eyes.

"I wanted to kill him," he said, dazedly.

He turned to Gloria and helped her to her feet.

"Are you badly hurt, Baby?"

She shook her head, trying to smile reassuringly, one hand to her bruised throat.

"It's my brother George," she said. "Is he dead?"

She stared down at the inert figure.

"He's all right," Chase Morgan said. "Look at him breathing. Probably got a few busted ribs, I hope so."

He began to breathe easier. He settled his collar and put his arm around Gloria again.

"Poor baby," he soothed.

She began to sob.

"That's right," he said. "Get it all out."

He glanced over at George.

"What did the bastard want?" he asked.

"M-money," Gloria said. "That's all my family ever wanted from me was money. When I wouldn't give it to him he said he'd tell you all about me—about the baby and everything. When I wouldn't give it to him he knocked me -down and was choking me."

216

"A little blackmail," Chase Morgan said.

He went to the telephone.

"What're you going to do?" Gloria asked.

"Call my friend, the Chief of Police," Chase Morgan said grimly.

"You're not going to have him arrested. You can't do that, Chase."

"I won't have him arrested," Chase said. "But I'll have him ridden out of this part of the country. You get upstairs now and wait."

"I don't want to."

"You get upstairs, Baby. Everything'll be all right. I'll be up in a few minutes."

Gloria had her dinner in bed. Afterward Chase Morgan sat down beside her, holding her hand.

"How'd you like to get married, Baby?" he asked.

She smiled up at him, silently, and gave his hand a quick little squeeze.

"I guess we might as well," Chase Morgan said. "I don't believe in marriage as a theory, but it's the only way to live in a social system that is based on marriage."

Gloria kissed his hand shyly.

"Hey, don't do that, Baby," Chase Morgan exclaimed.

He bent and kissed her ankle. Then he kissed her knee.

"I wish I'd been good," Gloria said wistfully.

"Why, you little skeezicks," he said. "You've always been good—only other people have been bad. You know I always think of you as chaste."

"What's chaste?"

"Well," Chase Morgan said, "it's something that kept you sweet and lovely and good, no matter what bad people made you do."

"Maybe that's why I was drinking—so I wouldn't know about it—huh?"

She gazed at him with the wide eyes of an infant.

"I always wanted to be good," she said.

"Don't worry," Chase Morgan urged gently, touching his lips to her ear. "You are good. And the first chance you saw to get out of the mess you were in you packed up and moved in on me, didn't you?"

Gloria smiled.

"I guess you were surprised," she murmured.

"Now about this marriage business," he said. "I thought we'd have some of my friends out here. Have a little party. Would you like it?"

She nodded, smiling. Putting up her hands she pulled his head down.

"Can you guess something?" she whispered.

"No," he said. "I'm a rotten guesser."

"Maybe we're going to have a baby," she whispered.

Chase Morgan raised his head and looked at her.

"You're kidding yourself," he exclaimed.

She wagged her head on the pillow, curls rippling around her pink cheeks.

"The doctor says I will," she said.

Chase Morgan kissed her and sat up straight.

"Well, it's a good thing we're going to get married, isn't it?" he said.

Gloria nodded, eyes wistful. She plucked at his coat lapel.

"I hope we have lots of babies, Chase," she said.

He made a sound as if he were about to say something, but he changed his mind.

"I know what you were going to say," Gloria said.

"What was I going to say, Baby?"

Her cheeks flooded with color, but her blue eyes met his squarely.

"But it's a lot different—having babies—when you love somebody," Gloria Boyd said.